"YOU'VE BEEN AVOIDING ME . . .

$2.50

"Why? Damn it, Susan, something *is* happening." Daniel took her face between his palms and his grip was not entirely gentle. "You feel it, I know you do."

She shook her head in denial.

"Hell and damnation, Susan, passion isn't a sin!"

"It is for a woman who has taken vows against the indulgences of the flesh."

"You haven't taken any vows yet."

"I will."

"Why? What in hell have you done that could be so bad you'd give up your entire life?"

When she started to flee, he grabbed her waist and hauled her tightly against him. Lifting her from the ground, he backed her up to the stall . . .

His mouth opened, his head tipped. His tongue bid entrance into her honeyed sweetness.

When she refused, he lifted away ever so slightly. "Please, Susan, let me taste you . . ."

Praise for
Silken Dreams

"Simply wonderful . . . Lisa Bingham breathes life into your wildest fantasies."

—*Romantic Times*

"*Silken Dreams* is a

D1431207

Books by Lisa Bingham

Distant Thunder
Eden Creek
Silken Dreams

Published by POCKET BOOKS

Most Pocket Books are available at special quantity discounts for bulk purchases for sales promotions, premiums or fund raising. Special books or book excerpts can also be created to fit specific needs.

For details write the office of the Vice President of Special Markets, Pocket Books, 1230 Avenue of the Americas, New York, New York 10020.

DISTANT THUNDER

LISA BINGHAM

POCKET BOOKS

New York   London   Toronto   Sydney   Tokyo   Singapore

This book is a work of fiction. Names, characters, places and incidents are either products of the author's imagination or are used fictitiously. Any resemblance to actual events or locales or persons, living or dead, is entirely coincidental.

An *Original* Publication of POCKET BOOKS

 POCKET BOOKS, a division of Simon & Schuster Inc.
1230 Avenue of the Americas, New York, NY 10020

Copyright © 1992 by Lisa Bingham

All rights reserved, including the right to reproduce
this book or portions thereof in any form whatsoever.
For information address Pocket Books, 1230 Avenue
of the Americas, New York, NY 10020

ISBN: 0-671-73950-6

First Pocket Books printing January 1992

10 9 8 7 6 5 4 3 2 1

POCKET and colophon are registered trademarks of
Simon & Schuster Inc.

Cover art by Ken Otsuka

Printed in the U.S.A.

To Caroline Tolley, my editor.

Thanks for believing in me.
Thanks for making me reach.
And thanks for the cover.

DISTANT THUNDER

Prologue

Southern Pennsylvania
March 15, 1865

It rained for three days. Thunder rumbled like cannon fire, lightning cracked and spit in the darkness. Then, when the storm's fury had weakened, the horizon lay bruised and swollen beyond the moist green hills.

Through it all, the stolid shape of the Benton House Memorial Orphanage stood bravely against the glowering sky. The tempest had passed. The crisp rays of dawn glinted on the new windows, and the house stared vacantly into space, waiting for the first of its charges to appear.

Sunlight trickled through the whipped clouds, illuminating the war-hardened face of a nine-year-old boy who emerged from the trees bordering the road. For several silent minutes he studied the hollow building before him. The set of his shoulders grew rigid, a manly stance for one so young.

"We're here, Annie," he said, speaking to the infant nestled in his arms. He held the tiny baby with a tenderness that belied his early years. "See how

1

pretty it looks? They'll take good care of you. You'll see.''

The infant didn't respond. Forcing back the panic that gripped him, the boy edged onto the dirt path. Hiking the blanket-clad body a little more tightly against his chest, he hurried down the puddle-strewn road leading to the front steps.

The tang of wet lumber and varnish lingered in the air around him. Rising on tiptoe, the boy reached for the brass knocker. By stretching as high as he could, he managed to flick it with his finger, causing it to rap on the anchor.

While he waited for someone to answer, he surveyed his surroundings with the practiced eye of an army scout. He noted the cleanliness, the order. And though he couldn't be sure, he thought he heard someone humming. Annie would be safe here. No one would harm her again.

Inside the house, the melody paused and he caught the sound of approaching footsteps. The door opened with the barest of squeaks, and the most beautiful lady he had ever seen stepped onto the porch.

''Yes?''

For a moment he couldn't speak. He could only stare at the woman's shining toffee-colored hair. An angel. God had sent an angel to help his baby sister.

The boy's hands trembled as he drew the dirty blanket away from Annie's face. ''Please, can you help my sister?'' he asked, his voice proud yet containing a thread of pain.

The woman touched the fluff of golden hair spilling over the baby's forehead. Gentle fingers traced the pale infant features and shattered jaw. She shook her head, her eyes filling with grief. ''I'm sorry . . .''

She didn't need to say anything more. He'd known all along. He just hadn't wanted to believe.

Bowing his head, he rested his cheek next to that

of his sister. He tried one last time to capture her sweet baby scent. Then he straightened and looked up at the woman, attempting to speak past the crushing weight that had settled in his chest. "May I borrow a shovel, then? And just a tiny piece of land . . . ?"

Beyond the dull pewter gleam of Simpson Pond, a jagged valley butted against the tumbling winter-dead hills, as if God had grasped a handful of earth and thrown it to one side, leaving a gouging scar. It was here that Jonathan Hurst had built a home for his bride and his children.

In the cool morning air, a writhing fog rose from the water and snaked through the trees toward the squat one-room farmhouse, painting the breeze with the dank smell of mold. And death.

Until that day war had remained a distant sound of thunder, a dull flash of lightning. While Union forces pummeled a beleaguered Confederacy hundreds of miles to the east, a band of deserters had raided the tiny farm, closing in upon it like a pack of wild dogs. When their thirst for blood had been slaked, the dissenters fled, leaving their victims to stiffen in the early-morning gloom.

In the trampled grass next to the house, Jonathan Hurst and Erin, his bride, were separated in death as they had never been in life, their bodies torn, their warmth seeping into the greedy earth. And beside them, crouched in the mist, knelt a four-year-old child, eyes wide, red hair streaked with mud. She paid no heed to the blood that stained her clothes or the cold that gripped her body. She could only gaze into nothingness, her lips forming the words that had become a dirge and a prayer: "Mama. Mama. Mama . . ."

Mr. Macauley, from the next farm, was the first to

stumble upon the scene. He'd heard the gunfire and had come to the Hurst farm as fast as his bowed legs would carry him. But as soon as the red-haired child saw him, she began to scream so fiercely he was forced to back away. Not knowing what else to do, Mr. Macauley summoned Father Gregory. The good father received the same inauspicious welcome.

Ruminating aloud over the situation, Mr. Macauley smacked his age-pursed lips together and regarded the priest helplessly. "What're we gonna do? We can't have her gettin' hysterical like that, poor mite."

"Get some womenfolk and a wagon. Perhaps they can calm her enough to take her away from this place."

"Where they gonna take her, Father? What with the war an' all, times is hard. Not many people got grub for their own kin, let alone another mouth."

Father Gregory squinted up at the murky patch of sun struggling through the frayed clouds. "Benton House. They'll take her."

Four hours later, the wagon rumbled to a stop in front of the orphanage. Drawn by the sound of hoarse screaming, a boy peered from inside the doorway. While the adults tried to calm a wild red-haired little girl, he watched her with unaccustomed interest.

A feeling of kinship came over him. Her cries were filled with grief and fury, bewilderment and frustration. He understood her anger. He knew just how she felt.

Heedless of the grown-ups who were trying to approach her much the same way a lion tamer would approach a wounded cub, Daniel Crocker strode straight toward her. Climbing onto the hub of the wagon, he swung his leg over the side rail. The little girl was so intent upon the people gathered around her that she didn't note his presence until he laid a hand on her head.

Her tirade stopped. Their eyes met—his an icy blue, hers a deep moss green.

"I know." They were the only words he said. Then, kneeling in the straw, he awkwardly put his arms around her shoulders.

She clutched at him, her body shaking with great silent sobs. But she didn't cry. In a cracked voice she whispered one word over and over again: "Mama."

1

Denver, Colorado
January 5, 1885

Susan Hurst pushed back a strand of auburn hair and
clutched her wrapper to her throat. If anyone found
her wandering the halls of Saint Francis Academy so
late at night, questions were bound to be asked. But
right now Susan had too many unanswered petitions
of her own to worry about such an event.

She paused only once in her trek. At the doorway
of the primary dormitory, she leaned inside to peek
at her charges. A dozen tousled heads rested serenely
upon feather pillows. Muttered snatches of dream-
talk filtered into the air, a sniffle, a grunt.

Susan envied their state. It had been weeks since
she'd slept through the night. Not that she'd had bad
dreams—to the contrary, in fact. Actually she would
have preferred the nightmares. At least then she
would have a reason for being afraid to lay her head
on her pillow and surrender herself to the sweet stuff
of her imagination.

Leaving the girls to their slumber, Susan ran down

the hallway to the steps beyond. Without a candle to lead her, she found the corridors black as pitch. But her feet knew the way through the twisted hallways that led from the living quarters of the academy past the cloister to the small private chapel nestled deep in the heart of the building.

Fourteen years ago Susan had come to Saint Francis as a student. After four years of schooling, she had stayed to begin her novitiate. But time had a way of catching up to a person. Susan could feel the future looming in front of her, forcing her to make decisions that would bind her irrevocably to a life that had become as familiar as breathing.

The door to the chapel swung open on well-oiled hinges, giving no clue to Susan's errand. Once inside, she hesitated, staring up at the elaborate stained-glass window behind the altar. Moonlight filtered through the tiny jewel-sized panes, bathing the room in muted color.

During the day Susan had no problems dealing with the choices she'd made. She had been happy at Saint Francis. Very happy. She felt a bond with the sisters that went beyond that of mere co-workers; she adored her students and her work. So it had only been logical to begin her novitiate with the intent of some day joining the order. Whenever she'd felt qualms, Susan had told herself that she had ten years to consider taking her final vows. Then she had ignored the passage of time with a desperate glee.

In the space of a few weeks her grace period would expire. Each tick of the clock pounded into her conscience with such force she couldn't deny that something was missing—some deeper devotion. Thoughts of officially joining the sisters caused a heaviness to grip her chest.

In the daylight she could push the foreboding aside, telling herself that such feelings were natural. A permanent step like this deserved careful consideration. She was acting as normal as a bride-to-be with last-minute jitters.

But at night she couldn't thrust away her fears. She couldn't forget that she would be marrying not a mere mortal but the church. And she couldn't ignore the fact that her commitment was a little strained. A part of her wanted . . . more.

Susan sank to her knees, seeking answers in front of the altar just as she had every night for the past few months. The dark shadows of the chapel pressed heavily upon her shoulders, cloaking her in an inky chill that sank into her bones. The stones of the nave were icy, their surface worn to a glossy smoothness by the penitent worshipers who had knelt in this same spot hundreds of times over the past twenty years.

Locking her hands together in fervent supplication, Susan Hurst began, "Holy Mary, Mother of God." But the vaulted ceiling swallowed the words whole, leaving a gaping emptiness. She doubted that heaven had even heard her plea.

Sighing, she rubbed her forehead and ran her fingers through the loose silky auburn tresses that hung unbound to her waist. Above her, the serene visage of the Virgin Mary looked down with guarded eyes.

The restlessness in Susan's heart swelled another degree. Why hadn't God answered her prayers? Why hadn't He taken away the longings? If she was to become a member of the order, she had to eradicate these half-formed yearnings from her heart. She knew that. Yet, she fought a wayward spirit that wanted things it could never have—in or out of the order.

Sister Mary Margaret had once told her that God's children gave energy to those wishes and desires they pondered the most. So for the past month, Susan had tried to think solely of her duties and her students. But she couldn't seem to stop the phantoms that came to her once she slept. Sweet passionate demons that made her body tremble and her arms reach out for . . . what?

A cool draft drifted across the floor at her feet, piercing the loose weave of her wrapper. A bout of shivering racked her body, and she stood. Hugging her arms tightly to her chest, she tried to warm herself as best she could. Saint Francis became as cold as an icehouse each night, trapping the winter's bite deep in its thick, irregular walls. Nevertheless, the rugged rock structure would soon become her home, so she'd best become accustomed to it. Something akin to panic gripped her at the very thought, and she stumbled closer to the statue, touching the Virgin's feet. "Holy Mary, Mother of . . ." The familiar prayer locked in her throat. "Holy Mary . . ."

Drawing back, Susan searched the shadows, seeking a measure of comfort. For years she had been coming to this altar, craving the balm it offered her aching spirit. But lately that peace was getting harder and harder to find. She couldn't stop the burgeoning mixture of anger and dissatisfaction that churned in her chest.

She whirled to challenge the blackness around her. "I don't belong here! Can't you see that?" The echoing ricochet of words on stone mocked the fervor with which they'd been spoken. A weary defeat colored her added confession. "But I don't belong anywhere else, either."

She stabbed the air with an accusing finger. "Why? *Why?* Why am I cursed with these . . . these *feelings?* Why am I tormented with thoughts of a man's arms and a man's touch when you know I can never . . . can never . . ."

When she couldn't even force herself to say the words, Susan ran down the aisle, her hair flowing behind her like a brilliant auburn pennant. At the last row of pews, she turned to confront the shaft of moonlight spilling through the stained glass and casting a pale pattern of stardust onto the floor.

"*You* did this to me. You killed my parents and my childish illusions. Now all I want is an answer. Either give me back my life or give me the serenity I need to surrender my future to the church."

Her only reply was silence. But Susan Hurst had become quite good at waiting. Maybe God wasn't ready to tell her now. He would, one way or the other. Only three weeks remained until the orphanage reunion, which would see her home to Ashton for a brief respite. Susan could only be grateful that the reunion would be held in Wyoming and not in Pennsylvania. Years ago, the headmistress of the Benton House Orphanage had married and moved the institution west, away from the crowded cities. Since many of the children had come with her at the time, most of them still lived within a few hundred miles of Ashton in the Wyoming Territory.

She intended to enjoy herself, to relax, and to think things through.

After the celebration, if Susan had not received some kind of sign that heaven was opposed to the idea, she would return to Saint Francis and take her vows.

Cheyenne, Wyoming Territory
January 7, 1885

The pounding on the door could have roused the dead, but it barely pierced the haze clouding Daniel Crocker's brain. Moaning, he rolled onto his stomach, dragging a pillow over his ears; but the blasted racket continued, offering him no choice but to get up and answer the door.

One hand reached blindly toward the bedside table, patting the unfamiliar assortment of items—lamp, key, matchbox—until he encountered the smooth contoured shape of his Peacemaker revolver.

"Go away." There was no need to shout or raise his voice. The pure rage that sizzled in the careful intonation of each syllable conveyed his foul mood clearly enough. Stuffing the pillow in a ball under his cheek, he held the Peacemaker at arm's length and sighted down the barrel with one fever-reddened eye. The steadiness of his aim and the hard cast of his jaw belied the weakness of his body.

"Mr. Crocker?"

"No."

"Mr. Crocker, I know it's you," a boyish voice called through the panels. "I saw you come in late last night. I'd recognize you anywhere. I've seen the pictures."

Daniel didn't answer. The gun didn't waver. Except for the steely gleam that entered his ice blue eyes, he showed no reaction.

"Mr. Crocker?" the voice came again, more hesitant this time.

"Who wants him?"

"Well, nobody—that is to say, I've got no business with you personally . . . I mean I've got a telegram for you, but I don't intend no harm." The person on the other side of the door waited a full ten seconds then tentatively added, "Please?"

Damn. Daniel released the hammer and set his revolver on the nightstand. Moving as gingerly as he could, he eased upright from the bed.

His head pounded. Cupping his aching side, he took a quick indrawn breath when the action pulled at the blood-caked strips of cotton wrapped around his waist.

Retrieving the revolver, he padded to the door. The mirror over the bureau eloquently testified that, except for the stained bandages, he was naked. However, the freezing air had little impact on his skin. He'd been fighting a fever for over a day now. Even the cold January weather couldn't seem to shake it loose.

"Mr. Crocker?" The wavering summons was followed by a soft tap. "I don't want to bother you, but—"

"Who are you?"

"Jordie. Jordie Davis. I work with Mr. Smythe down at the telegraph office. I do all his running. I've also got some medicine Doc Goddard ordered for you. He said to bring it straight here."

"Stand back."

"Beg pardon?"

Before the boy had a chance to speak again, Daniel opened the door and leveled the gun at a spot in the center of the boy's forehead. Jordie Davis stared at him with eyes as round as marbles. Swiftly Crocker checked the hall in either direction then pinned the boy with a penetrating glare. "What do you want?"

Jordie gulped, cowering beneath the loaded pistol like a cornered rabbit. Daniel Crocker's reputation had preceded him. "Ruthless" would have been a kind word to use in connection with his work for the Pinkertons. Last summer Jordie had seen the gruesome newspaper photos taken after Crocker apprehended the murderer Mackie Beeb. Beeb had worn a serene expression. Had it not been for the pennies over his eyelids and the bullet hole through his neck, no one would have guessed how swiftly he'd been sent to his Maker.

Jordie gnawed at the inside of his lip. Why, oh,

why, had he agreed to make the deliveries to this man? Nine times out of ten, telegrams meant nothing but bad news. Fear inundated Jordie in sleeting waves. He had the rotten luck to bring sad tidings to a man who appeared as touchy as a grizzly roused from a long winter's nap.

"I didn't mean to get you up—honest!" He took in Daniel's sleep-mussed hair and stubbled jaw, then noted his bare chest, makeshift bandage, and naked thighs. Silently he thrust a small package and the folded paper into Daniel's free hand, then backed away.

"Boy!"

Jordie froze, standing ramrod stiff next to the flocked paper on the hotel wall. "What?"

"You deserve something for your trouble."

"No! No, no. No trouble at all. No trouble. None. Honest!" Then, scrambling toward the staircase on the far side of the building, he disappeared from view.

The weapon became too heavy for Daniel to hold. Dropping his arm, he backed into the room and shut the door. Setting the gun and the telegram on the nightstand, he drew the covers over his legs and settled onto the bed. The sheets were speckled with streaks of blood from his restless night.

Flinging an arm over his eyes to block out the light streaming through his window, he ignored the crumpled scrap of paper waiting for his perusal. He didn't want to look at it—didn't *need* to look at it. No doubt the missive held a summons from Jedidiah Kutter, his superior. Since Daniel had taken a knife in his side while apprehending Grant Dooley and most of his gang, the last thing he wanted to think about was going back to work. This past year he'd been on a horse more often than not. He'd been beaten, shot at, and cursed. He'd traversed most of Wyoming Territory tracking the Dooleys, and most of the Mountain West trailing the Beebs, and if the Dooley gang had been trouble, the Beeb brothers were his personal nightmare. Daniel was tired. Bone weary. Not just of the last few weeks, but of everything: his job, his routine. His life.

Squeezing his lashes closed, he willed his body to settle into the arms of sleep. But sleep had never come easily to Daniel Crocker, and right now it seemed an impossibility. The presence of the telegram burned into his consciousness.

"Damn." He shifted his arm and rolled his head on the pillow. The paper beckoned him like the crooked finger of a practiced whore, promising the sweet fulfillment of his curiosity, yet mocking him with the emptiness of that same fulfillment.

Knowing he would have no rest until he read the contents, Daniel stretched to take the note between two knuckles. He held it up in the light as if he could read through the paper, then finally tore it open.

There was no return address, no signature. Just one simple line: "She will take her vows."

" 'She will take her vows,' " he read aloud. He crumpled the telegram in his fist. If he closed his eyes, he could see that bitter October day when he had helped little Susan from the train and handed her over to the care of a special friend, one of the new novices at Saint Francis. He had persuaded himself and her guardians at the orphanage that Susan would need to stay at the academy only a few years in order to receive her education. In the meantime, Belle would watch over her and protect her—something Daniel could no longer do.

But Susan had not left Saint Francis four years later. She had stayed to begin her ten-year novitiate. In all that time, Daniel had visited her once, on the day of her graduation. He hadn't seen her since. He'd contented himself with infrequent reports from Belle.

This most recent telegram was no different from any other he'd received over the years. Except for the message.

She will take her vows.

"Like hell she will," he ground out between his teeth. He rolled to his feet and reached for his trousers.

As soon as he'd cleared the building, Jordie ran down the front steps. The man was waiting for him, just as he'd said he would.

"Well?"

"I gave him the package; now leave me alone. I've got to get back to Mr. Smythe or he'll have my head."

The stranger reached into his pocket and withdrew a twenty dollar gold piece. "For your trouble," he said.

Surprised, Jordie reluctantly took it. Twenty dollars was a lot of cash. More than he could make in months and months of running.

But as he stammered his good-byes and raced down the street, he couldn't shake the feeling that he'd just been paid blood money.

2

In Susan Hurst's opinion, Saint Francis Academy for Young Ladies became as sterile as a tomb once the girls went to bed. She missed the restless energy and the sound of muffled laughter. She longed for the faint trace of forbidden toilet water that sometimes wafted into the air. But most of all she yearned for the company of another human being.

As one of the few novices serving at Saint Francis, Susan was given duties that kept her busy long after the sun set in the sky. Most of her assignments required solitude, providing her with the time and opportunity to ruminate over her upcoming admittance into the order. Yet sometimes the loneliness became unbearable.

Arching her back to relieve the weary crick that had settled low in the nape of her neck, she made her way through the night-blackened corridors to her room. Her footsteps echoed against the vaulted ceiling. The frost, condensed on the surface of the stones, lent a bite to the draft that snaked beneath her skirts.

For nearly thirty years Saint Francis had been the motherhouse of the Ursuline nuns who had founded the academy. During her own association with the institution, Susan had never failed to admire the dedication and commitment of the women who served here. That was why she'd tried so hard to be like them. She wanted to belong to something important. She wanted—*craved*—a place where she was needed. Yet the doubts would not go away. A hollow spot had appeared in her heart, feeding on itself day by day.

Perhaps she just needed a rest. There had been so many details to finalize before Susan could leave for a few short weeks to attend a reunion of children who had once stayed in the Benton House Memorial Orphanage. She'd been working from dawn to midnight each evening, preparing lesson plans, outlines, and lecture notes for her substitute. Her shoulders ached, and her head throbbed. But she couldn't allow herself the luxury of easing her pace. Until tonight, when she'd discovered every possible task was finished and one long empty evening remained before she left for Ashton in the morning. One lonely, never-ending evening.

Susan rounded the corner and frowned. A finger of light stroked the bottom edge of her chamber door and inched into the hall. Her steps faltered.

As assistant to Sister Mary Margaret, headmistress of Saint Francis Academy, Susan had the unaccustomed luxury of a private room. Special records and accounts were stored in her desk drawer, so her quarters were kept locked at all times. No one would have a reason to be inside without permission. No one but the mother superior or one of the other nuns accompanying Max, their handyman, who sometimes brought her a bunch of wildflowers or an extra armful of wood.

Tiptoeing forward, she reached for the handle. The knob remained firmly in place. Whoever waited for her on the other side had locked the door. Neither the mother superior nor Max would have done such a thing.

Susan dug into the deep pocket of her skirt and removed a worn brass key. As noiselessly as possible, she slid it into place and released the latch. Then, cautiously, she opened the door.

A glass lamp on the far side of the room dispelled the darkness, but the wick had been adjusted to a shallow glow. Enough light illuminated the narrow space to reveal that her bed remained tautly made, her pillow fluffed. The single straight-backed chair was unoccupied; her trunks were untouched. No one was there.

Summoning her courage, Susan stepped inside. She had just cleared the threshold when the door slammed shut behind her and an arm wound itself around her neck, a broad hand clapping over her mouth. Susan instinctively clawed at her captor, her lungs gulping air to scream.

"Don't. It's me."

As quickly as the terror had seized her, it drained away. The fingers that had been digging into his arm eased. She knew that voice—the husky, gravelly timbre, the familiar inflection.

The second he released her, Susan whirled to face him. "Daniel!" It took a few seconds for her to absorb the sight of his lean, angular frame. But what she found made her wince. How long had it been since she'd seen him last? At least ten years and he'd changed so much! His wavy ash blond hair hung past the taut lines of his shoulders. He'd gained twenty pounds in muscle alone, and his body was tempered by time and hard living. The huge calf-skin coat he wore couldn't mask the strength of his torso and the whipcord length of his thighs.

"Hello, Susan."

"What are you trying to do?" she demanded. "Scare the life right out of me?"

He shrugged and uncocked his weapon. Susan hadn't even known it was ready to fire.

"I left the light on. I wanted to come earlier. But I'm not the sort of person the good sisters would let pass through their gate, let alone visit one of their little lambs."

The statement was harshly spoken—and Daniel was right. Most of the sisters at Saint Francis would disapprove of any association with Daniel Crocker. He was a man no delicate woman, especially a novice, admitted to knowing. He cursed; he drank. He'd killed. But the most telling characteristic of all was his eyes. They were angry. Bleak. Long ago they had turned flinty and cold, and no amount of feminine fussing could ever thaw them. Susan didn't remember when the change had occurred, but Daniel couldn't have been very old. Tonight they seemed even bleaker.

"You look awful, Daniel." The glow from the lamp cruelly outlined the craggy indentations of his cheeks and the square line of his jaw.

"It's nice to see you, too."

Susan wanted to touch him, soothe the deep furrow of tension that lined his brow, but the stiff way he held his body told her he wouldn't welcome such an overture. Daniel had never taken to coddling of any sort. Even from her.

"You don't look as if you've been taking very good care of yourself."

"I've been busy."

"Too busy to sleep?" She noted the weary lines

that slashed from his nose to the corners of his mouth. A gray pallor dusted his skin.

"I'm fine."

Susan had a different opinion, but she knew it would be useless to argue. "Why are you here?"

He'd never visited on her birthday or on a holiday or during a vacation—not once in ten long years. She knew he thought about her. Their childhood bond had not weakened over time. Even now she had the eerie feeling that Daniel had somehow sensed how much she needed him. Her childhood confidant. Her protector. The only male she'd ever allowed herself to trust.

Daniel stepped toward her, his eyes intent on her face. "I've heard some disturbing news."

She nervously cleared her throat. "News?"

"Why didn't you send word and tell me?"

She retreated from him. "Tell you?"

"Damn it! Don't play games. You know exactly what I mean. A *nun*." He said the word as if it were dirty.

So he knew the truth. "How did you find out?"

"Does it matter?"

"I think it does."

"Then let's just say a little angel appeared in the dead of night, perched on my shoulder, and whispered your plans in my ear. Hellfire and damnation, Susan, have you lost your mind?"

Defiantly, she lifted her chin a notch. "It's an honorable calling."

"Maybe for someone else, but not for you."

"I think I'd make a fine nun."

"Well, you're not getting the chance." He crossed toward the small wooden trunk that Saint Francis Academy had supplied to hold her meager belongings.

"Just what do you think you're doing?"

"Packing. I'm taking you away from here." He flung open the lid.

"You are not."

In the dimness of the room, his eyes flashed with icy crystals of determination. "Watch me."

"I'll scream."

"Fine." He began pulling petticoats and drawers free. An empty carpetbag she had borrowed for her trip to Ashton lay on the floor, and he scooped it onto the bed and began stuffing it with clothes.

"Stop it!" An angry blush stained her cheeks. When he returned to the trunk and removed the tray with the intent of rummaging through her outerwear, she batted his hands away and slammed the lid shut. "What in the world has come over you?"

He leaned close, his nose almost touching hers. "I'm doing what I should have done years ago. I'm taking you away from here."

"And just where do you plan on going?"

"To the orphanage. You can live there from now on."

"The orphanage! I don't need charity. I'm not a child anymore."

"You're sure as hell acting like one."

"Why? Because I've found a way to support myself? Because I've managed to keep a roof over my head and food in my belly without living off the goodness of other people?"

"No. Because you're not facing your problems; you're running away. I knew you were still afraid of men, but I didn't think you'd take things this far."

She gasped as if he'd struck her.

"It's perfect, isn't it? Not a male around, except Max, who might as well be a child. You'll spend the rest of your life shut inside your precious stone walls with no one to talk to but a gaggle of women."

She slapped him hard across the cheek. The crack of flesh meeting flesh ricocheted through the room.

Daniel's head snapped back from the force of the

blow. When he looked at her, he knew he'd gone a step too far. Susan stood trembling in front of him, her skin glassy white, her dark green eyes wide and haunted.

Damn. Why hadn't he been more careful? He'd pushed her past the unspoken emotional boundaries that had been drawn the first day he'd met her, a terrified red-haired little girl. Since Susan was so afraid of men, the neighbors had surmised that she had witnessed the attack on the farm and on her mother, but she'd never volunteered an explanation. She refused to speak of that day, even though it still colored her entire life.

"I'm sorry."

She didn't react. She could have been carved from ivory, so rigid had she become.

He'd come to dread that look. It made him feel helpless. And mean. Daniel had been hated by a lot of people. He'd grown used to scorn and betrayal, and it rarely affected him. But he couldn't bear to have Susan gaze at him with hurt or disapproval.

His own fears had made him reckless. Normally he was able to keep a tight rein on his emotions, but seeing her now, so pale and unhappy, he felt the old familiar urge to make things right, to fix her hurts and right her wrongs. He had to make her see that her decision to enter the sisterhood was a form of desperation, not devotion. He had to keep her from making a mistake she would regret for the rest of her life.

"Susan?" His voice held an uncharacteristic trace of tenderness. At an early age, Daniel had been forced to fend for himself. He'd developed an instinct for emotional survival. Despite the few happy years he'd experienced at the orphanage, he'd soon grown bitter and cynical. It had been so long since he'd felt any emotion other than anger, he'd forgotten how to be gentle. His feelings had atrophied when he left

Susan with the nuns at Saint Francis and joined the cavalry. There he'd been plunged back into the only world where he'd ever belonged. One where pride and a stubborn strength of will bred a generation of men like him: men born to take the brunt of the world's fury—before giving it back again in full measure.

He reached out to comfort her, but she jerked back.

"Don't touch me."

"I'm sorry. I shouldn't have said—"

"I think you'd better go."

"Damn it, Susan, you're too good for this kind of life!"

"I don't want you here."

"You're sweet and kind and loving. Don't shut out the world."

"Go away!"

He knew he should do what she asked. Who was he to tell others how to conduct themselves? He'd had no luck following his own code. But at the mere thought of Susan, his little Susan, locking herself into a convent . . .

The minute she took her vows, she would be lost to him completely. Maybe he was being unreasonable. He hadn't sought her company for over a decade. He'd wanted to. He'd always known he could. He'd kept a record of her progress; he'd thought of her every day. But he kept thinking he would visit sometime in the future, once he'd proven himself and become a better man. But he'd only grown harder and more cynical.

Now he was faced with the fact that once she became a member of the order, she could no longer be his in any way whatsoever.

No. He wouldn't let it happen. He couldn't. For too long he'd served as Susan's protector, either in person or through the help of friends. He couldn't stop playing that role now, even if it meant saving Susan from herself.

He moved closer to her. "Come with me. Leave Saint Francis. You don't belong here." He spoke with silky persuasion, but it didn't ease her rigid stance.

"You were the one who brought me here in the first place! Why are you so dead set against my staying?"

His slight control snapped. "I brought you here because you needed to learn. You refused to go to school with the other children at Benton House. You hid down by the creek each day because the schoolmaster was a man."

"So you took me hundreds of miles away from home and abandoned me."

"Abandoned? Abandoned! I left you with good women who could teach you. I couldn't help you anymore, Susan. Dear God, I wanted to, but I was only a boy myself. I knew the sisters would be able to offer you some guidance and some confidence. I left you here for your own good."

"And you never came back."

"Hell, this is a convent! They wouldn't have welcomed me here."

"You could have visited if you'd wanted to. You could have skulked through the shadows as you did tonight. You didn't have to leave me here thinking you'd forgotten me."

"Forgotten you?" He repeated the phrase as if he found the thought inconceivable. "How could you think such a thing? I sent you letters."

"Two. In the fourteen years I've been here, you sent me two letters, both of which held fewer than three lines of writing—while I wrote every month or more. If it hadn't been for letters I received from

Esther Reed and the other children at the orphanage, I wouldn't even have known you were alive."

"I thought about you every day."

"Did you? I doubt it. But it doesn't really matter. I've built a life for myself. One that doesn't include you. From now on I'll make my home with God and the other sisters."

They'd come full circle again, and he hadn't swayed her a bit. "Why are you so determined to do this?"

"It's none of your concern."

"It *is* my concern." He grasped her elbows. He tried to ignore the way she flinched at his touch. "Tell me. Tell me why you've decided to become one of them."

"I don't have to tell you anything."

She was correct in that regard. He'd surrendered any rights to her secrets by leaving her to fend for herself.

"Tell me anyway."

He saw the way she crossed her arms defensively in front of her, but he showed no outward reaction. He didn't release her, either. Not when he could feel her trembling like a frightened sparrow.

"The sisters have been very good to me."

When she didn't continue, he prompted, "And?"

"And I enjoy working with the children."

"Female children."

Once again he'd said the wrong thing. She wrenched free and crossed to stand behind the corner of the bed, effectively putting a barrier between them.

"There's nothing inappropriate about my choice, Daniel. I'll be doing good, honest work. Work that is rewarding and challenging. I will be supporting myself and not living off the charity of others."

Daniel knew Susan's interest in taking her vows was logical. It showed a great deal of thought and

25

devotion. And she was right. Her association with the sisters would be fulfilling.

But he couldn't bear to see her do it. If she were to don the heavy habit of the order, the thick all-encompassing woolen skirts and veils would choke the last vestiges of spontaneity and passion from her character as surely as they would strip away her worldly mien. Daniel could have kicked himself for not realizing what was happening, for trusting her care to others instead of guaranteeing her happiness himself. So much joy had already been taken from her. Why did she want to give away what little she had left by joining such a restrictive life?

Daniel knew some women flourished in the religious calling, but Susan wouldn't be one of them. Deep in his heart he believed that to be true. Susan needed a different kind of existence. She needed gaiety and laughter and passion. She needed children— not borrowed for a season, but to rear as her own. Daniel had become so lost in his work, his own hellish way of life, that he'd become blind to Susan's needs.

"I'm good at what I do, Daniel."

"I know."

"I'm one of the first novices to be given such responsibilities."

"You've always been a fine teacher." He continued forcefully, "But you don't have to stay in the order! You could go anywhere you wanted."

"You don't understand," she said bitterly. "You don't *want* to understand."

"I'm trying! Damn it, I'm honestly trying." He touched the sides of her face, the nape of her neck, in an effort to calm her. Fiercely he absorbed the delicacy of her bones. He wanted to yank off the heavy scarf she wore, wondering if her hair was still the color of fire. But he couldn't. Not without scaring her completely. So his arms dropped impotently to his sides. One hand cupped the knife wound in his side. An ache had been simmering there all day.

"You don't think I have the capacity for such a commitment, do you, Daniel?"

"I think you have the capacity for more than Saint Francis can offer you."

"I would be working with God and his children. What more could there be?"

Daniel advanced around the bed. "You're ignoring a whole gamut of sensations."

"With men?"

"Yes, with men!"

"From what I've seen of the masculine sex"—she shot him a pointed look—"I'm not missing much." She backed away from him until her palms touched the wall. "I've already given this a great deal of thought. I've made my peace with myself. It's what I intend to do."

"And you have no doubts whatsoever?"

She opened her mouth to affirm. But the words remained dammed in her throat. How could she lie to Daniel? How could she lie to herself?

"It's a waste."

"That's your opinion."

"I won't let you do it."

"*Why?*" She pushed free of the rough stone wall and edged past him so that she wouldn't feel so cornered. And threatened. "Why can't you give me your blessing?"

Daniel sucked in a bracing draft of air and steadied himself, then looked at her. "There's so much waiting out there for you, Susan. You know that. But instead of facing your problems head-on, you'd rather bury them and retreat to some ivory tower where people can't scare you or worry you or touch you."

"And you're the expert on how a person should live?"

The words stung. More than they should have had the power to. His arm dropped from its support, and he forced himself to straighten to a proud height.

"Daniel, I'm sorry, I didn't mean that."

"Yes. You did. And you're right." He crossed to the door and reached for the knob. "Maybe I'm just trying to keep you from making some of the same mistakes I've made."

"You're not leaving!"

He paused and rested against the jamb. "Goodbye, Susan."

"When will you be back?"

He met her worried glance, but his own was inscrutable and hidden in shadow.

"Daniel, things don't have to change between us. You'll still be my friend. I'll enjoy seeing you and talking with you. Once I become an official member of the order you won't have to sneak into the academy."

He sighed in resignation. "I don't think you'll welcome a visit from someone like me once you become a nun."

"I will always welcome you, Daniel."

"Maybe. But I couldn't come to you that way. I couldn't stand to see you so . . ." Shaking his head, he said, "Never mind." He rubbed one knuckle down the curve of her cheek. A tingling effervescent trail followed its path. "It's late. You need your rest." He gazed at her long and hard, his expression masked in secrets yet filled with a heart-wrenching regret. Then he began to walk out of the room.

"No, Daniel. Don't go!" She reached out to stop him.

Her palm encountered a hard, contoured body.

A masculine body.

She recoiled, startled. Suddenly her vision of the past was stripped, and she saw Daniel not as the boy she'd adored but as a man. A *man*.

Her breathing became quick and shallow; she felt a clamminess gather between her shoulder blades. When had it happened? When had the last shreds of adolescence melted away? When had Daniel become a man?

"Susan?"

Daniel eased forward, alarmed by the white cast spreading into her cheeks. His frustration mounted to an exploding point. He'd been content to humor her about beginning her novitiate. He'd known Saint Francis would be a good place for her to nurture confidence and grow emotionally. But damn it all to hell! He hadn't thought she'd go through with it.

His frustration blazed into anger, anger into resentment, resentment into hatred—of the men who'd left her with such deep psychological scars, and of Susan for surrendering to the memories. But most of all, anger at himself for not understanding how much she'd needed him.

No!

He gripped her face, his palms flat on her cheeks, his fingers splaying beneath the scarf and tangling in her hair. "Don't do this. Please don't do this."

A mewling whimper escaped from her throat, but it barely registered on Daniel. He saw the shards of fear forming in the liquid depths of her eyes, and for once he couldn't find the patience to deal with her terror. He wanted to ram his way through her defenses. He wanted her to awaken to reality. He wanted her to experience the pleasure as well as the pain, the joy as well as the fear.

Backing her against the wall, he leaned heavily into her body. "Feel, damn it. Stop cowering like a soft little mouse in a safe black hole. Look at me and really see me. Touch me. Hate me. Scream at me. Anything is better than just giving up. Don't wither and die inside. Life has too much to offer—yes, it hurts sometimes. And I know you've been hurt more than your share. But that doesn't mean it always has to be that way."

She held his wrists, but didn't push him away. Instead, she clung to him as if he were her anchor in a tempestuous storm. Tears welled, but hung on the ends of her lashes as if trapped.

"I want . . ." She blinked against the tears that threatened to spill onto her cheeks. "I can't . . ."

"You can."

"It's so . . . cold."

He saw the way her eyes focused—not on him but on the past. She shivered—whether from the draft or from her memories, he didn't know.

"Tell me." He shook her. A terrifying flurry of expressions flashed by, and he knew she relived painful recollections, but she didn't speak. "Tell . . . *me*," he repeated intently.

"No, I can't."

"Please."

"No, don't make me, Daniel. Please don't make me."

She threw her arms around his neck and held him so tightly she could have burrowed inside him.

Daniel gulped, torn between pure male astonishment and regret that he'd pushed her so far. The body that clung to his own was soft and shapely. He could feel her breasts pressed to his chest. As his arms shifted, he blindly roamed the gentle slope of her shoulders, the strong back, the delicate spine. Beneath the enveloping skirts he felt the tiny waist, the shapely hips. Then, the one sensation he'd never thought to feel with Susan gripped him. Desire.

Shocked, Daniel hung motionless, unable to force

her to stop, afraid to pull her closer. When had she ceased to be a child? When had she become such a vibrant, beautiful girl? No—woman. Somehow she had sailed past coltish adolescence and straight into full-grown adulthood. She was so beautiful, so feminine. She should have been leading men on a merry chase. She should have been breaking hearts and dashing hopes.

She must have sensed his hesitancy, because slowly she retreated. Before she could move too far out of his reach, he stopped her.

"Susan?" Her name held a note of panic and wonder. As she trembled in his grasp, Daniel admitted she unsettled him—even scared him a little. More than he wanted to admit. Her eyes clung to his own with the intense hunger of a woman who yearned to be kissed. And heaven help him, he wanted to satisfy her. Not only with his lips, but in the most intimate way a man could satisfy a woman.

No! It was wrong to think that way. *Wrong.* She wasn't his for the taking. She deserved more than he could ever give her.

But her eyes were wide and dark, her lips moist and slightly parted. The desire he felt grew stronger, flooding him with a sudden unbearable heat. "Don't look at me like that."

Her features remained filled with a desperate entreaty. He doubted she knew what she wanted from him. Regardless, he found himself powerless to resist. He knew he would scare her. She would probably hate him. But he couldn't refuse.

Cradling her face in his palms, he tipped her head to one side. Her breathing came sharp and fast, as if she'd just run miles instead of standing sheltered next to the strength of his body.

He bent to within a hairbreadth of her lips. Her eyes widened. Stroking the pads of his thumbs over her cheekbones and uttering soft shushing noises, he quieted her.

Giving her time to adjust to him, he inhaled her sweet feminine scent. Once, twice, his nose brushed her skin.

"Please?" she begged, more of a question than a demand.

"Shh."

She whimpered. Every nuance of her being became imprinted in his memory: the dark uncertainty of her eyes, the pallor of her skin, the velvety texture of her mouth. How had he stayed away from her for so long? If he'd seen her like this once during the past few years, he never would have found the strength to keep away.

He touched her lips with his own. She started as if scalded, but did not back away. Encouraged, he increased the pressure.

She tasted of innocence and springtime. Femininity and forbidden delights. A burst of temptation led him on. He wanted to crush her body to his own. He wanted to drown himself in her sweetness. His body urged him to sate his cravings. His kiss grew demanding and impatient.

Too late he discovered he'd taken a step forward, crushing her between himself and the wall. Before he could control his instincts, Susan wrenched free and fled to the opposite side of the room.

"Susan . . ."

Her fingers curled into a tight ball. "Go away."

Self-recrimination quickly doused the fires inside him. "I didn't—"

"Go! You don't belong here. But I do. This is *my* choice, *my* way of life, and nothing you can say or do will change my mind!"

Regret had a bitter flavor. Daniel had experienced it so many times that he shouldn't have found it so unpalatable. But it had never lingered so dank and heavy on his tongue as it did now.

Susan retreated into the corner. Accusation and confusion radiated from the stiff way she held herself, making him feel lower than the lowest worm. How could he have treated her so roughly? She would never look at him the same way again.

He sighed. "I'll go." The pain in his side was nothing compared to the sorrow that cloaked him like a somber cloud. "I guess this is probably the last time I'll see you, then."

She couldn't meet his gaze. Daniel had always been her rock, her foundation. Now he'd committed the ultimate betrayal: he'd grown up and become a man. He was no longer safe, and that terrified her.

"It's for the best."

Her statement hung starkly between them, forming a chasm that had never been there before, even when time and distance had separated them.

He reached out to touch her cheek, but she cringed and he abandoned the overture. He walked from the room, his wide shoulders filling her vision. As the door closed behind him, she heard, "Sweet dreams, little one."

He hadn't said that to her in years. Not since, as a child, he'd held her in his arms and chased away the demons.

3

The sounds of Daniel's footsteps had not completely faded away when Susan's chin began to tremble.

She shouldn't have sent him away.

But she couldn't let him stay. Not after he'd kissed her.

The memory returned. She'd wanted the embrace to occur. Just once she'd needed to feel a man's arms around her. She'd longed to know what it was like to be kissed. She'd hoped it would be wonderful and awe-inspiring.

Then it had actually happened. With Daniel. And it had been terrifying. Not because he'd hurt her, not because he'd changed, but because he'd left her wanting things she wasn't capable of having. Daniel. Her childhood friend. How was it possible that he could arouse such a storm of emotions with one single kiss?

Her mind conjured up the image of Daniel as clearly as if he stood in front of her. The fear could not be completely dispelled. Daniel had grown so harsh, so fierce, since last she'd seen him. How could a person change so much? How could the years have robbed him of all that had been so familiar to her? She didn't recognize the stranger with long flowing hair and angular features. She didn't recognize the broad shoulders and molded torso. The rigors of his job had taken their toll, wiping away the laughter, the joy.

However, if she was honest with herself, she would admit that life had not changed him so much in the last decade. She had simply refused to believe her own eyes. She'd carried a mental picture of Daniel as an adolescent, and she'd been unwilling to abandon it. Until tonight—when she'd touched him, smelled his rich musky scent, absorbed the deep whiskey texture of his voice—and the evidence of her senses could no longer be refuted.

Her hands shook in delayed reaction, and she tightly clasped them in front of her. At one time she had dared to hope that she could someday have a healthy relationship with a man. But Daniel had nullified that myth with a single kiss. Deep down, she'd always known that Daniel was the only male she could trust enough to unlock her secrets. But instead of assuring her that she could be whole, Daniel had frightened her even more. She might have responded favorably to the old Daniel, but not to the man he'd become. That man scared her. She felt overpowered in his presence. Insignificant. Overwhelmed. Confused.

Time was the true conqueror. Right now Susan felt defeated. Her last hope of being normal had been shattered and had dissipated into blackness.

The chill of the room forced her to move. Unless she lit a fire on the cold grate, the room would prove unbearable throughout the night.

The kindling box next to her bedside table held a

precious cache of crumpled paper, so she went there first. Then, deciding that the room needed whatever cheer she could muster, she reached out to heighten the wick on the lamp.

Her fingers came away sticky. Wet. Frowning, she glanced down to find them coated with a crimson stain. Though a shred of foreboding wafted into her head, it took several minutes for her brain to grasp its meaning.

Blood.

Concern immediately warred with an unaccustomed fear. Susan restlessly searched the room, certain that some other dreadful sight would come leaping to the fore. But her quarters appeared the same as they always had. Small, cramped, and empty.

Dread filled her heart. She'd turned on Daniel, cowered away from him like a frightened bird, then sent him into the cold without even offering him something to eat or a few minutes' rest.

But she hadn't known that he was injured! If she had, she would have . . .

What? His very presence had sucked the air from the room, leaving her shaky and unsure. And when he touched her, she couldn't think.

That wasn't his fault. It was her own. Hers and her stupid, illogical fears. Why couldn't she find a way to control them or banish them completely?

Susan's remorse quickly blossomed into shame. Daniel had needed her help, and she'd failed him. She'd lashed out at him for no more reason than an attack of nerves. Silly, womanish nerves.

She had to find him. He couldn't leave like this! Maybe he'd only pricked his finger, but she had to find him and reassure herself. Most of all she had to smooth the harsh words that had passed between them. He would hold true to his promise never to see her again—that man could be as stubborn as a mule when he wanted to be—and she would never forgive herself if they parted in anger.

Yanking open the door, Susan ran into the dark corridor, searching for his avenue of escape. She thought of logical exits, trying the rear hall and checking each window for clues of tampering. There was no sign of his passage. No matter which way she chose, she found no sign of Daniel Crocker's visit. He could have vanished into the air around them, if not for the streak of blood that stained her skin.

He'd scared her. He'd seen the way the fear had dimmed her usual spirit like extinguishing a kerosene lamp, and there hadn't been anything he could do to stop it.

Daniel propped his back against the concealing corner between the chapel and the cloister. He squeezed his eyes shut, partly because of the thrumming in his side, but mostly because of what he'd done.

He'd seen the way Susan reacted to men a hundred times over the last twenty years. As a child, she'd screamed whenever a male entered a room. By adolescence, she'd learned to control herself, but her aversion to a man's touch and the haunted shadows remained.

Now for the first time she'd been that way with Daniel. By kissing her he'd scared her even more. He'd been lumped into the same pile as every other male. He'd become a threat.

Damn.

Damn, damn, *damn!* Daniel pushed away from the wall and strode through the echoing halls of the academy, intent on retrieving his horse and leaving this place. He'd come with one single goal in mind: to stop her. But he'd failed. He'd behaved like an idiot. He hadn't dissuaded Susan from her purpose; he'd pushed her even deeper into her decision—the wrong decision!

A *nun*. His little Susan a nun! The knowledge burned like a hot brand, filling him with a bitter irritation he'd never known before—more so after experiencing the sweetness of her lips and the softness of her body. He'd never dreamed he would want her the way a man wanted a woman, but now he couldn't seem to banish the idea.

Daniel didn't have anything against nuns or against the church. He and God hadn't exactly been on speaking terms lately, but he had no problems with those who were. Eventually he could probably have reconciled himself to Susan's plans if she had made them for the right reasons. But he knew she was running away.

If only he could get her to see there was so much more to life than the stone confines of Saint Francis. If only she would give herself a little more time.

If. What a useless, stupid word. She wouldn't have anything to do with him now. She wouldn't listen to reason. Anything he said would only drive her farther away from him.

Great bloody hell.

At the end of the hall Daniel eased a heavy oak door open and slipped inside with an accustomed silent ease. The thick plank floors muffled his passage as he closed himself into the tiny bedroom. His entry had been so quiet, he would have bet money that the woman kneeling in prayer had not heard his approach. But when he opened his mouth to speak, she held up a restraining hand and continued, "God bless Sister Mary Catherine, Sister Mary Simon, and our dear reverend mother. Bless Susan, Millie, and Max . . ."

Impatient at the delay, Daniel prepared to leave, but her next words stopped him: "And God bless

Daniel and help him not to make a fool of himself any more than he already has."

Leaning against the wall, Daniel bowed his head and waited, knowing that the woman would say her piece, one way or another. He might as well stay and get the whole thing over with now.

Sister Mary Margaret finished her prayer, crossed herself, then rose to her feet and turned. After taking one look at him she stated, "You've argued."

"It was hard not to. Susan refused to listen to reason."

"Did you try to reason with her, or did you demand that she comply?"

Daniel didn't bother to speak.

"Just as I thought." She sighed and began to unfasten the ties that held her veil in place. "It's my own fault, I suppose. I shouldn't have sent a man to take care of such a delicate situation."

Daniel speared her with an icy glance. "Are you suggesting that I don't have the skill to drum some sense into her thick skull?"

"I'm only suggesting that you sometimes lack . . . tact." She folded the heavy cloth over the edge of the trunk butted next to her bed and nimbly began removing her wimple.

"I'm leaving."

"Of course you are."

"She's determined to go through with this."

"I told you that in the telegram."

"Damn it, Belle!"

She ruefully shook her head, a secret smile toying with the corners of her lips. "Why is it that I can avoid my past for years, and with one careless word you bring it all rushing back?"

"I thought Saint Francis would have drummed the memory of the Starlight Social Club right out of your head."

39

"Some memories can never be dimmed."

Looking at her, Daniel barely recognized the girl he'd known so long ago in Pennsylvania. At nine years of age, Daniel had stumbled into the Starlight Social Club looking for food for his baby sister. To his dismay, he'd discovered the establishment was not a café, but a brothel. But Belle, sweet lonely Belle, had taken him under her wing and helped him to hide in the shed behind the house. Two or three times a day, she'd sneaked food and water and milk to his sister and him, until her mother, the madam of the house, had discovered their clandestine activities and punished Belle for depleting the precious wartime rations. Although Daniel had been forced to take his little sister away, he'd kept in touch with his friend and savior. When Belle's mother sent her to a fancy convent school in Denver, he hadn't forgotten.

She drew the wimple from her head, exposing a face with exquisite bone structure that had grown more beautiful over the last twenty years, a long graceful neck, and black, black hair that had been shorn so close to her head that Daniel could see the gleam of scalp through the baby-fine stubble.

"God, Belle, what have they done to your hair?"

"I would appreciate it tremendously if you would avoid taking the Lord's name in vain."

"Aw, sh—"

"And cursing, too," she interrupted calmly. When he clamped his mouth shut, she inclined her head in silent approval. "Now tell me what happened. Is Susan still determined to take her vows?"

"Stubborn would be more like it. Stubborn, pig-headed, and misguided." He glared accusingly. "*You* did this."

"I?"

"I brought her to you to learn."

"She stayed to teach."

"Then you forced her into this decision."

"And where were *you*, Daniel, when she needed answers?" He remained mulishly silent. "Do you really think so little of me? After what we've been through?"

He shifted uncomfortably.

"I helped you and Annie when you were a little boy. When you ran away from the orphanage years later and followed me to Denver, I hid you here even though I knew it was wrong. I had only just entered the convent, but when you brought Susan to Saint Francis Academy, I watched over her—and continued to do so even after I took my vows. I don't think I deserve your censure."

Some of Daniel's anger drained away, but not all of it. A portion still lingered in his stomach, coiled and ready to flare at the least provocation.

"She doesn't belong here."

"Maybe not, but if you leave now, who's going to stop her?" Her words hung poised in the air like a gauntlet being thrown.

"What am I supposed to do? Sneak into Susan's room night after night?" He clenched his jaw, fighting a betraying grimace when a spasm of pain gripped his abdomen.

"That's hardly necessary when she'll be traveling to Ashton tomorrow morning for the reunion. The seven o'clock train." She delved into the deep pocket of her habit and held out a small envelope. "I've already purchased your ticket."

"I hadn't planned on attending. It won't do any good, anyway. She won't listen to me now." He remembered how he'd left her; she'd been cold and shaking.

"Maybe you should try another method of persuasion. If you attended the celebration, you would have ample time to talk to Susan. Work with her—side by side. Become acquainted with the woman she's become. That's one of the reasons I sent for you. You've been away from her for too long."

He snorted in derision, not wanting to admit to himself or to Belle that she was right.

"She's offered to decorate the house and help with the children. You should have time to talk with her if you volunteer to assist."

Daniel shook his head. "I don't know anything about that kind of work."

Mary Margaret's eyes twinkled. "As I recall, you were always very good with your hands. You may have been fifteen at the time . . ."

He knew she was referring to those weeks he'd spent in Denver after running away from the Reeds and the orphanage. Belle had been a rebellious student at the academy. Filled with defiance against the strictures of the church and the shame of her own background, she had introduced Daniel to a few creative sensual pleasures.

Some of his shock at her statement must have shown on his face, because she chuckled. "I'll let you in on a secret, Daniel. I have mended my ways, but I'm not dead. I remember how things used to be between us, though I'm sure most people would be horrified that a nun could have such a checkered past. Especially with a boy nearly five years her junior."

A flush teased his cheekbones. "What if Susan refuses to change her mind?"

Mary Margaret patted his arm and crossed to the door. "Don't mistake my methods as disapproval of Susan's intentions, Daniel. I think she'd make a fine nun. But this isn't a literary club or a tea meeting. This is a spiritual calling. If Susan isn't comfortable with taking her vows, her service will never give her the fulfillment she deserves. She would be cheating herself. And God."

Daniel stepped into the hall, but before she could close the door, he turned and stroked Mary Margaret's satiny cheek. "Do you ever regret the life you chose?" His eyes flicked to the stubble of her hair.

Mary Margaret glowed with an inner peace. "I only regret not having accepted it sooner."

"And you don't feel . . . stifled?"

"No. Not at all."

And Daniel knew by the passionate fervor of her voice that Belle—Sister Mary Margaret—had never cheated anyone with her decision. Not even God.

4

Cheyenne, Wyoming Territory
January 10

"Well? Where is he?" Jedidiah Kutter rose from behind his battered desk and glared at his new underling who had dared to appear for his first day on the job in a suit—a suit for hell's sake!

"I-I don't know, sir."

The pimply-faced youngster couldn't have been more than nineteen. Kutter suspected that the idiot had run away from home, seeking glamour and fame while his parents wondered what could possibly have happened to turn poor Timmy Libbley away from religion, home, and his mother's cherry pie.

"What do you mean you don't know?" Kutter growled. "I told you to go to his room and wait in the hall until doomsday if necessary."

"But he wasn't there!"

"So what are you doing back here so soon?" Kutter shouted, losing all patience with the boy.

"I-I had the desk clerk let me in. Crocker wasn't there. His things were gone. *All* his things. No one's seen him in a couple of days."

44

"Blast!" Kutter slammed his fist down on the desk, making the chipped enamel cup and a motley assortment of desk supplies dance. "He's not supposed to go anywhere—*anywhere*—without notifying someone." He speared the air with an accusing finger. "Remember that!"

"Y-yes, sir."

"And don't stammer. It shows weakness. Makes people think you've got a yellow liver. If you plan to be a Pinkerton, you can't let anyone see you flustered, got that, boy?"

Timmy Libbley nodded as meekly as a choirboy. It was pitiful. Absolutely pitiful. If Kutter couldn't get Timmy whipped into shape in a week or two, the boy would probably have his fool head shot off by some vengeful, half-crazed grandmother.

That was another reason why Jedidiah had sent for Daniel Crocker. From the time Crocker had been discharged from the cavalry and had come to work for the Pinkertons, he'd been as cool and mean as a block of ice. Kutter wished he had a dozen more like him. If he did, he could have cut his work in half and retired by now. But no, he had a passel of employees like Timmy Libbley. Mealy-mouthed mama's boys who were still wet behind the ears.

"Did they tell you where he went?"

"No, sir. No one saw him leave. He never even bothered to check out of his room."

Kutter squinted at him. "Any signs of foul play?"

"Some blood on the sheets."

"Lots of blood?"

"Just a bit here and there."

Kutter grunted. "Crocker took a knife in his side apprehending Grant Dooley. Let's hope that's all it is and they haven't managed to find him yet."

"Excuse me?"

Kutter snatched a paper from the desk and waved it beneath the boy's chin. "They've escaped!"

"Who, sir?"

"Don't you listen? The Dooleys. The Dooleys! Grant Dooley and his brother Marvin escaped from DeMont Prison before they could be tried. That means every scruffy, no-good, lying, cheating Dooley from here to Saint Louis will be converging on the area." He leaned forward until he stood nose to nose with Libbley. "Know why?"

"N-no, sir."

"Don't stammer!"

Libbley snapped to ramrod attention. "No, sir. I-I mean yes, sir!"

"I'll tell you why," Kutter returned to Timmy's earlier question. "Because we've still got one brother—Baby Floyd Dooley, the stupidest namby-pamby Dooley it will ever be your pleasure to meet. Grant Dooley won't let him hang. Not while that shrew of a woman he calls a mother is prodding him every step of the way. Unfortunately for us, Baby Floyd was apprehended in Nevada, which means we've got to transfer him here to Cheyenne for his trial in two weeks."

"The Dooleys will try to get him first."

"Hell, yes!" Kutter swung away and crossed to the window. Leaning against the splintered frame, he glared outside. "And that's not our only problem. We've got to find Crocker—and fast. The Dooleys have had a vendetta with him for years; they won't let him slip away with just a knife wound this time. They'll spend their time waiting for Baby Floyd's arrival by hunting Crocker down like a rat in a hole. We've got to think of a way to trap the Dooley gang—again—before that happens. Then we can bring Baby Floyd into Cheyenne slick as you please." His lips thinned. "If we could only . . ."

"Use Crocker for bait?" Libbley hesitantly provided when Kutter didn't continue.

Jedidiah Kutter lifted his head. Turned. Stared. Then he began to laugh. A rich, booming laugh that rebounded off the rafters and rattled the windowpanes.

Libbley retreated when the older man advanced, but Jedidiah caught him by the shoulders and shook him in delight, stating, "By dang, we just might make a Pinkerton of you yet!"

5

The train huddled next to the station, belching great plumes of smoke and steam into the bitter January cold. A fresh layer of powder had fallen the evening before. Huge drifts of snow bordered the track, their windswept mounds already dingy with coal dust.

Even so, a breathless excitement hung about the eager travelers. Well-dressed matrons in bustles and plumed bonnets milled with farmers in homespun and work boots. Trunks and carpetbags littered the platform, mixed with canvas sacks and wooden crates.

Susan could barely take in the sights as Sister Mary Margaret, Max, and she plowed through the crowd of passengers. The breeze whipped at the hem of Sister Mary Margaret's veil, causing the edges to flap like the wings of a great bird. Perhaps that was why the other people who had gathered under the awning shifted to allow her to pass—a feminine Moses parting the sea of humanity so that she and her disciples would not miss their train.

They walked quickly. Trailing behind them like a gentle giant, Max carried the trunks of supplies Mary Margaret would take to the convent in Ashton.

Since Sister Mary Margaret had made most of the arrangements for the journey, Susan was content to let the older woman worry about such things as tickets and baggage. Susan concentrated on the thrill of the adventure ahead of her and the box of oatmeal cookies she'd brought for the children at the orphanage.

"Susan, would you be so kind as to stay here with Max and watch my bag while I inquire about the track conditions and our estimated time of arrival?"

"Of course, Sister." Susan took the valise, not surprised in the least to find it relatively light. As she watched Sister Mary Margaret approach the conductor and interrogate him like a general drilling a cadet, Susan thanked heaven that the reverend mother had seen fit to send Sister Mary Margaret as her traveling companion. Susan didn't know what she would have done if she'd been forced to spend the whole day with the dour incommunicative Sister Mary Simon, or the befuddled Sister Mary Catherine. Now the hours spent traversing the three hundred miles to Ashton in the Wyoming Territory didn't seem quite so long.

"Thank you, my dear." Sister Mary Margaret retrieved her bag. "According to the informative Mr. Digby, we should arrive shortly after suppertime, weather permitting." She turned to Max, waiting for him to focus on her and to clear the perpetual cobwebs from his mind. "Max, take the trunk to the rear platform," she stated slowly and succinctly. "Then return here so that you can join us for the train ride."

Max eyed her blankly for a moment, then offered a shy, boyish smile that belied his forty-plus years. "Yes, Sister Mary Margaret. Miss Susan."

Susan watched as he lumbered away. Gentle, sweet Max was what the sisters called "special." Head injuries sustained during the war had caused Max to return to a kind of second childhood. At times he could be as lucid as any man; then his expression would become vague and he would trail people around the academy like a little brother. He doted on Susan with an endearing charm and had been so upset to see her leave the academy, even for a short time, that Sister Mary Margaret had arranged for him to accompany them, take care of their bags, and help her once she arrived at the abbey in Ashton. Since the nuns at the convent were a cloistered order with little or no contact with the outside world, they relied upon Ursalines from other areas to help them exchange supplies and distribute the honey and medicines they made each year.

Susan automatically watched Max's progress, making sure that he placed the trunk in its proper place. Then, straightening, he waved to her with his hat and came back.

Sister Mary Margaret consulted the watch hooked to the metal chatelaine on her cincture. The chatelaine, with its half dozen chains suspended from a bronze clip, held the watch, a tiny pair of scissors, a brass key, a thimble, a needle case, and the minute whistle she used to call the academy students to morning devotions. "Once in Ashton, I will see you safely to the doors of the orphanage. Then Max and I will journey to the nearby convent where I am scheduled to exchange supplies and information." Dropping the timepiece against her long dark skirts, she asked, "Ready?"

"Yes. Yes, I am." Since leaving the academy walls earlier that morning, Susan had been filled with exhilaration. Grabbing the iron handrail, she pulled herself up to the first step leading into the rear car. She had just attained her position when she felt a strange tingling sensation. The hairs at the back of her neck pricked slightly. Glancing over her shoulder, she scanned the crush of people, but the feeling of being watched could not be confirmed.

"Miss Susan? Is something wrong?"

She offered Max a comforting pat on the shoulder. Shaking away the disturbing notion, she selected one of the few empty benches and slid next to the window to make room for Sister Mary Margaret. Max completely filled the bench on the opposite side.

Max peered out of the window with the eagerness of a spaniel. "Where are we going?" he asked for at least the hundredth time.

"Ashton, Max. In Wyoming Territory."

Susan was going home.

Daniel waited until he saw Susan and her companions safely swallowed by the interior of the passenger car. Then, ignoring the stabbing pains shooting into his side, he led his horse toward a boxcar filled with sweet-smelling hay. After securing his sorrel gelding, Chief, and supplying him with a healthy measure of oats, Daniel eased into a mound of straw and tipped his hat over his brow. Settling deeper into the heavy warmth of his huge calf-skin coat, he prayed for sleep to come.

But he found himself thinking of Susan. She was wearing the sober uniform of a novice—severe black dress, black shoes, black cape. Even her hair was completely swathed in the heavy ebony scarf she wore around her head to hide the coils of auburn beneath.

The sight of her had hit him like a mule kick to the gut. Not because the inky garb had drained the color from her pale, delicate features, but because Susan had spent the last few years hiding away from the world he took for granted. Unless he did something soon, it could become a permanent situation.

He willed himself to relax, to sleep. He hadn't decided what he would do once they both arrived in Ashton, but he knew one thing for sure. If Susan wanted to lock herself away from the male sex, so be it. But not before he was sure, damned sure, that he'd wiped the fear from her eyes.

The train made several stops for water and passengers on its way to Wyoming. At each station, Daniel roused himself enough to melt into the crowds of people. He watched Susan and Mary Margaret, glaring at anyone who rudely stared at them or jostled them. Several times Susan turned as if sensing his surveillance, but Daniel had learned too well how to fade into the background.

Only once, when Susan, Mary Margaret, and their beefy bodyguard disappeared into a café did he adjust his tactics. The throbbing in his side and the pounding in his head warned him that he wouldn't stay standing too much longer. He'd just taken his medicine, but so far it hadn't eased the pain; it had only seemed to make him weaker.

Knowing he couldn't withstand the cold in his present condition, he climbed into the rear passenger car. On his way through, he paused at Susan's seat. Seeing the strings of her reticule trailing onto the floor, he frowned at her carelessness and tucked them more firmly into the depths of her carpetbag. In doing so, he dislodged the lid of a box nested carefully on the floor.

Cookies. Oatmeal raisin cookies.

Something inside him warmed, and Daniel tried to attribute it to the medicine and not the fact that, as a child, oatmeal raisin cookies had been his definition of heaven.

Regretfully, he placed the lid back on the box. He took a step away, two, three. He stopped. The siren song of freshly baked cookies held him captive.

He tried to shrug the impulse off. He tried to ignore the sweet scent that lingered in his head.

Then he succumbed.

Looking around him to ensure that he hadn't been noticed, he lifted the cover. The cookies gleamed up at him with a golden warmth. Studying them more carefully this time, Daniel could see they contained a double batch of raisins and were still soft and chewy. Just the way he liked them.

He took two. Then four. Then eight. Then, peeking out the window to ascertain Susan's whereabouts, he snatched the entire box and dodged down the passageway until he'd put several railway cars between Susan and him.

One empty bench remained this far forward. Wincing, Daniel sank into the seat. Though the journey had not yet resumed, the smells rising from the box became irresistible.

Prolonging his anticipation of the pleasure that lay ahead of him, Daniel waited until the train was again under way. Then, deliberating his choices with great care, he took one big raisin-studded delicacy. He inhaled. He broke it in half and appreciated the texture. With the care and patience of a true connoisseur, he bit off one succulent, savory piece. Manna from heaven could not have tasted so good.

For the next few hours he rationed each bite. Over a half dozen cookies kept him company, easing the aches and pains of life as no liquor or drug ever could. And if anyone questioned the sight of a long-haired, pale-cheeked, dangerous-looking man huddled over a cache of cookies like a miser guarding his gold, he never glanced up long enough to find out.

*   *   *

The train was fifty miles from Ashton when the snow began to fall. Not idle drifting flakes but a lashing, sleeting snow driven by gale-force winds. Therefore the passenger cars didn't creak to a stop in front of Ashton's platform until well after midnight.

Exhausted and aching from the long journey, Susan was one of the last people to step from the railway car. When she emerged onto the top step, and found Esther and Donovan Reed standing in the darkness, she felt a sting of tears threatening to fall.

"Susan! Susan, welcome home!"

Essie rushed toward her and clasped Susan close in a welcoming embrace. "I thought your train would never arrive. I nearly popped from the worrying." Her gray eyes glinted with delight. "I'm so glad the sisters allowed you to come home for a few weeks. You haven't had a chance to visit since Sarah's wedding three years ago."

Time hadn't changed Esther Reed. Not really. She still stood tall and slim and proud, her toffee-colored hair shining in the pale light emanating from the station windows. She turned to the man who lingered in the shadows pooled beneath the awning of the station house. His dark brown gaze followed their progress as they tromped through the snow toward him. The possessive gleam in his eye had not abated in the last twenty years.

Essie spoke over Susan's shoulder, issuing orders and welcoming Sister Mary Margaret and Max to Ashton. She insisted that they stay at the orphanage rather than try to reach the convent so late at night. Donovan hunted for their trunks and inquired about Susan's trip. Throughout the bustle and talk, Susan discovered this was the very thing she had been longing to experience for the past few weeks. She'd needed the comforting embrace of a family. In many ways, the Reeds were closer to being her parents than the hazy shadow figures she remembered from her childhood. The only person missing from the reunion was Daniel.

Daniel.

But she probably wouldn't see him again, after the way they'd parted at the academy. Once again she frowned when she thought she was being observed. But the sensation passed as the next few minutes were filled with laughter and exuberant chatter.

Just when the cold began to nip at her toes, Donovan Reed helped Susan, Max, and Sister Mary Margaret into the rear bench seat of a sleigh. He covered Susan's knees with heavy furs and woolen blankets and squeezed her mittened hand saying, "We'll be home in no time at all."

Home. When had such a simple word begun to sound so inviting?

From several yards away Daniel watched the homecoming. He heard Essie's fussing and fretting and Donovan's good-natured complaints about baggage and feminine frippery. He knew that Belle had agreed to spend the night at the orphanage and that she would enjoy coming to the reunion in a few weeks. Most of all, he'd seen the expressions that had flitted over Susan's face: joy, anticipation, relief.

Turning to collect Chief, Daniel knew that he'd made the right decision in following her here. Susan might not know it yet, but she wouldn't be returning to the academy or going to any other convent. In her mind she had already made the decision. Now it was up to him to make sure her heart agreed.

Daniel took his horse into town, boarded it at the livery, then walked the familiar few blocks to the Delta Saloon. At the desk he ordered a room and supper.

The clerk was already well acquainted with Daniel Crocker and was not surprised by the request. Once or twice a month, come rain or shine, this tall, fierce man arrived in Ashton, stayed one night, then disappeared again. The clerk knew Crocker had ties with the orphanage, had even lived there once, but he never stayed at Benton House when he was in town. Rumor had it that Crocker owned some land up Trapper Pass. The clerk didn't know if that was true, but he thought it might be.

Daniel's limbs were trembling as he climbed the staircase and entered the corner room. He set his rifle against the wall and his saddlebags on the floor, then stripped off his coat and shirt. The fresh stain of blood on his bandage made him wince, but he ignored it for now.

A soft tap on the door caused him to grasp his rifle. "Who's there?"

"I've got your supper, Mr. Crocker." The feminine voice sounded as weary as his own.

Daniel opened the door. The old withered woman barely acknowledged him as she handed him the tray.

"Leave it outside when you're done," she said, then retreated down the hall.

In the next hour Daniel picked at his supper. But the pain in his side had increased and his stomach roiled threateningly. So he took his medicine and washed it all down with a shot of whiskey. His stomach balked at the liquor's fire, and he admitted he felt empty inside. Alone.

Though he didn't know why, he suddenly found himself rising from the bed. He donned his clothes, took his saddlebags and his rifle, then collected his horse.

Dawn was still over an hour away when the gelding beneath him snorted and trotted to a stop at the gate in front of the orphanage. Automatically, Daniel took the Winchester from the saddle scabbard and eased to the ground. Grasping the reins, he led Chief into the barn, bedded him for the night, and gave him a measure of oats from Donovan Reed's grain bins. Then, grasping his saddlebags, he decided he would spend the night on one of the settees in the parlor.

The cold air stung his cheeks as he returned to the whitewashed house in the center of the yard. In the darkness he managed to decipher the small sign above the gate: Benton House Memorial Orphanage.

Daniel walked forward. The cold of the iron gate seeped through his gloves, the hinges creaking softly as he passed.

Vainly he tried to restrain the tumbling avalanche of emotions. But try as he might, he couldn't ignore the familiar rush of pleasure . . . and regret. For a few short years he'd been a resident of this orphanage, a part of this world. An older brother to the other children, a self-appointed protector to Susan Hurst.

Daniel climbed the front steps and turned to hold the newel post, his eyes sweeping over the inky wash of blues and blacks that bathed the snowy yard, taking in the barn and the smaller outbuildings.

His shoulders shifted as he recalled memories of those precious few years at Benton House. He'd been a boy here, a carefree boy. But at fifteen he realized he didn't belong. Not really. He'd always been uncomfortable with being loved, and he grew even more uncomfortable when he found himself wanting to love others in return. Hardening his heart and his resolve, Daniel had yearned to become a man—something he couldn't do if he continued to take charity. So Daniel had packed his bags and left Benton House for Denver. But he'd never forgotten the warmth and the love.

Nor had he been able to forget a frightened little

girl who hid in the bushes to avoid her schoolmaster. Or the way she'd watched him leave with wide tear-filled eyes. So he'd returned a few months later, then had taken her to Saint Francis. Even though Belle was only a novice at the time, he'd known she would take care of Susan, just as she'd once taken care of Annie in Pennsylvania.

Annie. It had been years since he'd allowed himself to think of her consciously. Remember her.

Exhaustion gripped his muscles and weighed down his eyelids. All at once he regretted the impulse that had driven him out of his rented room. He couldn't seem to summon enough energy to think straight. If he could find a quiet hole to rest in for an hour or two . . .

Digging under the layers of clothing, he unhooked his watch chain. Dangling from the end was a pair of keys. Choosing one, Daniel let himself into the orphanage.

Immediately he was inundated with familiar smells and impressions—fresh bread and lemon oil, polished wood and sparkling walls. He ran a palm over the rail where he'd taught the other boys to slide down the banister. Prowling the dark halls, he explored the parlor and the kitchen. There he found a half-eaten dried-apple pie. The sight made his mouth water, but he didn't have the strength to do anything about it.

He was about to return to the parlor when he noticed that the door to the hall next to the boys' dormitory room was ajar.

The guest room wasn't occupied.

An idea that couldn't be banished sprouted in Daniel's head. The thought of sleeping in a bed with freshly laundered sheets, hand-quilted covers, and woolen afghans beckoned like an angel's summons. He couldn't resist.

Minutes later he was snuggly cocooned beneath a wealth of quilts, his saddlebags draped over the rocker, his rifle propped against the dresser, his Peacemaker under his pillow.

And the box of cookies hidden safely beneath the bed.

6

Dawn tiptoed forward as the last few stars glittered in the sky like bits of mica embedded in steel. Defiantly ignoring each advancing tick of the clock, the hotels and shacks surrounding the freight yards seemed to grow bawdier, seedier. Daylight clashed with the night. Virtue with vice.

The man who waited in the shadows smiled.

Crocker would die soon.

The thought brought a kind of pleasure he had never imagined. A sweetness coated his tongue like the lingering kiss of fine wine.

Soon, soon.

Noiselessly he climbed the back staircase leading from the kitchen to the upper halls of the Delta Saloon. In his opinion, Daniel Crocker's affection for Ashton had made the Pinkerton agent careless. Crocker had returned to the rear corner room of this establishment with the nesting instinct of a wounded animal, unaware that he would sleep here, then bleed.

Then die. An echo of voices in the stranger's head repeated the words over and over again.

Treading in careful, silent footfalls, he eased down the hall toward the room assigned to Crocker. The narrow passageway was cloaked in long purple fingers that feathered his shape into obscurity until he resembled a hazy shadow rather than a man. With each step his impatience grew. Only a few days remained before Crocker would succumb to the poison coursing through his system. But the time couldn't pass swiftly enough.

He wanted Crocker dead.

Stopping at the door at the end of the hall, he listened intently for any sounds. He'd already bided his time in planning Crocker's demise. Long, endless months. Like a hunter, he'd set his traps, one by one, day by day. It hadn't been easy. Crocker had always been careful. Too careful. Like a wild thing he seemed to sniff out any impending threat.

But the man had woven his web so carefully that the Pinkerton had sensed nothing.

Nothing.

He could hear no noises—no rustling, no grunts, no moans of pain—and his brow creased in confusion. Either Crocker had succumbed to sleep . . . or the arsenic had worked more quickly than anticipated, thinning the man's blood until he bled to death from his wound.

His heart began to pound. A clammy sweat gathered in the hollows of his palms. Glancing down the hall to make sure no one was watching, he rapped on the door.

His years with the Pinkertons had given Crocker the nerves of a mountain goat. The muted tapping should have caused some reaction, a sound.

Nothing.

The stranger's heart rate intensified; the blood rushed

to his extremities, making him tremble with excitement. Indecision bubbled and churned in his brain. He imagined all sorts of pleasing scenes: Crocker delirious from pain or unconscious or lying cold and forgotten.

Throwing caution to the wind, he drew a brass key from his pocket. The key had cost him a rather unimaginative tryst with one of the chambermaids. The cold metal bit into his skin as he inserted it into the lock and released the latch. Then, stealthily, he opened the door.

His first sight of the room reassured him. A rumpled bed. Bloodstained sheets. Satisfaction settled deep, warming him.

Pushing the door open wider, he absorbed the sight of a half-touched plate of food on the dresser, a soiled facecloth, and a corked bottle of whiskey. With each added inch exposed to his gaze, the satisfaction quickly turned to bitter fury.

Slamming the door against the wall, he stormed inside. The room was empty. Empty!

He paced the narrow confines and frantically searched the corners as if disbelieving the evidence of his own eyes. Before he'd finished his circuit, he knew Daniel Crocker was gone.

His fury exploded. Grasping the bottle, he lifted it over his head, blindly aiming at the opposite wall in an effort to vent his frustration. Just in time, he reined in his temper. He couldn't be found here. Not now. Not yet. Not until Crocker had suffered the ultimate defeat.

Slowly he lowered his hand, growing more determined to reach his goal. Crocker would still die. Judging by the amount of blood on the sheets, he was well on his way to Judgment. He merely had to find Daniel in order to finish the job.

Turning, the man left the room and disappeared as

quietly as he'd come. There were people who would help him find his prey. In the meantime . . .

His lips tilted in a cruel smile. The voices crowded into his brain and repeated the same thought over and over again like a worn-out refrain.

Bleed, Crocker. Bleed and die.

7

Accustomed to early mornings and work-filled days, Susan rose at dawn, despite her late arrival. Excitement had made her sleep restless and light. She'd awakened again and again to peek at the black square of the window like a child willing the first kiss of Christmas Day to appear.

Because she would be taking her vows soon, Susan had been granted some time away from the academy to tie up her affairs and bestow on others the last of her worldly goods. In the meantime she would help Essie prepare for the reunion of children who had once lived at Benton House. The event would occur the first week in February.

Not wanting to miss a minute of her stay at Benton House, Susan tugged at the strings of her corset, pulled on two petticoats and a black wool dress, then wound a heavy scarf around her head.

The room she'd been given was the same dormer room she'd used years ago. Essie had thought the time spent at Benton House deserved a special touch. She'd put dried flowers on the dressers and embroidered sheets and pillowcases on the bed.

If she closed her eyes, Susan could nearly believe that the years had melted away, that she was still a child. But a glance in the drawers would eloquently confirm that the bedroom belonged to another pair of girls now. Time could not be dismissed so easily.

Sneaking from the bedroom, Susan eased the door closed behind her, then stole down the familiar hallway. Descending the back staircase, she discovered that she remembered where to step to avoid any betraying squeaks. She emerged in the kitchen where Donovan was stoking the stove in preparation for the day's cooking.

"You're an early riser. Not even the chickens are up yet."

She shrugged and leaned close to kiss him good morning. "Habit." The familiar peck on the cheek came naturally to her. She had indeed progressed since, as a child, she had screamed whenever Donovan entered the room.

"Miss Essie's not up?"

"She's feeding one of the babies in the nursery."

"Do you think she'd mind if I started breakfast?"

"I think she'd be delighted."

Less than a half hour passed before the smell of coffee, bacon, and oatmeal lured most of the children downstairs. They gulped their food, then scrambled outside to complete their chores before returning to gather their schoolwork.

"Lilly? Could you take this tray to Sister Mary Margaret in the guest room for me?"

The teenage girl nodded shyly and grasped the copper server, then crossed toward the rear hall carrying the tea, toast, and butter with such care they could have been made of fragile porcelain.

Susan was a little surprised that Sister Mary Margaret had not yet risen. The woman had always given the impression of having the constitution of an elephant. Susan couldn't remember ever having beaten her to her chores. Still, even a nun suffered from exhaustion now and again.

"Good morning, Susan."

Susan started when Sister Mary Margaret spoke from a spot right behind her shoulder. The nun was immaculately attired and bright-eyed. Judging by the toddler curled into her arms, Susan wasn't the only one who had settled into the orphanage routine.

"I thought you must still be sleeping."

"No, no. I wouldn't dream of missing the best part of the day." She tweaked the child under the chin and spoke to it in nonsense talk, then said, "I've been getting to know the children. This little one woke me quite early, insisting on a story."

"I'd hoped that the guest room would give you some privacy."

"The guest room? No, I slept in the main bedroom with the young girls. I insisted that Mrs. Reed not go to any fuss on my behalf since I would be moving on to the convent soon. Besides I believe the guest room is already occupied."

Susan's brow creased. "Occupied?"

"I'm quite sure I heard snoring when I passed," the nun confided.

"But I'm sure Essie said the room was free . . ." Susan's words trailed away. A niggling warning began to worm its way into her mind. Susan wasn't able to decipher its meaning. Something wasn't quite right. She twisted to peer at the corridor leading into the rear of the house. The guest room was situated behind the kitchen, three doors down.

Strange. First, eight dozen cookies had disappeared—

A scream pierced the quiet of the morning, followed by the unmistakable sound of broken crockery.

Daniel!

Susan didn't know how she knew he was responsible for the scream, but she did.

"What in the world?"

Susan ignored Sister Mary Margaret's gasp of surprise. Hiking her skirts well above her knees, she ran down the hall.

Sure enough, the guest room door was ajar. Susan skidded to a halt. Shy little Lilly stood in the midst of the rubble caused by a dented copper tray, a shattered teapot, cup, and saucer, and a growing puddle of tea. Her expression was comically shocked— mouth open and gaping fishlike for air.

Across the room, propped against the headboard, a sheet barely covering his chest, lay Daniel. He held a monstrous revolver, and judging by his fixed aim, he had been ready to use the weapon.

"Lilly?" Susan eased through the door. When she spoke, she used the same tone one might employ with a frightened toddler. "Lilly, why don't you go back into the kitchen? I'll see to the mess; then Mr. Crocker—Daniel—and I will be right along."

If Lilly found it strange that Susan knew the stranger's name and had suddenly decided to take control of the situation, she showed no sign. She nodded and raced from the room.

Susan waited until the girl's footsteps had faded into the kitchen, then she shut the door and whirled to face Daniel.

"Just what do you think you're doing? Have you lost your mind *completely?*" But her fury died a premature death as soon as she came face to face with her longtime friend. Daniel was really here. He'd followed her to Ashton!

Susan was faced with the first really good look at

Daniel she'd had in daylight for years. He had dropped the revolver and sat with his head flung back to rest against the wall, his eyes closed. Sunlight spilled through the multipaned windows, playing over the arc of his throat and the sloping span of his shoulders. A fine sheen of sweat covered his skin, highlighting the sweeping ridges of his collarbones and the sharp crease that separated the planes of his breast. Two dark masculine nipples gleamed above the washboard ridges of his stomach. His navel rested in a streak of gold-brown hair that arrowed down, down, ever down. . . .

Susan felt the color draining from her face with excruciating clarity. She averted her eyes from the sight of the fabric wrapped low around his hips and one muscular thigh bent free of the covers.

But she knew that ignoring Daniel would not make him go away. Spying his saddlebags and clothing heaped untidily on the floor next to Essie's favorite rocker, she snagged his trousers and a chambray shirt and tossed them in the general direction of the bed.

"Kindly clothe yourself before the rest of the orphans come storming in. Then you can explain why you're here."

Long minutes ticked by in silence. He finally said, "I can't."

Susan planted her hands on her hips and, forgetting herself, glanced at him. After confronting those coin-sized nipples so brazenly naked to her view, she looked away.

"You *will* explain. Whatever possessed you to—"

"I can't . . . dress."

His words halted her tirade.

"I don't think I can stand up. If I could, I'd . . ." He stopped in mid-sentence, gulped, then gurgled, "I think . . . I'm going to be sick."

The choked quality of his voice convinced her he

wasn't lying. After teaching children for several years, Susan had dealt with enough coughing, sniffling, and vomiting to know when the malady was real. She managed to reach the clean ceramic chamber pot and hold it under his chin just as Daniel leaned over the side of the bed, his body shuddering with dry heaves.

She braced the back of his head, tangling her fingers in the golden strands that grew there. Funny, but until this moment, she'd never known how silky his hair could be, how . . . enticing.

Daniel heaved again, causing the muscles of his back and torso to ripple and flex. Susan knew she should commiserate with him, but she couldn't help watching in fascination. Daniel's flesh was pulled so taut over his lean frame that each thrust and parry of bone to muscle could be seen clearly.

Daniel braced himself against the bed. After setting the pot on the floor, Susan grasped his shoulders and helped him to sit upright. The texture of his skin was like nothing she'd ever felt before. Smooth, yet with the supple strength of fine leather. Even when he'd regained his bearings, she couldn't pull away. Bit by bit, she became conscious of the way the heat of his body nearly scalded her own. Frowning in concern, she raised a palm to his forehead. "You're burning up!"

He shook his head. "It will go away. It has to go away. I've been this way for too long already. I have to get better."

Too late Susan remembered the blood she'd found in her room. "How many days have you been this way?"

He shrugged, but the movement lacked the energy and vitality Susan had always associated with Daniel Crocker.

"Seven. Eight."

"Days!" she retorted. "You've had a fever for over a week and you haven't done anything about it?"

"I saw a doctor. There's some medicine in my saddlebags. But it doesn't seem . . . to help."

"That's because you've been gallivanting all over creation, sneaking in and out of buildings, and making me addlepated."

That remark warranted a ghost of a smile.

Susan reached for the pitcher and washbasin on the dresser beside his bed, then chipped away at the ice crystals that had formed on the top and filled the basin with water. After wetting a cloth, she laid it on his forehead.

"Hell's bells! That's cold! What are you trying to do, kill me?"

"No. Although I probably should after all you've put me through." She wiped his cheeks and mouth, rinsed the scrap of fabric, and patted at his neck. But even though she knew he needed relief from the intensity of his fever, she couldn't force herself to go any lower.

Grabbing his wrist, she smacked the cloth into his palm so he could take care of the job himself, then retreated to the relative safety of the window.

"What are you doing here, Daniel?"

Despite his obvious discomfort, his lips lifted in a rueful half-grin. "I've come for the reunion."

"The reunion isn't for weeks yet. You have a job in the meantime—with the Pinktertons, remember?"

He shrugged. "I'm on holiday."

"You can't stay here."

He peeked at her from between his eyelids. "Why?"

"It's . . . unseemly."

"What's unseemly about staying here in the house where I grew up, with more than two dozen other people?"

She folded her arms and frowned at him. "But you haven't come with honest intentions. You've come because of some ulterior motive."

"I wanted to visit with old friends."

"According to the letters I received from Essie, you haven't really visited in years. The children who live here now are strangers to you."

"All the more reason to stay."

"You could sleep at a hotel."

"Maybe I haven't got enough money."

"Don't play innocent with me, Daniel Crocker. You seem to be the favorite subject of correspondence for a half dozen of our old friends. I'm well aware of all the bounty work you've done with the Pinkertons. I should think you'd be richer than Croesus by now."

"I spent it."

"*All* of it? On what?"

He remained stubbornly silent. Wincing, he gripped the muslin sheets. Susan realized she was arguing with a sick man. A sick and *injured* man judging by the bandage she kept seeing as the hem of the bed-clothes shifted.

Forcing herself to study him once again, she inspected Daniel from tip to toe. Much of him was bare to her examination, but she could see nothing physically wrong with him.

Sensing her scrutiny, Daniel tugged the sheet higher. Susan gasped when a bright patch of red began to ooze through the cloth.

"What have you done?" Her words quavered with horror.

He sighed. "Go away, Susan. I'll be fine in a little while. I just need some rest."

"You'll rest yourself right into a grave if you've been bleeding like that for long."

He refused to answer.

Susan didn't know what to do. He had to be tended to as quickly as possible, but if Essie saw him like this, there were bound to be questions. Awkward questions. Yet Susan didn't think she could care for him herself. Not when he was so . . . so . . . naked. At the mere thought, she feared her knees would buckle.

But this was Daniel, *her* Daniel. How many times had he eased a bump or scrape for her? He'd soothed so many aches. Not only the physical ones but the emotional ones as well.

The pallor of his skin decided the issue. If she didn't do something soon, he would pass out and the fever would be that much harder to control.

Pushing her misgivings aside, she opened the door. "Don't let anyone else in until I've returned." Not bothering to wait for a reply, she slipped into the hall. Halfway along the corridor, she met Sister Mary Margaret.

"Sister!"

The baby Sister Mary Margaret held squirmed at Susan's cry, but the nun remained calm. "I thought I'd better see what caused such a commotion."

"Nothing. A visitor. Since Lilly was expecting you to be staying in the guest room, Mr. Crocker . . . startled her, I think." She led Sister Mary Margaret gently but firmly back into the kitchen. "Mr. Crocker is not feeling well, I'm afraid. The cold draft in the guest room has given him the ague. I was going to fetch him something warm to drink."

"Do you need my help?"

"No, no. It will only take a few minutes to steep the tea."

Mary Margaret regarded her curiously. Not for the first time Susan was struck by the older woman's timeless beauty. "Very well. I suppose I should return this young lady to the nursery. Since I am not needed at the convent until tomorrow, Mrs. Reed has kindly invited Max and me to stay another night." Her voice became musical as she spoke to the toddler. "Are you ready for your bath, hmm?"

As soon as Mary Margaret had disappeared, Susan peered into the pantry and retrieved a battered wicker basket from one of the shelves. Esther had served as a nurse during the war, and her storeroom was more adequately stocked than most women's. Susan was relieved to find an abundance of ointments, tinctures, and other medical supplies Essie had gathered over the years.

Returning to Daniel's room, she closed the door behind her. He hadn't moved. He still lay big and broad and half-naked on the bed. She spread a dish towel over the dresser surface and laid out an assortment of bottles as well as a roll of bandages.

"What's that for?" Daniel asked suspiciously.

"You."

8

A murderous scowl spread over Daniel's face. The materials she'd pulled out of the basket looked complete enough to allow her to perform surgery. He wasn't about to have her spread him out on the floor and poke and prod at him with a serrated knife. "What the hell do you plan on doing?"

"I plan on doctoring you."

"I've already seen to that, thank you."

"Evidently not well enough."

He settled back against the pillows. "There's nothing wrong with me that a few hours' sleep won't cure."

"I don't believe you."

"When did you become so bossy?"

Instead of acting insulted, Susan beamed. Her new-found assertiveness was much more admirable than the way she used to react shyly to confrontations or avoid them altogether, but Daniel didn't think that gave her the right to appear so damned smug.

"I've been taking lessons from the sisters. They can be quite . . . persuasive when need be." After taking a stack of folded muslin strips from the basket, she sat on the edge of the bed.

The heat of Daniel's feverish skin sank into her skirts, but she pushed any recognition of the sensation out of her head. She had a job to do. She couldn't let her own insecurities get in the way.

"Let me see your wound," she said, indicating the spot on his side where she believed the blood had come from.

Daniel clutched the covers to his chest. "No."

"You're being childish."

"I'm being smart." When she lifted one brow in inquiry, he continued, "I don't think it's such a good idea for you to do this."

"Whyever not?" But Susan knew what he meant. She could feel the tension pulsing around them. Phantom memories of their intimate embrace hung like gossamer ribbons tickling her nerve endings. She had only to reach out and touch him to satisfy the forbidden curiosity that had welled inside her since their kiss. The seclusion of the room offered a perfect haven. Not a soul would disturb them. She could indulge her wickedness for a few stolen moments and no one would ever have to know.

Daniel groaned. "Go, Susan. Leave," he urged, so softly that the words were almost inaudible. His deep, raspy voice throbbed with a blatant warning. The rich, clear color of his eyes grew cloudy and dark.

"I'm not doing anything wrong."

"Are you convincing me or yourself?" At her stricken look, Daniel relented and teased her wrist with the back of his index finger. "No. You're not doing anything wrong. You won't be struck by lightning for touching me."

Daniel's feather-light caress invaded her senses. She felt drawn to him even as his maleness frightened her. She forced herself to remain still and silent beneath the tender exploration, but uncontrollable tremors began deep in her muscles and spread outward. Her body trembled. She opened her mouth, preparing to offer some half-formed explanation about her chill being caused by the cold hearth and the icy room, but she knew the lie would be useless. He knew what was happening inside her. He *knew*.

He must have guessed the reasons for her reaction because he added, "You saw something in me the other night."

Don't say it, Daniel. Ignore it. Deny that it ever existed and it will go away.

But he didn't stop.

"I frightened you."

No. Not a sound emerged from her throat, but her lips formed the denial.

"I never meant to scare you."

She folded her hands tightly in her lap. "I know." She stood and walked to the window, then stared out into the crisp January morning. Snow lay piled in frozen mounds, obscuring the gentle earth. So cold. So bleak. So barren. Just as Susan had been for so many years.

"I've touched you before, kissed you before."

"Not like that."

"I didn't do anything you didn't want me to do."

"I know. But—"

"You don't have to be afraid of me. I'm the same person who always watched over you."

"No. You're not."

The silence became painful, but she knew he wouldn't let her go without explaining. She forced the words out of her throat. "You aren't a boy anymore."

"We all grow up, Susan."

What could she say? That she didn't want him to get any older? That she wanted to retreat into the safety of their childhood?

Seeking to lighten the conversation, Susan returned to the supplies she'd arranged on the dresser. "Let me see what ails you."

But Daniel wouldn't let the subject pass so quickly. "You grew up, too, Susan."

How was it possible that with a single deliberate statement, he could affect her so deeply?

"Do you know what I see when I look at you?"

She shook her head, unable to speak.

"I remember the little girl who followed me like a shadow. She had carrot-colored braids, grass-green eyes, and a button nose covered with freckles. But now . . ." The harshness of his features eased. "Do you have any idea how beautiful you are?" He added slowly, "That's why I followed you to Ashton. I couldn't let things end between us like that. I had to follow you and make things right."

His admission was startling. Disconcerting. But it was his compliment that piqued her attention. "I'm not beautiful," she insisted. But she wished she were. And she hoped that what he said was true, that he had come after her just because he cared for her in some little way. Then she might know that he was just as deeply affected by her femininity as she was by his masculinity.

"Yes. You are." He leaned forward in emphasis. "Maybe that's why God is tempting you to hide away. Maybe he thinks no earthly man is good enough for you."

"That's absurd."

He continued more passionately, "But your beauty goes deeper, Susan. You're kind and good—inside, where it counts."

"You make me sound like a custard pie."

He eased back against the headboard. "I give up. You never would accept a compliment. Go ahead and think whatever you like."

"Good." Needing to dispel the sober mood that had settled around them far too quickly, Susan took hold of the sheets. "Let's have a look at you."

"No. Go get Essie."

"If I do, you'll have to answer some awkward questions." When he didn't relent, she elaborated. "Such as how you were injured, how you came to be here without anyone knowing, and how you managed to take such poor care of yourself in the first place. Then Essie will fuss and fret, badger you about your job—you know how much she hates the risks you take—and feel guilty about taking time away from overseeing your convalescence to prepare for the reunion."

"Leave the supplies here and I'll bandage the wound."

"Daniel!" She huffed in irritation when he refused to give in. "Drat it all, are you afraid of what I'll see?" As soon as she'd asked the question, she wished the floor would open and swallow her. She had been referring to viewing the seriousness of his wound, not . . . not anything else. But judging by the gleam that entered Daniel's eyes, he'd assumed something entirely different.

"Why, Susan, I never dreamed you thought of me in that way." There was a caution to his teasing, as if he were treading on thin ice by saying anything at all. Susan felt encouraged enough to respond in kind.

"Even if you were worried, there's no need," she plunged on bravely. "I've seen it all before."

His brows rose.

Though she could feel her face flame, she explained, "The other girls and I used to play by the creek. Sometimes we caught sight of you and the other boys swimming."

"Susan, we weren't allowed to swim unless we wore our drawers."

The heat she felt in her cheeks could have singed hair. "I'm not asking you to . . . strip. You can keep your drawers on."

She thought she detected a slight hint of color on his own cheeks, but his response was silky smooth. "I'm not wearing any."

"Oh." The images that rushed into her head nearly pummeled her with their strength. The thought of his being bare to the world except for the bedclothes brought forth a rush of warmth and a chilling awareness. Fire and ice.

He reached for the bandages she'd dropped on the bed. "Let me—"

"No. I told you I'd take care of you, and I will. Just . . . uncover a little." But he was already uncovered quite a bit as it was. More than was proper.

"Susan—"

"I won't go away until you do." Her chin jutted out at a stubborn angle. "You can either humor me or bleed to death while I wait."

He sighed.

"I mean it."

"And damned if I don't believe you," he conceded. It was apparent that even this much of an argument had taxed him. "Fine. Do whatever you want. Sell tickets, but get the peep show over with so I can get up."

"There'll be no getting up yet. Not until you've had a good long sleep. I told Sister Mary Margaret you had the ague. As soon as I've taken care of you, I'll pass the same news on to Essie. She won't need to know the extent of your foolishness, though I'm sure you'll still have to answer to her for sneaking into the house like a thief." Dipping the facecloth in the cool water, she ordered, "Uncover, please."

In those few brief seconds before he moved, she steeled herself for what she might see. But her imagination could never have prepared her properly. As a child, Susan had been so shielded from the male sex that except for the boys at the swimming hole, she had never seen so much as one shoulder exposed.

Right now she was afforded with the sight of more male flesh than she had ever dreamed she would view. Taut, masculine flesh. Daniel could have been carved from marble or bronze, his musculature was so clearly defined.

Just when she felt she couldn't bear seeing another inch of exposed skin, Daniel stopped lowering the sheet, revealing a long, wicked gash that sliced into the spot where his waist butted against his hips.

"What have you done?" she breathed.

"I was whittling, and the knife slipped."

The hard edge of his flippant reply warned her that he wasn't going to tell her the truth. And the pale crisscrossing of faint scars proclaimed that this was not the first time he had been so incapacitated.

The sight of so much maleness, so much blood, caused a wave of nausea. Old and bitter memories crowded into her head, bringing the odors, the visions, of faded horrors.

Swallowing back the rising gorge and fighting the memories, Susan stood and rushed to the dresser to soak the already wet facecloth and to hold her hands in the freezing water, concentrating on the bite of the liquid.

"You should go back into the kitchen."

"No! No. I'm fine." She offered him what she hoped was a dazzling smile. "I wasn't expecting so much . . ."

"Blood?"

"Yes. That's it."

But that wasn't the complete problem. And they both knew it.

Determinedly she returned to the side of the bed. Concentrating on the wound with a vicious intensity, she tried to forget whom she tended. She tried to forget everything but her task.

"This has already been stitched."

"I told you I'd seen a doctor."

"It isn't binding together. When were you hurt?"

"A week or so ago."

She touched the angry skin around the wound, and he hissed, his abdominal muscles contracting. She could see each rippling strand of tissue as it tightened beneath her fingers.

Drawing a tight rein on her thoughts, she turned back to the dresser. "You said you have some medicine?"

"It's in my saddlebags, but it's almost gone."

"I'll find a way to run into town and have the alchemist restock your supply. In the meantime some of the skin is a little too red and inflamed for my liking. You may be developing an infection."

He offered her a thoughtful look. "You appear to know quite a bit about this."

"The sisters have taught me several skills in addition to teaching." She took a jar from the basket and carefully unsnapped the wire hinges that held the ceramic stopper in place. "This will sting."

"I'm sure it will. I've never known any kind of medicine not to."

She placed a folded towel on the bed at his side, then gingerly rested her hand above the wound. Hard, yet tensile. Issuing no further warning, she doused the inflamed area with the pungent liquid.

"Aaagh!" Daniel's hips lifted off the bed, and he grabbed great fistfuls of bedding. "What the—"

"Turpentine," she supplied, knowing what he'd been about to ask.

"Turpentine! Hell and damnation, woman, what are you trying to do to me?"

"Heal you."

"Maim me, you mean. Damn it, you knew it would hurt!"

"I warned you."

"You said it would sting—*sting!* Not eat away at my flesh like the fires of perdition."

Susan didn't dare tell him that he'd only suffered the first step of the process. Quickly she uncapped a squat jar and poured some granules on the afflicted area.

Daniel's face drained of all color. The breath he took rasped in his throat in a surprised half-yelp, half-gasp. He squeezed his eyes tightly shut and all but reared completely from the bed.

"Salt," she said with a smile.

He pried open one eyelid and glared at her in reproach. "You did that on purpose."

"It's the best way to cleanse the wound and stop the bleeding."

He fell weakly against the mattress. "You're enjoying this, aren't you?"

"No . . ." Her lips twitched at his dazed expression. "Well, maybe a little." She retrieved a length of muslin and, after helping him to sit up, swiftly wrapped it around his waist. Then, after tying the ends in a bow as she did for the children at the academy, she gathered her supplies and stowed them in the basket. "I'll be back later with some broth and a cup of tea. Tonight I'll sneak in and bring you a poultice to draw out the rest of the infection."

"What are you planning on putting in that? Ground glass?"

"A handful." At his startled grunt, she laughed out

loud. Having Daniel at her mercy this way was a novel experience. He was always so calm, so cool, so controlled. But today the icy reserve he usually wore had cracked a tiny bit.

"Get some sleep," she urged, her voice gentling. She could have been a mother speaking to a child. Or a woman whispering to her lover.

When she tucked the blankets beneath his chin, it was with a reverence, a tenderness like none she'd ever felt before. As she settled the folds around his chest, her knuckles brushed the winged ridges of his collarbone. Skin as smooth and firm as velvet over steel enticed her, even as a clammy, familiar regret sank into the pit of her stomach.

"Get some sleep, Daniel." Shifting her attention away from the tormenting lines of his shoulders, she tested the heat of his fevered brow. Yet that couldn't explain why she paused to cup his cheek, touch his chin.

He remained still during her explorations. Still and intent and wary.

"Daniel, I . . ." But she didn't finish. She wasn't even sure what she wanted to say. She could only frown beneath the emotions roiling in her, each fighting for supremacy: fear, need, doubt.

Daniel's knuckles lifted to hover at the side of her face. Susan inhaled sharply, willing herself not to flinch and resisting the instinctive urge to recoil. She could touch, but still shied away from being touched. She needed to feel she was in control of the situation and had an avenue of escape if she needed it. But Daniel's caress was so fleeting and tender as he stroked the delicate curve of her jaw that she didn't retreat. It tugged at her heart to see the way he shook with the effort it took to complete the simple task. Next to her chilled flesh, his finger burned. The rough texture of his skin lightly abraded her own.

"Little Susan," he whispered. "You've changed."

"I'm still the same," she insisted, thinking he found something lacking.

"No. You're different. Stronger."

"Not strong enough," she stated regretfully. Then, as if to prove herself wrong, she leaned forward, slowly, hesitantly, eyes wide open.

Her lips grazed his, gently, a mere wisp of pressure. Even so, her pulse began to thunder in her ears. Wrenching away, she gathered the medicines and ran from the room, closing the door behind her.

Daniel stared at the door. A yearning twisted in him. A need. Not so much physical, not so much emotional, but a combination of both. As he lay in silence, he could feel the careful walls he'd erected tremble, crack.

Though his body ached and his mind wanted to escape, he summoned enough energy to lean over the side of the bed and grasp his saddlebags.

Moving with a weariness that sank deeper into his bones each day, he delved inside the bag and withdrew a leather envelope. His thumb rubbed the flap in indecision. Then he opened it and withdrew the stiff daguerreotype.

The three women in the picture were dressed identically in the somber uniforms of Ursuline novices, yet Daniel had no trouble whatsoever finding Susan Hurst. Even as a child she'd been strikingly pretty, with her fiery red hair, deep green eyes, and fragile features. But while the other two women stood tall and proud in the photograph, their lips tilted in secret, peaceful smiles, Susan stared soberly into the camera, her face filled with a wistful entreaty.

When Belle had sent Daniel the picture in care of the Pinkertons a few years earlier, he'd been drawn to the photo in a way that had astounded him. He'd been taken by surprise at how swiftly she'd grown into a woman. But he'd never pursued his attraction. He'd known she wouldn't want a man like him. A man so hardened. So lost.

Even so, he hadn't been able to wipe the photograph from his thoughts. He'd wondered if Susan's hair was still the color of raw carrots and her skin as pale as buttermilk. But most of all he'd wondered if some man would ever manage to banish the fear and draw her away from her self-imposed exile from the world.

Exhaling a careful gust of air, Daniel sank deeper into the pillows, his thumb tracing the sober woman on the right. With a bitter laugh of self-recrimination, he found himself thinking: *No, her hair's the shade of autumn, her skin ivory, her eyes a deep moss green.*

And suddenly, more than anything in the world, he wished *he* could be the man to eradicate the wistful expression and replace it with a woman's fiery desire.

9

"Mr. Kutter! Mr. Kutter, sir! We found him!"

"What the hell are you doing back so soon?" Jedidiah Kutter whirled around from the map he'd been surveying on the back wall. Scowling at the red-haired, freckle-faced Timmy Libbley, he clamped his cigar into his mouth in irritation and snapped, "I thought I put you on a train with Braxton Hill and told you both not to come back until you had some good news?"

"But we found him! We found Daniel Crocker!"

Kutter's jaw dropped, and the cigar almost tumbled from his mouth. "The hell, you say."

"Yes, sir. We went to Ashton, just like you said. We found him there."

"He's gone to his farm?"

"No, sir. He's at the orphanage. Benton House. Turns out there's some kind of reunion for the youngsters who used to live there. I guess he decided to go."

"By damn. By double ding damn." Kutter turned back to his map in excitement. "Do you know what this means, boy?"

"No, sir."

"Come take a look at this."

Surprised at his superior's uncharacteristic expansiveness, Timmy edged forward.

"We need to bring Baby Floyd from Nevada to Salt Lake City, where he'll be held until our men pick him up for the transfer to Cheyenne. Somehow he has to be taken from here"—his stubby finger pointed to the Salt Lake junction—"to here"—he speared the railway hub at Ogden—"to here." Holding his cigar between two gnarled knuckles, he slid an imaginary line across the map to the star that signified the city of Cheyenne. He pounded the map with the side of his fist and let out a whoop. "That's how we'll catch the sons of bitches, I tell you."

Timmy eyed the map, Kutter, and the map again, wondering where he'd missed some important shred of information. He had no idea of what Kutter meant. "Excuse me?"

"Here, boy. Here! Are you blind?" Kutter jabbed at the map with a nail-bitten digit. "Can't you see it?"

Timmy leaned close enough to see that Jedidiah pointed to the city of Ashton, a mere speck on the map and not much to crow about.

"The rail lines. Look at the rail lines!"

Timmy squinted at the hen scratches that marked the route of the Wasatch Territorial. The squiggling trail snaked through the narrow pass that separated the Utah and Wyoming territories, moving through the small town of Ashton and following the jagged path of the creek. But then the lines terminated their eastern route, butting against those of the Humboldt and Western.

"They change at Ashton."

"Well, of course they change at Ashton." Kutter's gray eyes snapped. "Perfect spot for an ambush." He chortled. "At least that's what the Dooleys will think. They won't know that we plan to ambush their ambush." He slapped the map. "We'll squash 'em like bugs in a trap. And those bastards will never know what hit 'em." Grinning, he clamped the cigar between his teeth. "But first we need some bait— something that will encourage the entire Dooley gang, not just a chosen few, to attend our soir-ee. Then we need a spy. Someone to leak the information to the Dooleys."

"But who?" Timmy straightened.

Kutter offered him a guileless smile and waited for the reactions to flash across Timmy's freshly scrubbed face. First surprise, then suspicion, then dawning, then dread.

"Oh, no, sir. I don't think—"

"You don't have to think, boy. You only have to do what I tell you."

"But how am I supposed to find them?"

"Let them find *you*, boy. Let them find *you*! That's the first law of good detective work."

Timmy cringed in dread at the almost gleeful expression on Kutter's face.

Slapping him on the back with the force of a loco-motive, Kutter said, "Welcome aboard the Pinkerton Express, boy. Welcome aboard."

10

Daniel had been ensconced in the guest room for little more than twenty minutes when Esther Reed discovered his whereabouts. The woman had a sixth sense or something, Daniel decided, because she marched through the door, scolded him for stealing into the house without a word of warning, then gave him an exuberant welcoming hug and demanded to see where he'd been wounded.

Susan, who had been hovering in the doorway, merely shrugged. Who could tell how Esther Reed garnered her information? When one of her little chicks had been harmed, she knew it.

Since then he'd been alone only when he insisted on privacy to relieve himself. Each time he awoke from a fitful rest, he found someone by his bedside—either Esther or one of the older girls. Daniel's activities were observed so keenly that he wondered if he'd been thrust back into the military. Essie and her ministering orphans kept tabs on how much rest he had, the amount of broth he refused to eat, and the number of times he asked to use the chamber pot. It was downright embarrassing.

Supper passed, his tray was gathered, and Daniel could tell that the children were beginning to prepare for bed. Earlier he'd heard singing in the parlor, and he'd felt a sliver of envy because Essie would not allow him to attend, but then someone had walked down the hall and propped the door open so that he could at least hear the music.

He must have fallen asleep after that because now, except for an occasional footfall, a murmured voice, and the creak and sigh of the house, silence reigned supreme.

After spending a day in bed recuperating, Daniel found himself wide awake and bored. Just when he was ready for some company, the rest of the orphanage had settled down for the night.

From the far end of the hall, he heard the rustle of petticoats. His pulse beat a little faster. Susan. She hadn't come all day. It had to be Susan.

But the head that peeked around the edge of the door belonged to Sister Mary Margaret. "May I come in?"

"Do whatever you want." Daniel hadn't meant to sound so brusque, but he hadn't expected to experience such keen disappointment, either.

Sister Mary Margaret stepped inside and closed the door behind her with utmost care. "How were the cookies?" she asked when she approached the bed.

"What cookies?"

She made a tsking noise and tucked her hands into the tabard of her habit. "Never lie to a nun, Daniel. We have a great talent for sniffing out the truth."

He glared at her and leaned over the side of the bed, pulling the cardboard box into view. Lifting the lid, he chose two cookies, then restored the cache to its hiding place. "Want one?"

"And become your partner in crime?"

"Light a candle or something."

"Your views on penance are sorely lacking." But she took the cookie nonetheless. After tasting the first bite, she lifted one shapely black brow. "No wonder you haven't been drinking your broth."

"Baby food," Daniel muttered.

"I see. And cookies are more adult?"

"What do you want?"

She chuckled and turned to leave. "I came to tell you that Max and I will be leaving for the convent tomorrow." She opened the door and added, "You have three weeks."

"Susan won't be going back to Saint Francis."

"That remains to be seen." Though her tone remained doubtful, her eyes sparkled. "Good luck."

"Belle!"

The door had nearly closed, but Sister Mary Margaret poked her head through the gap. "Yes?"

"Why do I get the feeling that you wouldn't mind so much if I persuaded Susan to abandon her vows?"

Quite seriously she explained, "You brought me a little hope during the war . . . and later you helped me to see that my background had nothing to do with my worth. You never thought I was trash or assumed that I was doomed to follow in my mother's footsteps." She smiled. "You made me see that my greatest enemy was myself and that my wicked ways were only making me more miserable."

He grimaced. "As I recall, I was an accomplice to those wicked ways."

"Mmm. Even now you could tempt a saint into forgetting all vows of chastity." When his mouth dropped, she chuckled. "But have no fear, Daniel my boy. I am quite happy in my calling and have great faith in your future. After all, the Lord works in mysterious ways. This quandary with Susan may be God's secret means of getting you to church."

His searing curse should have singed her ears, but Sister Mary Margaret merely laughed and shut the door.

Sister Mary Margaret met Esther Reed on her way to Daniel's room. Judging by the medicinal contents of her tray and the determined glint in her gray eyes, Essie was intent on seeing to it that Daniel Crocker healed in minimum time.

Mary Margaret stopped her, wondering if she was overstepping her bounds, but somehow sensing that the slender woman could become her ally. "I don't think you want to go in there."

Esther frowned. "Excuse me?"

Checking behind her to make sure no one lingered nearby, Sister Mary Margaret continued, "Susan is very knowledgeable in the healing arts."

"But—"

"She would benefit a great deal from the practice. And I think Daniel would appreciate her company."

Esther was not a stupid woman. Mary Margaret could see that at once. The slow-dawning pleasure that spread over her features proclaimed the woman's true feelings easily enough.

"You aren't saying that—"

"I think so."

"Daniel and Susan?"

"Yes."

"But they haven't seen each other in years."

"I think that fact is merely serving to enhance the situation."

"Nooo," Essie drawled in disbelief. Her lips lifted in pleasure, and she leaned forward to whisper, "Really?"

"Mmm-hmm."

"And you think the two of them are . . . could . . .''
She made a vague gesture.

"Time will tell."

"But Susan intends to take her vows."

Sister Mary Margaret slipped the last bite of cookie
into her mouth and chewed. "Does she?"

Esther straightened, looked at the closed door to
Daniel's room, then back at Sister Mary Margaret.
"I'm feeling awfully tired."

"You've had a busy day."

"And there are so many preparations for the
reunion."

"You mustn't wear yourself out."

"Susan might be kind enough to finish this task for
me."

"Undoubtedly."

The two women chuckled softly together and crept
back into the kitchen.

Susan tapped lightly on Daniel's door, then entered. Obviously he had not been expecting her,
because he quickly scrambled to pull the covers a
little higher on his chest.

"Miss Essie was busy and asked me to help. Am
I disturbing you?"

"No! No." He pushed himself into a sitting position, wincing as he tried to turn and rearrange the
pillows.

"Here, let me," Susan interrupted quickly. She
placed the tray on the dresser, then bent to pull the
cushions free. Unintentionally, she let her hands skim
over the firm contours of Daniel's back. The warm
friction caused a flurry of sparks to rush through her
veins. Hungrily she absorbed the lean expanse sec-
tioned in half by the slope of his spine. Why, if she

peered down from the proper angle, she could see bare skin all the way to his . . .

Yanking her thoughts back into a more appropriate channel, Susan plumped the pillows with a savage thoroughness, then set them back in place.

Daniel relaxed against the bolster she'd created and sighed in relief. "Thanks."

"Feeling better?"

"Yes. I told you I just needed some sleep."

Susan found that highly doubtful, but didn't comment.

"So what has Essie sent as my latest torture? Gruel? Oatmeal?"

"Actually, she wants you to shave and cut your hair."

"And why is that?"

"She says you look like a hoodlum."

"I am a hoodlum."

"Be that as it may, she doesn't want you to *look* like one."

Daniel smiled and ran his finger down her forearm. "You're getting better at this."

Susan jumped at the unexpected, tormenting caress. "What?" she asked breathlessly.

"Banter. Teasing. I remember a time when you wouldn't answer me unless it was with one syllable. Yes or no. But I suppose you don't recall doing that?"

"No."

At her monosyllabic reply, he chuckled, a dry, rusty sound that came with some difficulty at first, then began to loosen up.

Susan was delighted. She couldn't remember the last time she'd heard Daniel laugh, and judging by his own astonishment, he couldn't either. Returning to the orphanage had been good for them both. The casual, easy atmosphere had allowed them to remember a happier time when being an adult hadn't seemed so difficult.

Susan poured the hot water she'd brought from the kitchen into the basin, then extended a towel and razor to Daniel. "You may as well shave first."

"No."

"What do you mean, no?"

He held out his hands. Despite his day of rest, they still shook. Such large hands. Big and broad and callused. But they could be gentle when they had to be. Or wanted to be.

"If I try to clear a path on my jaw, most likely I'll lay my throat clean open. Tell Essie I'll do it tomorrow. Or the next day."

"I suppose *I* could do it."

He waited a beat of silence before saying, "You could." His voice dropped an octave, stroking some hidden corner deep in her soul.

Susan avoided his keen slate-blue gaze. Idly she touched the supplies she'd arranged on the tray. "Why do you keep looking at me that way?" The question was little more than a whisper.

"I keep wondering about your hair."

Unconsciously she smoothed the heavy wool wrapped around her skull. "My hair?"

"I haven't seen it loose in years."

"I'm not allowed to leave it uncovered."

"Why?"

"A woman's hair is often a reason for vanity."

"You had beautiful hair. Thick and rich and flowing—something to be vain about."

"Don't."

"Don't what?"

"Don't talk like that." She snatched the shaving cup from the tray and beat at the froth inside with renewed fervor.

"They'll cut your hair, Susan."

Whip. Beat. Beat.

"They'll cut it down to a stubble if you take your vows."

She couldn't let him see how his remark pained her. Her hair might not be a source of vanity, but it was *her* hair. She wasn't sure she wouldn't feel naked and exposed without it. "It's easier to take care of that way," she insisted—to him and to herself.

He grasped her elbow. "It would be a crime."

"The only crime here is your appearance. Now shush while I tend to it!"

Needing to stop anything more he might say, she slapped the cream over his face and chin, applying much more than was necessary.

Daniel tried once to speak and earned a mouthful of lather for his trouble. After sputtering and swearing, he snapped his lips shut, leaned back, and contented himself with watching the way the lamplight revealed a flush on her cheeks. He loved to provoke her into blushing. It reminded him that there were still pockets of innocence in the world. Beauty had not been completely eradicated by corruption. Not yet.

Susan carefully stropped the razor, then held it up to the light. "I believe it's probably sharp enough, don't you?" She tested the blade with her thumb, recoiling when it bit into the pad, drawing blood. Susan yelped and stuck the injured digit into her mouth to suck away the crimson beads. Daniel's body reacted immediately. But not with revulsion. With something much more base and primitive. He'd had one glimpse of a pink tongue. Her mouth had opened. Her lips were moist.

Sensing his regard, she drew her thumb free. "Well?"

Daniel felt a thread of suspicion. "Have you ever done this before?"

"Cut myself?"

"Shaved someone."

"I've lived the last fourteen years in a convent. What do you think?"

"Damn it!" Daniel snatched the razor from her hand. "Don't you touch me with anything sharp, you got that?" he ordered. "I've already been skewered once. I'm not in the mood for a repeat performance."

She grinned. The carefree joy of her smile transposed her sober features, making her more beautiful than any woman had a right to be. Especially when she was swathed from head to toe in scratchy black wool.

"Hold the mirror," he demanded brusquely.

"Yes, sir."

She took Donovan's shaving glass from the tray, then sat on the side of the bed. Daniel tried to shift away, but she wriggled across the mattress and nudged her thigh firmly against his own.

"Go on. I'll watch."

And he knew she would. He knew she'd follow each move he made with those big green eyes. He trembled even more—and not from the weakened condition of his limbs.

"Higher. Hold it higher."

While he still had some control left in his body, he began to scrape the four-day stubble from his chin. To his infinite relief, Susan didn't tax his concentration any further. And with the mirror held the way it was, he couldn't see the way she followed each stroke of the blade.

But he knew he'd counted his blessings much too soon.

"Does it hurt?"

The blade nicked the underside of his chin, and he jerked. "Does what hurt?"

"Shaving. It sounds terrible. I can hear your beard scraping the razor as you cut it."

He grabbed the towel slung around his shoulders and dabbed at the nick on his chin. "No, it doesn't hurt."

"But you're bleeding!"

"It's nothing. Honest." He dropped the cloth and began again.

"How many times do you do it?"

"Do . . . what?" Why was it that each time she asked a question, his mind formed a much bawdier interpretation.

"Shave."

He gave the blade to her so that she could rinse it in the warm water. This time, when she returned to sit on the bed, she brought the bowl with her and nestled it in her lap, causing her thigh to push even more tightly against his. For the time being, her delight in his company seemed to have sent the past to the back of her mind. Yet he feared that it would rush back if he dared to touch her.

"How many times, Daniel?"

He pulled his attention back to her earlier question. "Unless my job requires me to appear . . ."

"Scruffy," she supplied.

"Scruffy?"

"Scruffy," she affirmed.

"Unless I need to appear . . . scruffy I shave every morning. Sometimes in the evening as well."

"Why in the evening?"

He opened his mouth, hesitated, then returned to his task. How could he tell Susan that there were times when he wanted to ensure that his beard didn't leave a mark on a pretty woman's skin? "Sometimes it grows a lot faster. When it's sunny."

"Oh."

Daniel managed to finish the job and avoid any

more mishaps. By that time his hands were noticeably shaking from the effort.

As soon as he had removed the last whisker, Susan forcibly took the razor. "I'll finish the job."

She retrieved another cloth from the tray, dipped it in the warm soapy water, then rinsed the lather from his jaw.

"Why, Daniel! You look almost handsome with a clean face."

And it was true. There were men who appeared naked without a beard. And some used their whiskers to hide a weak mouth or skinny lips. But Daniel's jaw was hard and square, with a slight cleft in his chin.

"Now we need to do something about your hair." She immersed her fingers in the golden brown tresses that hung past his shoulders. To her infinite surprise, the strands spilled through her fingers like sunshine. Warm and silky and clean. It was a bit of a shame she had to cut it.

Susan frowned at that idea, but she really did regret having to trim his long hair. Though she had never approved of men who let their appearance run wild, Daniel's "ruffian" looks piqued some latent fascination deep inside her. The long golden waves were slightly pagan, primitive. As if the civilized veneer Daniel wore had been stripped away, revealing the primeval man beneath.

"Susan?"

"Hmm?" She'd been staring. Susan cleared her throat and stood up. Water from the basin she held sloshed onto the floor, but she paid it no heed. What was happening to her? Why was she thinking these inappropriate things?

But how could she avoid such thoughts when the room seemed to be closing in on them both? Memories of other stolen glances, other caresses, kisses, hung like incense in the air.

"Maybe we'd better finish this another time."

"No. No, now is as good a time as any." She surveyed the room as if she'd never seen it. It took a minute to focus on what was actually there.

"This would be easier if you sat somewhere else. I don't want to get hair in your bed." She marched from the room and into the kitchen.

There she leaned against the ladder back of a chair. Curling her fingers tightly around the top slat, she gathered her composure, then returned to the bedroom.

"Here we are!" she proclaimed brightly.

Daniel wasn't interested in the chair she brought with her. He watched her with a cat-eyeing-a-canary look that made her uncomfortable.

"You don't want to be a nun."

She slammed the chair onto the floor with evident pique. "I don't want to have this conversation. Now, are you going to sit here or are you going to spend the evening sleeping in little bits of hair."

Grumbling, he swung his legs to the floor. "Turn around."

Susan paled. She'd forgotten. He didn't wear any drawers.

Her skirts swirled around her ankles in her haste to offer Daniel her back. She heard the rustle of bed-clothes, the shuffling of feet.

"All right. I'm ready."

To Susan's infinite relief, Daniel had wound the linens around him several times and now held the folds securely beneath his arms. Even so, those flat copper nipples were exposed to her view.

Daniel wasn't the only person in the room who had begun to tremble. As she gathered the sewing shears and another towel, Susan wondered how she would survive the next few minutes without dissolving.

Approaching him from behind, she held out the scissors. "Would you hold these, please?"

After he'd taken them, she draped the towel around his neck. Through the cloth, she could feel the taut expanse of skin and muscle.

"I take it you've cropped hair before."

"Yes." But she didn't tell him that she had cut the sisters' hair. There was no skill involved in trimming their tresses as close to the scalp as possible.

"I'll hurry so you won't get cold," she murmured. Though a fire now burned on the hearth, a draft snaked around the window frame and across the floor.

He didn't answer. The chill air wasn't the only thing that sifted tantalizingly between them. A burgeoning intimacy snuggled into the small room, arousing a gamut of unfamiliar emotions. Susan could feel the same tension being emitted from his body that was emanating from her own. But how could such a simple task take on such sensual overtones?

As Susan took the shears and began to cut away the rich golden hair, she wondered what had happened to her strength of will. Her piety. When she had agreed to help Essie, she hadn't thought that the bounds of her endurance would be tested so severely.

Working as quickly as she could, Susan tried to divorce herself from the nature of her task. She snipped and cut, trimmed and evened. And through it all she ignored the heat of his body, the texture of his hair, the sheen of his skin. She didn't allow her gaze to drop and trace the crease of his chest or the molded shape of his breast. She didn't try to analyze the irregular pattern of his breathing.

When the last hair had been cut and combed into place, she stopped.

"Finished?" Daniel shifted, and the towel around his neck shivered, clung, then dropped to the floor.

He bent to retrieve it, and Susan stopped him, saying, "No, I'll get it." Unwittingly, she reached down to keep him from bending. Her hand encountered the naked masculine flesh cradled between his neck and shoulder.

She blanched even as she pressed the golden expanse. But she couldn't draw away. She was melded to the spot.

"Susan?" Her name was a whisper. A promise.

She shifted, rubbing the swell of muscle that ran down his neck to the ridge of his collarbone. Like a blind woman, her exploration filled her senses with sights she had never imagined. Her pulse thrummed. Her heart lurched against her ribs as if in an effort to spring free.

He didn't move beneath her caress, but she could feel the raggedness of his breathing and the irregular beat of his pulse.

Growing bolder, she spread her fingers wide and plunged down, down, until her thumb grazed the nub of his nipple.

Daniel's head arched back. His eyes were closed, though whether in pleasure or in pain she didn't know.

Once, twice, she brushed the sensitive kernel. A heaviness flowed into her limbs, robbing her of the ability to do anything more than feel. *Feel.*

She hadn't felt in so long. So long . . .

Brackish memories swam to the fore.

Mama!

Susan, run, you hear me? Run as fast and as hard as you can. Run!

Daniel's eyes opened. They were filled with age-old masculine desire. They burned into her, awakening a part of her she hadn't believed existed. But with the arousal came a pain like none she'd ever known. It sliced through her body with a piercing swiftness, tearing free years of scar tissue and exposing the ache beneath.

"No." The word bled from her lips. Shuddering, she drew away.

"Susan?"

Daniel tried to control her, but she fought him like a wild thing. The memories came more strongly now, crumbling the blessed mantle of forgetfulness she had struggled to wear for so long. Her sins were laid bare. Her deficiencies hung naked for all the world to see.

Moaning, she tore free and ran to the door. But Daniel caught her, slamming his hand against the wood before she could open it.

"Don't. Don't punish yourself this way."

She tried to free herself. His body pressed her against the door, closing in on her in a way that was threatening and completely male.

"Don't!" He hissed at the pain arcing through his side, but ignored his own discomfort and held her shoulders, turning her to face him. "What you're feeling isn't wrong! It isn't wrong."

Her expression grew tortured. Huge tears hung like diamonds on her lashes, but she refused to let them fall and humiliate her further.

"You make me think things I shouldn't. You make me want things I can't have."

"Why can't you have them?"

She told him sadly, "No one would want someone like me."

When he opened his mouth to refute her statement, she continued, her voice dead. Quiet. "A part of me has been amputated. It's gone. I know it's not there even though I feel its spirit. And a phantom pain." Her chin trembled. "But it's gone. It's gone."

She pushed him away. Not with her body, but with the depth of her withdrawal. Drawing her pride about her like a visible shield, she forced him to take a step back. Then she opened the door, walked into the hall, and disappeared into the blackness. A shadow of a woman being swallowed by shadows.

11

Susan retreated to the darkness of her own room—
yet not her own room. As she closed the door behind
her and studied the familiar arrangement of the bed,
rocker, dresser, and nightstand, she knew that things
had changed. *She* had changed. She wasn't the same
young girl who had left Benton House years ago to
begin her training at Saint Francis Academy.

And she wasn't the same woman who had left Saint
Francis only days ago.

She reached for the black bone buttons that closed
her gown from neck to waist. One by one she slipped
them free.

For the first time in as long as she could remember,
she yearned for the caress of silk or taffeta or faille.
There were times when she thought the black wool
she wore day in, day out, would smother her. She
hated the prickly heat of the fabric in the summer
and the scratchiness in the winter.

Feeling confined, imprisoned, she tore the gown

from her body and threw it carelessly on the floor. Then, taking deep gasping drags of winter-kissed air, she tried to rid herself of the sensation that the walls were closing in on her.

Quickly she stripped the rest of her clothes away until she stood bare and shivering in the cold. Needing to avoid any feeling of confinement, Susan pulled her simplest linen nightdress over her head. Three sizes too big, it hung loose and flowing.

Not bothering to fasten the buttons, she tore the heavy black scarf from her head. *Free.* She had to be free.

Her fingers trembled with her urgency, and she yanked at the tight plaits and coils that were pinned in a thick twist at the nape of her neck. The *ping* of hairpins striking the floor pierced her conscience, reminding her of the pitfalls of vanity, but she didn't care. One by one she unbraided the rich fiery strands. Ferverishly she worked until her hair spilled over her shoulders and down her back in a tangled cape.

"Susan?"

Her name was a stark whisper of sound in the silence. She turned, seeing the way the moonlight streamed through her window and limned the solitary figure in the doorway.

She clutched at the gaping edges of her gown, then found herself rooted to the spot.

Daniel stepped inside, closing the door behind him. He had abandoned the sheet and had put on a minimum of clothing. Though the trousers were fastened, his shirt hung open and unbuttoned. His feet were bare.

Susan couldn't speak. She couldn't move. She stood rooted in tense silence as he walked toward her. At first his gaze clung to her face with such blatant hunger that she could scarcely credit her own interpretation. His eyes then dipped, skimming the fabric of her nightgown now clutched against her breast. Then his stare centered on the auburn waves tumbling wildly about her shoulders.

"Your hair." The two words held the reverence of a prayer. "Look at your hair."

As if drawn by some unseen power, he edged closer until they stood a breath apart. His large callused hands reached out, hesitantly at first. One knuckle slid over a stray curl, then lingered. Next he rubbed a strand between his thumb and forefinger.

"Your hair," he breathed again, more to himself than to her. He cupped her head in both palms, tilting her face so that she couldn't avoid his rapt expression as he savored the texture of the braid-crimped strands.

Something magical spread through Susan's body with each second that passed. He worshiped her. He made her feel special. He made her feel . . .

Whole.

Daniel's hands shifted, and the neckline of Susan's nightdress parted ever so slightly. A masculine nipple grazed her breastbone.

Both of them froze. Susan focused on the firm contours of Daniel's chest. In the firelight, the gilded muscles seemed even broader and more muscular. The smooth expanse was broken by the faint markings of old scars—evidence of his rigorous way of life since he'd left the orphanage.

Susan's eyes widened as she took in Daniel's form. There was something frightening about a man's body. It was so hard and angular, where her own was smooth and curved. Men were so . . .

She squeezed her eyelids shut, trying to block out the past that crowded into her mind, the return of the horror, the fear.

Mama? Mama, I heard you call!

Susan, get back in the cellar!

Mama?

Stay, little girlie. Stay or I'll cut your ma with this knife, see?

Susan! Go back!

"Look at me!"

Daniel's rough whisper brought Susan back from the web of the past. Her lashes flew open, blue eyes met with green. He took her fingers and pried them loose from his waist. With a rush of shame, Susan saw she'd squeezed his side so hard she'd pained him.

Moaning deep in her throat, she tried to jerk free and run from the room. Daniel anticipated her intent and, despite his discomfort, snapped his arms around her waist, holding her fast. Folding her in his arms, he absorbed the brittle quality of her stance and the unintelligible sounds that spilled from her lips.

Susan bucked and squirmed. He wouldn't let her go! He wouldn't let her go! Reality swam in front of her, mingling with the sounds and shapes of her childhood, distorting, twisting, until it wasn't Daniel who held her, but another angrier male.

"Susan. Susan, stop it!"

She felt him shaking her. She gradually focused on Daniel's face, and she grew still, shivering against the cold that crept into the marrow of her bones.

A choked, tortured sound escaped from the tightness of her throat. "Let me go. Please."

Daniel's eyes became dark and inscrutable, filling with an echo of her own pain. His hold abated, but he would not allow her to pull completely away.

When he knew that she would not try to escape, he reached for the buttons of her nightdress. Awkwardly he fastened the disks into their delicately edged holes.

"I won't hurt you. You know that."

But Susan felt differently. Every move he made

affected her, making her doubt herself and her future. She wondered if he knew that he blazed a trail of fire and ice through her frame. Anticipation and fear. Though her body cried out for the sweet absolution of Daniel's caresses, her mind would not free her from the prison of past horrors.

Daniel's fingertips teased the hollow of her throat, and the last button slid into place. A warmth spread from that spot, flowing into her entire being with an inexplicable enticement.

His thumb traced a tempting circle before slipping up to her jaw, skimming her chin, and coming to rest on her lower lip. He lowered his head.

"Just this once," he whispered.

She made a faint murmur of protest, but he paid no attention. He stroked her lip with his thumb, then replaced it with his mouth. His tongue.

Her fists pushed him away in refusal even as her feet took a hesitant step forward. She wanted him to hold her close and ease the pain in her heart. She wanted him to step back and leave her alone. The constant pull in two directions filled her with an unbearable confusion and an unspeakable hunger. She didn't know how much longer she could bear the warring feelings, but the thought of abandoning his touch left her with an even bleaker image.

When the kiss ended, Susan's knees threatened to buckle. The warring emotions grew, blossomed, overpowered her. Memories, dark and dank, crowded the room. Haunting scents filled the air. Phantom screams. Distant thunder.

"No!" Her hand swung out in a purely instinctive reaction. Sobs rose to choke her throat, lying trapped there in a burning ball of fury and regret.

Daniel caught her and twisted her arm behind her back. "I'm not one of those deserters, Susan! I wouldn't hurt you or your family."

She didn't try to deny what he'd read in her face. He knew her too well.

"You're a Pinkerton."

He didn't speak.

Her voice throbbed with barely concealed disgust. "You've killed."

His mouth grew taut and sad. "Yes."

"Those deserters killed my mother. And my father."

"Yes."

"So what makes you any different, Daniel?"

Her accusation hung suspended in the bleak stillness of the room. A self-deprecating pain splintered in Susan's breast. A terrifying remorse. What had she done? Why had she said such a horrible thing? She wished she could retract the words, but it was much too late. With a damning wave of shame, she discovered she'd hurt him deeply. Although the set of his features did not change, she knew she'd hurt him.

"I'm no different." He stepped away.

"No, Daniel, I—" She tried to stop him, but as she grabbed the edge of his shirt, the words died in her throat. The skin beneath her knuckles was naked.

Susan's glance clashed with Daniel's. He watched her intently.

Though the intimate contact caused a flurry of unease, she refused to back away. She forced her hand to uncurl and rest on the indentation of his breastbone. Long minutes stumbled by. Long tension-fraught moments while she concentrated not on the past but on the present. Not on some band of nameless men who had shattered her life but on Daniel.

The tight constriction binding her lungs eased.

The warmth returned.

"No," she whispered again. "No, you're not like

those men. Are you?'' The last was said almost to herself.

Trembling, Susan stepped closer until the folds of her nightgown brushed his thighs. She laced her arms behind his neck and hugged him.

"I'm sorry." She clung to him, her nails digging into the fabric of his shirt. "I'm sorry."

"Shh." The sound was a sigh. A question. A benediction. He held her so tightly that she and Daniel could have been one flesh, one mind.

One heart.

"I'm . . . sorry." She squeezed her eyes closed against the regret that threatened to consume her.

She felt him hesitate. He pressed a kiss into her hair. "Tell me, Susan. Tell me what happened that day."

"No." She shook her head.

"Please."

Susan trembled in his arms. She had never told anyone the whole truth. She couldn't. Not now. Not ever. As a child she had buried the demons deep in her head. Every year she'd added another lock to their tomb. Each time the phantoms strained to break free, she forced them back. She couldn't release them. They hovered in her mind for a purpose. To remind her of all she'd done.

She could never be forgiven.

She could never be absolved.

She could never be restored.

"Help me, Daniel." Susan wasn't sure if she had actually spoken the words aloud, but her heart kept repeating them over and over again. "I don't know what to do. I don't know what"—her chin wobbled, and she gulped air into her lungs to push away the strangling tightness of her chest—"to do."

"Shh. Shhh." Daniel held her trembling frame. "Shhh."

His body offered a sanctuary she craved, but Susan couldn't escape the phantoms of her mind.

Mama. Mama. Mama . . .

"It hurts, Daniel. It hurts."

"Shh."

"I don't want to be this way."

"I know, Susan. I know."

Stroking the length of her hair, Daniel gentled her, soothing the aches that had burrowed so deep into her heart that she hadn't known their extent. He buried his face in the auburn waves of her hair and rocked her back and forth, back and forth.

And suddenly she found herself crying against his chest. Her tears fell on his skin, wetting the hard warmth that pillowed her cheek. The sobs soon became uncontrollable, stripping her of her dignity and her reserve. Her emotions lay naked and vulnerable.

But it didn't matter.

Daniel understood.

12

Timmy Libbley felt like an ass. He staggered from
the Dewdrop Saloon, reeking of whiskey, sweat, and
stale cigar smoke. In the last three days he'd been
jostled, cursed, and ignored.

Breathing deeply of the pre-dawn air, he tried to
clear his nostrils of the stench. But most of the stench
came from Timmy Libbley, so what could a man do?

Despite his exhaustion, he began to jog, then run,
toward the edge of town, where he'd been told to
meet Kutter at the abandoned homestead office
behind the schoolhouse. Knowing Kutter would have
his hide if he didn't, he purposely took a twisting trail
through the alleys to elude anyone who might have
seen him or followed him. Then, with one last peek
over his shoulder, he barreled into the rickety building and slammed the door behind him.

"Well?"

He wasn't surprised that Kutter was waiting for
him.

113

"Grant Dooley wasn't there." Timmy was already tearing off his disguise. He was sure that Kutter had stripped the clothes off some dead sheepherder and let them ferment for a month or two.

"What do you mean he wasn't there?"

Timmy was sure he'd heard this conversation somewhere before. Not bothering to unbutton the shirt, he dragged it over his head and began to unfasten his trousers.

"He wasn't there. He wasn't there, damn it!" He threw the pants to one side and, despite the freezing temperature of the cabin, began working on his union suit. "I stayed for days in that pit of hell, and he never came!"

"He was seen there at the beginning of the week."

"Well, he's not there now."

"Damn it, where could he be?"

"Ashton," Timmy supplied, crossing to the corner of the room where a pail of fresh drinking water waited.

Kutter's eyebrows rose in surprise. *"Ashton?"*

Snatching the bucket from the floor and a washrag from the shelf overhead, Timmy turned with a grin. "Talked to one of the other Dooleys an hour ago. I let loose with the information about the exchange and the dynamite being shipped through town, just like you said. Then Nate Dooley decided to introduce me to some of his family. The Dewdrop is crawling with 'em. They were planning on meeting up with Grant and Marvin in a day or two and skipping for the Mexico border."

"The hell you say."

"I think I managed to dissuade them from leaving right away. I told them that Crocker had gone to Ashton to oversee Floyd's transfer. I also let slip that the Pinkertons would be shipping a crate of dynamite through town the week before. When I left, the

Dooleys were lathering at the mouth. They were planning on amassing a regular Dooley brigade to help their cause." He grinned. "You were right. The promise of a shipment of dynamite only whetted one or two appetites. But the promise of bagging a Pinkerton has them falling all over themselves to get to Ashton. Come the end of the week, I'd say the whole clan will be hidden in the hills around town."

Kutter whooped with glee. "We got 'em! By jiminy, the whole dad-blasted family is about to take the bait!"

Timmy waited until he had Kutter's full attention. "What I want to know is how Grant and Marvin found out about Crocker being in Ashton. I thought you wanted *me* to leak the information."

"Baby Floyd has kept tabs on Crocker for years, kind of a personal vendetta. My guess is that they remembered some of Floyd's old tales and looked for Daniel there when they couldn't find him in Cheyenne." He clapped his hands together in overt delight. "But who cares, boy? As long as the information's been leaked." Kutter reached out to chuck him under the chin, but halted a few feet away. "Whew! You stink like a pigsty."

Timmy glared at him.

Kutter only chuckled. Braving the smell, he grabbed the bucket and upended it over Timmy's head—ice and all.

Timmy bellowed in shock and outrage, but Kutter laughed even harder. "Get yourself washed up, boy. We've got a train—and some Dooleys—to catch."

13

In the crisp winter days that followed, Susan had little time to think back on the night Daniel followed her to her room. While she had the strength to push the memory away during the day, in the dark of her room, before she slept, she often found herself remembering the heat of his skin, the scent of shaving cream and soap, and the unnamed yearnings that felt like the rush of spring after a long hard winter.

Her guilt grew stronger each day, feeding upon itself, until the weight became unbearable. A young unmarried woman was not supposed to entertain a man in her bedchamber—especially when he was partially unclothed and ill and she was one step away from a lifetime with the church.

A lifetime.

Why did her future seem bleaker than before? Why couldn't she tamp down the desires that had increased tenfold? She had thought some time away from the academy would help her decide what to do. But she had merely become more confused than ever.

"You look very pretty, Susan."

Daniel.

The sudden pounding of her heart reminded her that they had not been alone since the night she'd checked his wound. Susan flashed him a shy smile. She meant to deny his compliment, since her black uniform made her feel like an old crow, but found herself saying, "Thank you. I'm going into town. I'll get your medicine refilled while I'm there."

He grimaced at her reminder. Susan was still quite irritated that he had stopped using the morphine powder nearly a week ago and hadn't bothered to tell anyone. She knew he didn't want to worry Esther or make her feel that he didn't value her own ointments and powders. Susan had found him dumping the contents into his commode and coerced him into admitting that he had not followed doctor's orders. He'd complained that the powder made him sicker. She'd insisted that statement couldn't possibly be true. Burying the medicine in her reticule, she had decided that she would have it refilled herself. Then she would force it down Daniel's throat if necessary.

Even so, she couldn't help admitting that Daniel had recovered well enough without the prescribed drug. Except for the way he cupped his side if he rose too quickly, and the twinge of pain that raced over his features if he made a sharp movement, he was nearly recovered. According to Essie, his skin was beginning to knit together nicely. He would probably have a permanent mark from the ordeal, but it would simply be one more to add to the half dozen already there.

"I guess I'd better go," she said finally, when Daniel didn't speak.

"Not yet. I want to give you this," he murmured, and when he smiled, Susan caught a glimpse of the boy Daniel had been. One who used to bring her surprises from the mercantile after he'd been paid for his work at the livery. She couldn't remember the number of times she'd run out to meet him on the road, hoping for his company, only to be offered a stick of peppermint or a horehound drop.

"What?" she breathed.

His free hand lifted in the slight space between them, his fingers uncurling.

Susan gasped in delight upon seeing the delicate gold locket nestled in his palm. "Daniel, it's beautiful! But I can't possibly accept it."

"Please?" The single word was not a demand but a request, shattering any protest she might have offered. "I want you to have it. It belonged to my sister."

His expression was hidden in the shadows of the hall, and yet Susan sensed Daniel's attachment to the locket.

"I never knew you had a sister."

"Thought I'd been hatched from an egg?"

"Well, no, I . . ."

He slipped the necklace into her palm. The action was filled with such sweet hesitancy, such tenderness, that Susan knew he must have cared for his sister very much.

"Annie died before I came to the orphanage." It was the first time Susan had ever heard him offer even the tiniest bit of information about his life prior to coming to Benton House. "Actually the locket belonged to my mother, but when Annie was born, Mama put it around her neck for luck." He firmly folded Susan's fingers around the piece. There was an odd note of farewell in his voice when he said, "I thought you should have it."

Susan stared at their hands. Daniel's were so large and dark and rough.

"Do I remind you a lot of Annie?"

She lifted her head in time to catch the ghostlike smile that hovered on his lips. "Not really." He paused, seeming to think back in time. "But she was sweet. Like you. Keep it," he urged again, then retreated toward the stairs.

"Daniel?"

He stopped. His brow lifted in silent inquiry.

"Will you help me put it on?" she asked softly.

Daniel reluctantly returned to her side. Susan gave him the locket and turned her back. She was acutely aware of his nearness.

The necklace dropped to rest on the tailored lines of her bodice, the gold glinting against the inky cloth. His feather-light touch was gone before she had fully registered the tingling it caused on the sensitive skin of her neck.

"How does it look?" Susan asked, facing him, her chin held high.

"As if it belongs there," Daniel answered, matching her light tone.

"Then that's where it will stay." She rubbed the delicate etchings on the front. "I'll always wear it, no matter what."

Daniel appeared pleased and a little embarrassed by her statement. He backed toward the stairs again. "See you later, then. After you get back."

It wasn't until he disappeared that Susan remembered: once she took her vows she would have to surrender all earthly goods—even a tiny gold locket that had once belonged to a child named Annie.

Susan slapped the reins on the gelding's rump and turned the sleigh onto the path through the pines that would take her into town in half the time it would take by the regular road.

Esther had asked Susan to drive to Ashton to collect supplies for the upcoming festivities. Since her errand would require several stops, Susan had also brought Daniel's vial of white powder to refill at the chemist's.

The sleigh rushed down the wind-carved slope into the valley below. Susan had traversed little more than half the distance to her destination when she discovered she wasn't alone. On the ridge above her four men on horseback stood etched against the dark green-black backdrop of the trees. Giving them little more than a quick glance, Susan encouraged the horse to hurry forward.

"You there!" One man separated himself from the group and galloped over to her.

Susan's fingers curled more tightly around the reins. The gelding, sensing her unease, skittered sideways, tossing its head. The sleigh faltered at the edge of a deep drift, then darted forward again.

Familiar dread swirled in Susan's stomach. She tried to brush aside her nervousness, telling herself that the man who rode toward her was merely one of her old neighbors. But as the figure approached, she knew she was wrong. He was a stranger.

The horseman bent from the saddle to grasp the traces of the sleigh, tugging until the vehicle came to a complete stop. Instinctively Susan shrank against the backrest of her seat. Her eyes flicked from the unkempt rider with his long, matted hair to the three other horsemen on the hill, then back again. The past few years had increased her confidence, but there was still something forbidding about encountering such a rough-looking character so far away from any kind of help.

The man straightened but did not release the bridle of Susan's horse. His gaze swept over her with a casual thoroughness before he dismissed what he'd seen. "Wondered if you could help me."

Susan fought her innate panic and stared pointedly at the man's grip on her horse.

The stranger ignored her silent command and smiled, his lips stretching over stained and chipped teeth. His pale skin was riddled with pockmarks, his features gaunt. "You from around here, ma'am?" Despite his smile, his expression remained cold and unreadable.

Susan forced herself to look at him. She sensed his wary interest, and something more. Something that echoed in the brittle cold of the air. Cautiously she held the butt of the whip that lay hidden beneath the folds of her skirts.

When she didn't speak, he continued, "My friends 'n' me have been on the road for some time. We seem to be lost."

Her pulse had begun to pound at the base of her throat with renewed force, but Susan struggled to remain outwardly calm. If she could only keep her wits . . .

"I hoped you could show us the road to Ashton," the man added.

Susan nodded toward the icy bluff where his companions waited. "Follow the trees west." Her instructions emerged low and tense. "You'll find the road directly past the creek."

Moving as if his joints pained him, the man straightened in his saddle. Just as slowly, he released her horse and tapped the brim of his hat. His gaze roved over her again. "Much obliged."

He pulled the reins to his mount, then paused in apparent indecision. "I hear there are some Pinkertons in town. Know where I can find 'em?" His eyes became hooded. "I've got a little job that needs looking after."

Susan gripped the whip even tighter. "You must be mistaken," she stated firmly. She didn't know why, but she couldn't bring herself to tell him about Daniel's whereabouts. "There are no Pinkertons in town. You could try—"

"Thank you kindly for your help, ma'am."

The man whirled his horse in the snow and galloped back to the other riders waiting on the hillside. Their dark shapes soon melted into the trees.

Susan shivered, releasing her death grip on the whip. Heedless of the distinct bite of the wind, she stayed in the valley for several minutes, allowing the riders a wide berth ahead of her.

From up above, hidden behind a screen of pines, Grant Dooley leaned on the pommel of his saddle and watched the sleigh skimming over the frozen snow.

His brother Marvin studied him consideringly, his face enigmatic and cool. The dark blocks of shade did little to enhance Marvin's flat profile. Since birth, his skull had been oddly shaped, as if someone had pushed the bridge of his nose into the center of his head. "You think she's the girl Floyd thought Crocker was trying to hide in that convent in Colorado?"

"Do you see any other nuns running around town? It's got to be her."

"So what're we going to do?"

"When are the Pinkertons bringing Floyd through?"

"Sunday next."

"That gives us over a week." Grant offered a feral smile, causing the pock-riddled flesh of his cheeks to crinkle and fold. He wanted Crocker dead, and his attempt at stabbing the man had failed. This time he would succeed—and he'd make sure the Pinkerton suffered first. For three years Crocker had dogged the Dooley gang like a bloodhound. He wouldn't rest until the last Dooley was dead or in jail, and Grant didn't intend to give him a chance to reach his goal.

"Let me kill him, Grant." Marvin's eyes gleamed

with malice. His own private war with the man had only intensified since he and Grant had been captured and sent to prison.

"What's the rush?" Grant eyed the last glimpse of the sleigh. "We've got plenty of time for a little fun. I say we drag him through his own patch of hell first."

"How?"

"I say we should have ourselves some fun with that little girl down there. Crocker's a tough bastard, but I think Floyd might be right. He said he snuck into the man's hotel room once and saw a photograph of some nun in his saddlebags. If she's the one, I think we could break Crocker like a twig."

Marvin's features settled into deep lines of disgust. He'd hated Crocker for years. Ever since he'd shot one of his cousins in a shootout in Cheyenne. Grant might have enjoyed toying with Crocker like a cat batting a mouse, but Marvin wanted to slit the Pinkerton's throat without all the fuss. He saw no reason to delay. If he saw his opportunity, he planned to take it. Soon. He wouldn't even blink at going behind Grant's back to do it.

Susan saw neither hide nor hair of the strangers once she arrived in Ashton. The busy streets were crowded with midday congestion: wagons, buggies, and townsfolk. Snow had fallen overnight, lending a crisp freshness to the air and a sparkling cleanliness to the wide store-edged boulevards.

Susan left the sleigh at the livery and, taking Essie's list from her reticule, began her errands, stopping at the alchemist's first.

The tiny brass bell above the door jingled as she walked inside. Susan had not been in Mr. Gibby's establishment for several years, yet the familiar smells of hair tonic and alcohol brought back a rush of childhood memories. She strolled around the room admiring the jewel-colored liquids in the display jars. Who would have thought that tonics, hair oils, and perfumes could make such a wonderful sight? As the sun spilled through the big picture window, they gleamed and twinkled, looking like kaleidoscopic patterns. Or stained glass.

"Good morning, Mr. Gibby."

The roly-poly gentleman who had been stacking supplies behind the counter turned. He gaped at her in astonishment, then beamed, his chubby cheeks flushing to the color of a bright persimmon.

"Susan? Susan!" His belly shook with a huge Saint Nicholas laugh. "You mean you've come all the way from that school in Colorado to attend the reunion?" He clapped his hands together in delight and trundled forward, enclosing her in a meaty, rib-snapping embrace. Then, standing back, he eyed her up and down. "My, don't you look pretty."

Susan doubted it, since she was once again wrapped in her black boots, dress, cape, and scarf. But Mr. Gibby had always been a flatterer.

"I've got some medicine here for Daniel Crocker. You remember Daniel, don't you?"

"Oh, yes."

"The morphine powder was given to him by a doctor in Cheyenne. I wondered if you could refill it for me, please."

"You don't have the prescription?"

"No. Daniel has lost it. Do I need the original paperwork?"

"We'll see what we can do. I'm sure I can determine the proper mixture." Mr. Gibby's chins quivered with excitement. Bending low, he asked, "Is he still working for those Pinkertons?"

"I believe he is taking a . . . vacation. He was wounded on his last assignment."

"No! Wounded?"

"Someone cut his side with a knife."

"Ohhh." Mr. Gibby gasped in horror, then took the vial. He peered at it from beneath scrubby brows. "The label's been torn, but I think I can read enough to get you what you need. I bet it's a basic morphine pain powder. You come back in an hour and I'll have it ready."

"Thank you, Mr. Gibby."

Susan spent the rest of the time gathering Esther's supplies. Nine out of ten shopkeepers recognized her right away—a phenomenon Susan found intriguing. They kept remarking on how happy and vivacious she'd become. As a child, Susan was always referred to as Benton House's "sober" orphan. Perhaps now they no longer found her so sober.

Susan had completed her last stop, retrieving a specially crafted bonnet the milliner had made for Essie, when she felt a tug at her skirts.

"Miss Hurst? Are you Miss Hurst?"

The little boy couldn't have been much more than five or six, but his sweet black face, curly hair, and shoe-button eyes glowed with excitement.

"Yes?"

"I thought you might be. He told me how to find you." He held up the vial that Susan had taken to Mr. Gibby earlier that day. "This is for you. The man paid me a penny to bring it to you, and I did."

Susan took the bottle and dug into the depths of her pocket. "And here's a penny for a job well done."

The boy's eyes widened to the size of saucers. "Thank you!"

"Don't spend it all in one place."

"No, ma'am!"

The boy ran down the boardwalk in the direction of the mercantile. Susan had a strong suspicion that his pockets would soon be filled with penny candy, even if he had to make two stops in order to keep his promise.

She slipped the bottle into her reticule, then frowned. She hadn't given Mr. Gibby any money for the medicine. Why had he sent it to her without letting her pay?

Since Susan didn't want to strain the bounds of Mr. Gibby's goodwill, she hurried back toward the shop. But when she tried the latch, she found it firmly locked.

"Mr. Gibby?" Cupping her hands, she peered through the window. The shop appeared deserted, yet it was far too early for lunch. "Mr. Gibby!" she called again.

No one answered, even though the sign at the door proclaimed that Mr. Gibby was open for business.

Shrugging, Susan stepped away. He'd apparently been called away on an emergency or some important business. She hesitated, rattled the knob again to make sure, then sighed and headed for the livery.

She would come back before the end of the week and pay him. In the meantime she had to hurry home. Daniel needed to take his medicine.

14

Each time she rapped on the door, the bell shivered, issuing a silvered sigh of sound. Inside the shop, he waited, knowing that she would soon leave. He felt torn, wanting to peek around outside to watch her confusion, yet knowing that she mustn't see him. Not until his plan was completed.

Crocker would die.

He heard the sharp echo of her heels striking the weathered planks of the boardwalk. Behind him the poor old alchemist sobbed.

"Hush. Hush." He turned, his lips lifting in a sweet, satisfied smile as he noted the way Mr. Gibby was sprawled on the floor trussed like a Christmas goose, his nose pressed against the splintered floorboards.

"You should have left well enough alone," the man whispered, leaning forward to grasp Gibby's collar and haul him close. "It never pays to be nosy. You should have simply filled the prescription without asking any questions."

Mr. Gibby sobbed again. His eyes rolled like a frightened steed's. But the man who hovered over him displayed no mercy. Mr. Gibby had interfered with the wrong person.

"You found out what was really in the vial, didn't you?"

Mr. Gibby shook his head from side to side, making unintelligible noises behind the barrier of the kerchief stuffed into his mouth and held in place with a length of packing twine.

"Come, Mr. Gibby. There's no need to lie."

He held up the jar Mr. Gibby had been using to fill Daniel Crocker's prescription. The label on the larger container of morphine matched the torn scrap of paper pasted to Crocker's bottle, but the powder inside was yellow, not white.

He slipped the bottle into his pocket. "Just in case," he whispered. Then he collected the box he'd used to top off the vial that was now securely nestled in Susan Hurst's purse.

"Crocker *will* die this time." He smiled. "My original idea was quite clever, don't you agree? Weeks ago Daniel Crocker was wounded. He summoned a doctor, who prescribed a pain-numbing powder. But before Crocker received the medicine, I altered the contents. Instead of morphine, he received a healthy dose of rat poison and table sugar. Just enough arsenic to make him slowly bleed to death."

Mr. Gibby recoiled in fear. The stranger watched him in disdain, then pushed him away and stood. "But I made one fatal mistake. I put all my trust in the arsenic alone. This time I won't be so careless." He stroked his chin in thoughtful delight. "This time I have assembled an army of men who believe in my cause. In little more than a week, they will ride against Daniel Crocker and the rest of the Pinkertons. I've given Crocker a smaller dosage of arsenic this time so that his suspicions won't be aroused—not enough to kill him, but certainly enough to weaken him. When next we meet I'll kill the man myself."

Mr. Gibby closed his eyes, tears of helplessness squeezing from his lashes. The figure snorted in disgust and kicked him in the ribs.

"You shouldn't have meddled," he stated again. In a sudden fit of violence, he took a broom from where it leaned next to the door and aimed it at the jars and concoctions lining the wall. The sharp odors of alcohol, medicine, and perfume filled the air.

"You'll be happier with your Maker, Mr. Gibby. And Daniel Crocker . . . well, he'll be plunged into hell." He struck a match and touched it to the corner of the cardboard box he still held. The colorful logo of a tiny dead rat lying on its side caused the man to laugh. "Imagine. Soon the poison will be coursing through his system—more subtly this time, since I halved the dosage. By midweek Crocker will feel an ache in his belly. Come Sunday next . . . he'll barely have the strength to stand. Then I'll shoot him right between the eyes. What an idea. What a clever, brilliant idea!"

He dropped the flaming box onto the floor and walked back through the front room. Once there, he paused to straighten his vest and run a hand over his hair. Then he reached for the sign hanging from the blind on the front door, turned it around, and went outside, locking the door behind him.

Once on the boardwalk, he glanced back at the building. Deep in the interior an eerie glow had begun to build. As if disturbed by some unseen force, the sign still quivered on its cord. He chuckled when he read the message: "Mr. Gibby regrets to inform you he is no longer open for business."

15

Daniel woke to the muffled noise of childish giggling. Still groggy, he frowned, then blinked. He'd spent most of the previous day helping Donovan Reed clear the barn of animals so the children could sleep in the loft during the reunion. The effort had taken its toll on his strength. Judging by the glaring sunlight pushing through the net curtains, Esther had let him sleep until noon.

The giggling came again, more clearly this time. And something about the sound caused Daniel's lips to twitch with a nostalgic smile. Basking in the texture of fresh sheets next to his skin and the faint scent of hot bread and coffee, he yawned, rolling onto his back and stretching his arms over his head.

The laughter came again.

Daniel stiffened. He felt a tingle of unease, as if he were being observed. Surreptitiously, he gazed around him, but the room was empty and there was little space left unused by the bed, dresser, and nightstand.

Deciding his mind had been playing tricks on him, Daniel settled a little deeper beneath the covers. Ten more minutes. It had been so long since he'd been allowed the luxury of a lazy day in bed. He'd give himself a little more time.

Once again he heard a muffled giggle. And once again Daniel had the distinct impression that he was being watched.

Daniel had trusted his instincts too long to shrug off the feeling a second time. Opening his eyes to a slit, he studied the room more carefully this time. He noted the iron bedstead, the pink and green flowered wallpaper, the crisp net curtains, an old oak dresser, a plain silver-framed mirror . . .

Mirror.

The high-pitched laughter came again.

Peering through half-closed eyelids so he could appear to be sleeping, Daniel saw that the mirror hung crooked. In the wall behind it was a good-sized hole.

He knew he'd caught a peeping Tom in the act of spying when he saw the looking glass swing back into place to the accompaniment of quiet shrieks and squeals.

Stifling a snort of surprise, Daniel scrambled out of bed, wound the quilt around his hips, and raced into the hall, intent on capturing the culprit—or culprits—who were hiding in the adjacent boys' dormitory room. He'd taken only a few steps when a door on the opposite side of the hall opened and Susan stepped out.

The two of them collided with a *whoosh* of surprise. Daniel reached out to steady her, but the quilt threatened to slip below his hips. He scrambled to save it from falling, immediately drawing her attention to the expanse of his chest and stomach.

She stared at him wide-eyed, and Daniel felt the heat of a blush seeping up his body.

"I'm sorry. I didn't know . . . That is, I didn't mean—"

"I can see that." She dug into her purse to remove a medicine vial. "I had this refilled for you."

He grimaced. "I told you I don't need that."

"Take it anyway."

He took the container and slammed back into his room.

Susan regarded the closed door in bemusement—partly from the impact of bumping into Daniel but mostly from Daniel's intriguing blush.

The door to the boys' room squeaked open, and Susan lifted a curious brow when she caught one of the younger girls peering into the hall. As soon as the child caught sight of Susan, she threw the door shut again.

Sensing that the youngsters were up to some kind of shenanigans, Susan decided to confront them. "What in heaven's name is going on in here?" she asked as she entered the room. Staring back at her were six too-innocent orphans in assorted shapes, sizes, and sexes, who sat innocently on the far bed.

"Nothing," one of them answered with a guileless grin.

Knowing she'd get no answers—yet—Susan continued. "Miss Essie wants you dressed in boots, hats, and coats and on your way back to the schoolhouse. As soon as the bell rings for the afternoon dismissal, she needs you back here for chores."

Grumbling and complaining, the children reluctantly filed into the hall. Folding her arms across her chest, Susan followed them as far as the doorway, just managing to catch one boy's whispered demand: "All right, pay up. Penny a peek."

Penny a peek?

Turning, she surveyed the room, wondering what kind of animal had been trapped in a box and was now being displayed like a circus sideshow wonder. As far as she could tell, the room was devoid of anything worthy of a penny's fee.

She was about to leave when she noticed the mussed covers of the bed and the crooked angle of the picture on the wall. Automatically she drew the quilts into line. She was about to straighten the frame when she caught sight of a peephole the size of a quarter. Something on the wall in the guest room covered the opposite side. Frowning, she tugged on the picture. To her surprise, when she pulled the picture down, the obstruction on the other side swung free.

Of all the ingenious little tricks. Those children had been spying on whoever stayed in the guest room since . . . only heaven knew how long.

Susan shrugged her shoulders at the follies of youth. And yet the temptation to look—to take just one peek—sidled into her mind with the artless persuasiveness of a favorite cat. She knew she shouldn't. She knew it was wrong. But she couldn't make herself back away.

Even though she knew the boys' bedroom was now deserted, Susan glanced over her shoulder just to make sure she was alone. Then she pressed her eye to the peephole.

Sweet Mary and all the saints! He was buck naked! Wide shoulders tapered down to slim hips, tight buttocks, muscular thighs.

She blanched and jumped away. But the sight of him—tall, muscular, and proud—was emblazoned on her mind. Fatalistically she knew she had to take one more look.

Once again she peered through the hole. This time it wasn't Daniel's body she saw, but one steel blue eye staring right back at her.

With a squeak of surprise she slammed the picture back into place, hiked up her skirts, and ran from the room.

A low, delighted chuckle followed her into the kitchen.

Once he'd dressed, Daniel retrieved his medicine and shook the prescribed powder into a cup of water. He took one small sip, grimaced, then regarded the bitter liquid.

He didn't feel sick enough to warrant drinking the brew, and he hated the way drugs of any kind clouded his judgment and made him feel weak. Deciding that he'd rather suffer the pain than endure the effects of the medicine, he tucked the vial into his saddlebags. It wouldn't hurt to have a little on hand for some future wound.

As the day wore on, Daniel's services were once again enlisted to help prepare for the reunion. First he helped Donovan assemble the spare bedsteads that had been stored in the attic. Then he cleared some of the furniture from the parlor to make room for dancing. Later the two men took the spare pieces into the barn and hoisted them into the loft.

Daniel worked throughout the afternoon, enjoying the heavenly smells coming from the kitchen. Essie had been baking since dawn while Susan bustled about the house supervising the work and helping the older children decorate the doorjambs and windows with pine boughs, red ribbons, and dried roses and statice. But Susan took great care to avoid any contact with Daniel. A grin spread over his lips when he thought about the reason why. After catching an eyeful, she was probably too embarrassed to face him.

A little after two a rider galloped into the compound searching for Esther Reed.

"Mr. Gibby's place caught fire, and he was burned

real bad," the young man told Esther. "Doc Patterson is up at the Fullertons' and won't be back until dark. We need you to come and help."

After nursing countless wounded during the war, Esther had grown used to being summoned to the town to help during emergencies. She quickly gathered her supplies and mounted the horse Daniel had saddled for her. "See to your own supper. I'll be back as soon as I can. And, Susan, make sure Donovan and the boys finish the list of chores we outlined for today."

Susan nodded, caught Daniel's glance, and flushed. Picking up her skirts, she hurried back into the house.

At five the men and boys were served a quick meal of cold meat and huge hunks of corn bread, augmented by tidbits of sweets and batter as Susan offered them samples, ordering, "Taste this and see if it's got enough molasses. . . . Taste this and see if it needs more spice."

After dinner Daniel noted that a few of the older boys had mysteriously disappeared. Looking at Donovan with a raised brow, he heard the older man murmur, "Grab that rug and meet us in the loft."

Curious about what secret activity was taking place, Daniel grasped the rolled-up floor runner and headed for the loft. The area was crowded with furniture, but he saw no evidence of Donovan or his helpers.

"*Psst!* Over here."

Daniel saw one boy peek around the edge of a breakfront. He set the carpet down and moved toward him. Once he reached the other side, he grinned.

Donovan and three adolescent boys lay sprawled on mattresses. On a dish towel between them lay two loaves of bread, a bag of raisins, a pile of walnuts, and a half dozen pieces of vinegar taffy.

"It's time we took a break from all that feminine nonsense," Donovan stated, his lips tilting mischievously. "Take a seat, Daniel, and cut the cards."

They'd only managed to play a half dozen hands when they heard someone in the barn below. Donovan held his finger to his mouth, motioning for them all to be silent.

"I know you're up there," Susan called.

One of the boys grimaced and threw down his cards.

"Miss Essie left instructions for the chores she wanted you to finish while she's gone."

The men looked at one another consideringly.

"All five of you."

"Damn," Donovan muttered.

"It will be dark in a few hours, and we need more pine boughs and firewood. And someone needs to start mucking out the stables, since the games will be held here."

"Dibs on the pine boughs," one boy challenged, gathering his sizable booty. His friends scrambled to follow.

"Now wait a minute!" Donovan threw down his cards and took his hat. Turning to Daniel he said, "I think that means you're in charge of the stables."

"Me?"

Donovan grinned. "You're the one who's losing." Gathering his own winnings he left Daniel with a measly half dozen raisins and a few pieces of taffy.

"Daniel?"

Susan's soft query stroked his senses like a subtle invitation—and not for mucking out stables.

"Daniel, I can find someone else to help—I know your wound must still pain you. I'll get one of the boys to—"

"I'll be right down." He stuffed his makeshift poker chips into his pockets and climbed down the ladder. As soon as he turned, Susan's face flushed to the color of a ripe tomato. She edged toward the door.

"You're supposed to be recuperating, perhaps it would be better if—"

"I'm not that sick."

"Maybe you should take some medicine first."

"Later."

"Daniel—"

"Later."

As he walked forward, she retreated until her back was pressed against the first stall. When she would have dodged past him, he grabbed her elbow. That single point of contact brought a rush of memories to them both.

"You've been avoiding me."

He noticed the way she couldn't quite bring herself to look at him. "No, I—"

"Yes. And not just today. You haven't really talked to me in some time." He took her other arm and turned her to face him. "Why?"

She touched her hair in a nervous gesture he recognized, but there were no stray strands to brush away. She had savagely combed the tresses and hidden them beneath the black scarf.

"I've been busy."

"Not that busy."

She took a step back. "I've got to go . . . change. I need a work apron."

Reluctantly he released her. "Fine. If you want to hide away from what's happening—"

She whirled in indignation. "I am not hiding!"

He felt a burst of irritation. "Then what do you call it? Damn it, Susan, I'm not any more comfortable with what's happening between us than you are. But something *is* happening."

"No."

"Yes!" He took her face between his palms, and his grip was not entirely gentle. "You feel it, I know you do."

She shook her head in denial.

"Hell and damnation, Susan, passion isn't a sin!"

"It is for a woman who's taken vows against the indulgences of the flesh."

"You haven't taken any vows yet."

"I will."

At her insistent reply, a spark of fury ignited in his gaze. "Why are you so hell-bent on that idea? You won't listen to reason. You won't even allow yourself to *consider* the other side of the issue."

He knew he had struck a nerve because she wrenched free. Her cheeks grew flushed with an emotion that could only have been guilt. The familiar ghost of panic appeared as well. "I have to take my vows, Daniel. I *have* to."

"Why? What sins are you trying to atone for? What in the hell have you done that could be so bad you'd give up your entire life?"

When she would have fled, he grabbed her waist and hauled her close. Before she could escape, he caught her and tipped her head back so that his lips could slant over hers.

She grew still, quiet, then shifted to participate in the intimate contact.

A burst of need centered low in Daniel's loins. She didn't know how her innocence and vulnerability stoked the fires in him even as his common sense begged him to take each step slowly. When her fingers curled over his shoulders and her breasts flattened against his chest, he couldn't think. He could only feel.

Lifting her off the floor, he backed her up to the stall, pressing his hips more firmly against hers. His mouth opened; his tongue sought entrance into her sweetness.

When she refused to part her teeth, he lifted away, ever so slightly. "Please, Susan. Let me taste you."

A broken moan burbled from her throat, but she did as he asked. Savoring each texture, each flavor, he took her mouth in a searing kiss.

Susan wrapped her arms around his neck and clung to him with all her might.

Daniel's hands explored her back, her spine. He memorized each subtle curve. He wallowed in the fresh scent of her skin. Then, when he thought he had broken through the walls she'd erected around her heart and her senses, she froze, so instantly, so completely, that he knew he'd gone one moment too long.

In a split second she became a terrified wildcat, wrenching free of him, her knee barely missing his groin.

"Damn it, Susan, stop it!"

Her glazed eyes were a rich black-green. But this time the fear and panic he saw were coupled with an overwhelming guilt.

Damn it. All her life Susan had been coddled and shielded—and Daniel had been her primary champion. But she had not emerged from her self-imposed isolation as he had hoped. Rather, she had retreated even deeper into her protective cocoon.

Daniel raked his fingers through his hair. He was tired of the way she kept fleeing—not only from him but from the truth. Even now she stood trembling, staring at him as if he'd become some sort of monster. All he'd done was kiss her, for hell's sake!

She wasn't meant to be this way. She'd been born with a passionate spirit. She deserved all the joys and desires inherent in daily living. She wouldn't be happy sequestered in a convent, shut away from life and love.

Advancing, Daniel stabbed the air with an accusing gesture. "If you take your vows, you'll be lying to God and to yourself," he warned. "You want more. Though you might not admit it, you want *more*!"

Susan glared at him, refusing to answer. And Daniel knew there was no response she could give him— without admitting he was right.

This time it was Daniel who turned and walked away.

16

How dare he! *How dare he!*

Susan marched to the stable door with the intent
of finding Daniel and giving him a piece of her mind.
But she had taken only a few steps when she stopped.

What could she say? He was right.

She did want more.

Guilt rode hard upon that thought. How had she
allowed her devotion to flag? When had she abandoned the precepts of God for the precepts of men,
or the precepts of one man—Daniel?

Doubt warred with responsibility, responsibility
with self-recrimination. She rushed to the back of the
barn and saddled one of the mares. Not bothering to
adjust the stirrups, she swung onto its back and galloped the animal into the snow, skirting the well-tram-
meled areas for the deep powder of the valley and
the huge stands of pine.

Daniel had been standing in the kitchen, peering
out the window to see how long it would take Susan

to follow him and admit that she had come to her senses. But she didn't confront him with her temper aflame. She didn't return at all. The minute he saw her racing out of the stables he knew he'd once again made a mistake.

Damn. When would he learn that he would never figure that woman out. He should just leave things well enough alone?

Ducking into his room, he collected his rifle and calfskin coat. Then, remembering that Susan had ridden away with little more than a sweater over her shoulders, he made a quick stop at her room, where he snatched her voluminous black cape from the back of the rocker. Still swearing under his breath, he hurried after her, hoping she hadn't gone so far or so fast that it would take him the rest of the afternoon to find her.

Susan didn't know where she was going until she arrived. Her horse trembled and snorted beneath her as she drew back on the reins and came to a stop in front of the high stone walls surrounding the convent of the Immaculate Heart.

She had returned to the arms of the church, where she had always felt comfortable and secure. The building itself didn't matter so much as the people inside. The sisters accepted her despite her deficiencies and never ceased to care for her welfare.

Susan slid from the saddle and, lifting her skirts free from the drifts, slipped and slid toward the front gate. She tugged on the chain that would summon one of the nuns.

Susan heard the rustle of skirts on the icy inner courtyard long before a cloaked figure appeared to answer her summons.

"Yes?"

"I've come to see Sister Mary Margaret."

It wasn't until the words fell from her lips that Susan remembered this was a cloistered order. Except for infrequent interaction with the Ursulines, these nuns rarely had contact with outsiders.

Either Susan's uniform or her desperate expression eased the woman's qualms, and she inclined her head and bade Susan come inside.

The iron gate squealed shut in harsh protest, testifying that very few people were allowed to enter, and even fewer left again once they'd come inside. Susan watched the solid metal shiver until it lay quiet next to its frame. She belonged here. It was her *duty* to stay. She couldn't allow Daniel's sweet temptation to draw her away from her original course. But a heavy pressure squeezed her heart and she experienced an overpowering urge to throw herself at the spiked bars of the gate and shake them until they opened and allowed her to escape into the sun and snow-drenched field beyond.

The sweetly smiling sister was waiting for her to follow, and Susan hurried across the compound. No words were spoken. The nun led her into the arched sandstone entrance of the cloister and through the thick double doors. Their wet shoes scuffed on the stone as they walked down the corridor.

With each step, Susan was plunged back into the world that had enfolded her in its gentle wings so long ago. Automatically, her footsteps lost their hasty gait. She pushed her shoulders back and adopted the regal posture she had admired in the nuns at the academy. She folded her arms, slipping her hands into the deep cuffs of her bodice.

She *belonged* here.

Didn't she?

She wasn't sure what she would say when she saw Mary Margaret. She didn't know why she'd come. To confess? To reaffirm her devotion? To hide?

The guilt grew stronger, more bitter. She shouldn't have come here until she had made peace with herself and with God. She knew that the doubts and feelings churning inside her would disappear once Daniel abandoned her again and she returned to the academy.

If she returned, a tiny voice taunted.

"Here we are." The nun's voice was little more than a breath of sound. "Please wait here and I'll tell her you've come."

The woman disappeared behind the heavy oak door, and Susan was left to wait in the hall like a penitent child summoned to face the headmaster. But she hadn't done anything wrong, had she?

Yes. She had. She had succumbed to the pleasures of the flesh. She had taken joy in the arms of a man. She had learned to care so deeply for Daniel that she couldn't imagine a day without him. She couldn't imagine years spent locked inside the walls of a convent.

Her heart continued its thunderous beat. She wanted to run outside and fill her lungs with a huge gulp of air. She wanted to hide inside the cloister in shame.

"She'll see you now."

Susan started. She had not even been aware that the tiny nun had returned.

"Thank you."

Hesitantly she stepped into a simple wood and stone cell. Except for a plain bed and a crucifix, the room was devoid of decoration. Susan had forgotten how bare a nun's quarters could be.

The door closed behind her, and Susan stood in indecision when she saw that Sister Mary Margaret knelt on the floor praying. But the other woman must have sensed her presence, because she crossed herself and rose to her feet.

A welcoming smile spread over her features. "I thought you would be the one who had come to visit me." Her eyes twinkled. "Daniel would not have done anything quite so conventional as announcing himself at the gate."

"Daniel?" As far as Susan could remember, Sister Mary Margaret and Daniel had met only once at Susan's graduation. Susan had sensed a rapport between the two at the time, but she had never thought Sister Mary Margaret would remember him years later.

"Never mind. Tell me why you've come. The reunion is about two weeks away, isn't it?"

Susan nodded. "Yes. I think preparations are going quite well. There's to be a huge celebration. I've been helping to decorate the barn for the children's games. And I've baked refreshments and . . ." Her words trailed away. This wasn't why she had come. But she didn't know quite what to say or do, especially since Mary Margaret always managed to strip through any kind of pretense. But how could she seek reassurance about her calling to the church when she wasn't quite sure that was what she wanted anymore?

Sister Mary Margaret patted the edge of the bed. "Tell me what has you so upset."

Susan sank onto the mattress, then bolted and crossed to the window, where she stared out at the courtyard and the play of blue and black shadows on stone and snow. Colors in the convent were muted because of the high wall that kept out a good deal of the sunshine. Yet, she couldn't deny the peace. The solitude.

But how much longer would she allow herself to feel trapped. . . .

Trapped? Was that how she saw her future in the convent—as a *trap*? If so, she wasn't serving God, she was hiding—just as Daniel had accused her of doing.

But she was meant to stay with the church. All her

life, she'd known she would have to serve God. There were debts that needed to be paid. She'd been content with her lot.

Until Daniel had stormed back into her life.

"What is it you wanted, Susan?"

"I just . . ." She rubbed the frigid pane of glass. She knew Sister Mary Margaret watched her keenly, but she still didn't know what to say.

"Tell me. I think you'll feel better."

When Susan didn't speak, Mary Margaret sighed and motioned for her to kneel beside the bed. Susan approached and sank to her knees on the hard stone.

"He can be very persuasive, can't he?"

"Who?"

"Daniel." Mary Margaret tipped Susan's chin up to the light. "Well, my dear, tell me what he's done to make you feel so confused, so unhappy, and so terribly alive."

"Alive?" Susan whispered.

Alive.

The revelation came to her quietly, not as a blare of trumpets or a burning bush. A part of her, deep inside, crumbled and dissolved. The guilt began to sift through her veins like fine sand until she was left feeling weightless and enervated. Gazing up at Sister Mary Margaret, Susan felt as if a heavy veil had been lifted from her sight. All at once she became conscious of the beauty of the woman in front of her, the rich shadows and light that played across the room, the diamondlike glint of the sun on the windowpanes.

How many years had she deluded herself into thinking this was her calling? Looking back now, she saw how much she'd cheated the order. She hadn't performed her duties out of love and joy; she'd completed them much the way a child reluctantly finished a dreaded chore. She had forgotten that life should include pleasure as well as pain.

She *didn't* belong here. She didn't.

Mary Margaret chafed Susan's chilled skin. "You won't be returning with me." It was not a question.

Susan opened her mouth to demur, but she knew she couldn't lie. "No." Saying the word seemed to lift her spirits. She wanted to confess everything that had happened in the last two weeks, but she couldn't speak to a nun about warm flesh, moist kisses, and a man's strong arms? How could she possibly explain to Sister Mary Margaret that she wanted to leave the order in exchange for the pleasures of the flesh?

"He's a fantastic man," Sister Mary Margaret prompted when Susan didn't speak.

"Yes."

"And he makes you feel . . ."

"Wonderful." The word burst from her lips, and Susan could no longer contain her eagerness. "He cares for me, Sister, I know he does. He's made me happy. When I'm with him, I don't think about anything but how much I love his company. When he leaves, all I wonder is when I'll see him again. And when he kisses me—" she broke off. The woman she was talking to was a *nun*. But Sister Mary Margaret smiled encouragingly. "When he kisses me, I feel as if I could conquer the world single-handedly."

"And you can."

"No." The panic rose as brackish memories threatened to overwhelm her. "No, I can't." Wrapping her arms around Sister Mary Margaret's knees, she hid her face in the folds of her skirts. Her exhilaration turned to dust in her veins. "I can't leave the order. I can't. God would punish me if I did."

Daniel's mount galloped into the valley, easily trailing the path of churned up snow leading away from the orphanage. The foothills of the mountains closed in, enshrouding him in a wintery silence until even the heavy breathing of his horse became an intrusion.

What in the world was Susan thinking, disappearing into the wilderness this way without so much as a by-your-leave? At the very least she should have told someone where she was going—should have told *him* where she was going.

But as Chief eased his pace and picked his way over a slippery frozen streambed, Daniel knew that Susan didn't owe him anything, especially since it had been Daniel's impatience that had driven her over the edge.

Why couldn't he learn to restrain his brutish instincts? Why couldn't he learn more tolerance, more diplomacy? More compassion?

Because he didn't deserve someone like her. He had surrendered any claim to a woman of her ilk long ago. His job had thrown him into a world of killers and desperate men. Although he worked for the right side of the law, Daniel had become more like the men he tracked than he cared to admit.

His horse had clambered up the steep embankment when a sharp sliver of warning seeped into his bones. He had been so involved in his thoughts that he hadn't paid much attention to his surroundings. No woman had ever managed to blunt his instinct for survival. Until now.

When he emerged into a clearing and a horseman rode toward him, he saw the extent of his folly. Soon another rider came into view a few degrees to the left, another to the right. The way they closed in on him left no doubt that they meant to stop him.

A sick feeling of dread settled into his stomach. If these men had encountered *him* so easily, they'd seen Susan as well. It wouldn't take a genius to conclude that he'd been following her.

Anger burned white-hot inside him. He whirled Chief in the snow, hoping to create confusion and draw the men away from Susan's path. To his horror, he found another half-dozen horsemen behind him.

The rifle slid effortlessly into his hand and he hunkered low over the horse's neck, castigating himself for letting a few days in a woman's company weaken him so completely.

"Crocker!" The name was followed by a shrill whistle. The circle of antagonists halted at least fifty yards away—far enough to make their winter-clad shapes indiscernible, but near enough to make Daniel an easy target.

With a keen eye developed over years of such encounters, Daniel picked out the leader of the band and raised his rifle.

"Shit, Daniel, can't you tell one of your own kind when you have to?"

The gravelly voice, coupled with the way the figure dived to one side and hugged the neck of his mount to avoid being shot, pierced the haze of anger clouding Daniel's judgment. His finger paused on the trigger. The tension began to drain away as quickly as it had come.

"Braxton, you bastard! What the hell are you and your men doing sneaking up on me like a herd of no-accounts?"

Seeing that Daniel had lowered his rifle, the Pinkerton eased upright, drawing his hat from his head to swipe away the sweat beading his brow. "Sneak! *Sneak?* A herd of buffalo could've tromped all over you without you payin' them any mind." Signaling to the other men, Braxton closed the circle.

Daniel regarded the toothless, scrawny man with something akin to pleasure. He'd worked on and off with Braxton Hill and most of the other men for the past decade. A strange bond had formed between them, one that went beyond friendship and yet held a curious emotional distance in case one of them should die in the line of duty.

Braxton chortled. "I saw the little filly you was chasin', Daniel—and I ain't talkin' 'bout the horse. Can't blame you if'n you got things on your mind."

A familiar possessiveness took hold of Daniel, but Braxton wasn't finished. "Got a message for you from Kutter. He wants to see you. Now."

"Kutter?" Daniel's brow creased, and he scanned the faces of the men present; they were the cream of the crop from a half-dozen western territories. "What the hell is going on?"

The men eyed one another uneasily, but none of them volunteered to speak.

"He's waitin' in that shack up Munster Fork we used last year," Braxton continued as if Daniel hadn't spoken. "We'd be happy to take you there."

Daniel scowled at them all. "I'm on vacation."

Braxton considered that point, shifted the tobacco he chewed to the other cheek, then spit on the ground. "Maybe you is and maybe you isn't," he muttered cryptically. "Make sure you see Kutter 'fore too long. I got no belly for his complainin' and groanin'." He leaned close to say confidentially, "An' I got no time to ferret you out at the orphanage so's you can keep your personal business . . . personal."

Snickering at his own verbal cleverness, he saluted Daniel with two fingers. "All right, men, head 'em up an' out. We got a thing or two t' do yet 'fore the sun sets."

The Pinkertons cantered away, leaving only the pitted snow and an eerie sense of unease.

The abrupt winter silence settled around Daniel as he thought of years of duty, a weariness for his rootless life. As the time ticked by, he acknowledged that

Susan was not the only one who had gradually lowered her barriers. Daniel had been so concerned about *her* feelings, *her* fears, that he hadn't admitted to himself that she'd punctured a few of his own.

The rifle slid from his numbed fingers back into the scabbard at his side. But it wasn't the cold January weather that held him in its strength-robbing grip. It was a strange, overpowering fear. Somehow he had allowed himself to need.

Squinting against the ebbing glare of sun on snow, he tried to ignore the panic. His feelings for Susan were becoming too strong, too intense, and he feared their outcome. Nothing could ever happen between them. Though he longed to possess her, she wasn't a woman to be kept like a bauble in a box and retrieved whenever he felt the urge. She was more like a flower that would need constant attention and care. She deserved a real home and a real husband.

The longing to provide that for her struck him with the power of a fist to his stomach. For one flashing instant, he considered hanging up his hat and becoming a normal man with a normal occupation. He could marry her, install her in his house up Trapper Pass, build a life for them. They could have chickens and milk cows and ducks. He could carry water for her, and she could cook for him.

But that kind of life was an illusion, a pipe dream. He didn't know if he could ever make it happen. He'd been involved with the Pinkertons too many years to untangle himself that easily. He didn't know if he could content himself with such a tame way of life, and he knew Susan couldn't survive in his harsh world. She would wither and die as surely as a daisy in winter.

Regret overwhelmed him. Their stolen embraces invaded his senses like fine wine. What had he done? To her and to himself? He had awakened Susan to a world of sensual pleasures and had removed her naive belief that entering a convent would wash away her problems. In doing so, he had failed to look at the future. He was too firmly entrenched in his ways to change. And his world held no place for a woman of her innocence.

Susan wasn't meant to live alone. She would find someone else eventually. And Daniel didn't think he could survive it when she did.

Nudging his horse in the flanks, he resumed his pace. Perhaps he should have left well enough alone. If Susan did enter a convent, she would be out of his reach.

But no one else could have her, either.

Sister Mary Margaret ran her hand over the top of Susan's head, calming her, but Susan barely felt the motion. Instead, she was grappling with the turmoil that threatened to consume her.

"I can't leave, Sister Mary Margaret."

"Don't you think that God has already made the decision for you?" She tucked a finger under Susan's chin, forcing her to look up. "Susan, very few people are called to such a service. That's why women complete a novitiate before they can become nuns—so that they can determine the truth of their own hearts. You haven't taken your vows yet. There's no shame in leaving the order if God has other things for you to do."

Sister Mary Margaret smiled at her, a smile that for some reason brought a hazy image of another beautiful woman. Visions of the past swam in front of Susan's eyes.

Mama?

Run, Susan.

She must have gasped, because bit by bit, she

noted the way Mary Margaret's palms framed her face, her thumbs gently wiping away the tears.

"Let it go, Susan. God isn't demanding your own life in penance for the past. Let it go."

The words struck Susan to the core. She *had* used her service at the academy as a form of self-inflicted punishment. And for what? Something that had happened to her as a child? An accident?

"I don't regret having served with the sisters."

"And you mustn't regret leaving them now that the time has come." Margaret reached out to pull her close, folding her in an embrace that smelled of wool and soap, roses and herbs. Susan tried to hold back the tears, but they bled through her lashes and silvered her cheeks.

"What am I going to do?" She managed to force the words from the tightness of her throat. "I don't belong out there."

Mary Margaret lifted Susan's chin again. "Oh, but you do. Don't you see? God has another calling for you, one outside the cloister walls. He will have prepared the way for you. You need only to find the courage to take the first step." She held Susan's cold hands. "Do you know that I had only just begun my novitiate when you came to the academy?"

Susan shook her head.

"I was a student at Saint Francis before that time—and I do believe I nearly drove the sisters to drink. My mother wouldn't allow me to attend school until I was nearly fourteen, so I was much older than the other girls. I was also wild and rebellious and angry with the world. I thought that Saint Francis Academy was the end of the world, and I was doomed to stay there until my mother remembered to fetch me. I fought with everyone. I even climbed over the walls and disappeared into town for days on end." Her chuckle was wry. "I probably broke every command-ment as I tried to survive those frantic years."

Susan couldn't imagine Sister Mary Margaret even treading on a flea, let alone breaking God's laws. Her eyes widened in astonishment.

"Then one day a friend came to me. He'd run away from his guardians and needed a place to stay. I was twenty at the time. I felt battered and dirty but I wanted to show him how worldly I'd become, how free. I think, deep down, I longed to shock him."

"And did you?"

"If so, he never showed it." Mary Margaret's eyes softened with nostalgia. "He never chastised me, never blamed me, but I could see that he was disap-pointed in what I'd become. To my infinite surprise, this young boy decided that I needed his help. He began to teach me things I had forgotten: that I was still a person of worth, that there were people in this world who cared for me, that I didn't have to become anything I didn't want to be. Soon after that I admit-ted that my behavior was a way of rejecting God before God rejected me—because I so desperately wanted to be a member of the order."

Encouraging Susan with a steady, kindly gaze, Sis-ter Mary Margaret reached for the ties and pins that held the heavy black cloth wrapped around Susan's hair. "Then he brought me a very precious gift."

Susan eyed her questioningly, somehow sensing what Sister Mary Margaret would say.

"A little bright-eyed girl with red pigtails and freckles."

"Daniel," Susan breathed. "You've known him all along. Why didn't you tell me?"

"He didn't want me to. He didn't want you to know that you had a guardian angel of sorts. And he thought you'd feel better about your accomplishments if you knew you'd earned them and they weren't the result of some sort of favor he'd done on your behalf.'' She touched her cheek. ''You know, the two of us aren't so very different. When I began my novitiate, I suffered through a turmoil of the spirit similar to what you're experiencing now. I had done some horrible, horrible things. I agonized over whether or not I deserved God's goodness. His forgiveness.''

She paused, then continued. ''I soon realized God was much more willing to forgive me than I was. It took some time and some training, but the day I took my vows and donned this habit I knew what it meant to feel truly free. I knew I'd made the right choice and God approved.''

The black scarf fell away from Susan's head, and Sister Mary Margaret began searching for the hairpins that secured the heavy coils of hair to her neck. ''Somehow I think those same vows would make you feel imprisoned.''

Susan wondered how Sister Mary Margaret had read her so perfectly.

''You're not slighting God by leaving the order, Susan. I think that particular path was ordained all along.'' Bit by bit, pin by pin, she loosened the heavy auburn tresses until they hung loose and flowing around Susan's shoulders.

''By releasing you from your obligations to the order, he heals not one heart but two.''

Sister Mary Margaret's quick smile held the joy of a woman at peace with herself. ''There, doesn't that feel better?''

Susan took Mary Margaret's wrists and kissed her palms. ''Thank you, Sister.''

''Nonsense. I haven't absolved you of anything— there's no need. I've simply helped you onto the proper course, the one you should have been following all along. If you need a reason, let's say I did it for a friend."

"For Daniel."

"No, Susan. For you."

Much later, after Susan had gone to the tack room to say good-bye to Max and wipe away his desperate tears, she eased through the squeaky convent gates and stepped into the sunshine. Pausing, she breathed deeply of the spicy winter air. Then she turned, intent upon her horse and home.

She had taken only two steps when she saw Daniel . . . and he saw her.

His gaze immediately leapt to the auburn tresses tumbling unencumbered about her shoulders. Slowly, as if he couldn't believe his own eyes, he dismounted and walked over to her, his boots squeaking in the snow.

"Why in the hell did you run off like that, Susan?"

She laughed at his scolding. Daniel was astonished at the way she glowed with childlike enthusiasm. She lifted her face up to the sunlight as if basking in the caress of the golden rays. Then, squealing, she threw her arms out and twirled on her tiptoes in the snow. Coming to a breathless halt, she grinned at him, her expression as eager and joyful as that of a new bride. "I won't be returning to Saint Francis. I've left the order."

Daniel had been trying to persuade her to make such an announcement for weeks. Now that it had actually come, he felt a burst of uncertainty. "Mary Margaret—"

"She knows." Susan didn't tell Daniel all that Sister Mary Margaret had revealed about him, about the way he'd protected Susan, even from afar.

Daniel didn't speak. He knew he should have felt

exultant. He should have been shouting his thanks to the skies. But he didn't feel very triumphant, especially when she stared up at him with big green eyes. Her exhilaration over her decision glittered in their depths, but he knew it wouldn't be long before it was dimmed by an old familiar fear. The panic would return. As soon as he touched her.

If he were a gentle man, if he knew the right things to say and the right way to approach her, the situation might be different. But he'd grown too cynical, too hard, too bitter. He didn't want to taint her joy with his own black moods.

But he couldn't let her go, either.

The cape he held swirled and snapped in a sudden gust of wind when he swept it around her shoulders. As she clasped the collar and fastened the metal hook, he pulled her hair free of the fastenings.

Fairy-spun silk could not have felt so soft next to his skin. Even in the open air, he was sure he could smell wildflowers and rainwater.

Susan reveled in his touch, closing her eyes as if to savor the contact. The guilt she'd felt in the past was gone. Daniel's caresses felt so wonderful, so right. She tipped her head back, filling his palm with the warmth of her skull and rich strands the color of fire.

Daniel knew he should walk away from the temptation that instant. He knew he didn't deserve her—and she certainly didn't deserve a man like him. But he couldn't resist. His hands roamed down her back to pull her tightly against him. His mouth crushed hers, his tongue plunging inside to sweep the moist velvet interior. Then, so that he wouldn't frighten her with the depth of his desire, he withdrew.

"Let's get back." If Susan noted how he had

avoided the word "home," she didn't comment. They both knew she had no place she could call her own—not the orphanage or the convent. She'd left her security and her childhood in the sturdy walls of the convent, just as she'd abandoned the thick woolen scarf.

17

Susan tapped on Daniel's open door and paused. A day had passed since their embrace outside the convent walls. Immediately she noted the changes. Where before Daniel had settled into the room as if he belonged there, now it had the appearance of being inhabited by a guest. His clothes had been tightly folded and tucked away in his saddlebags. His coat, holster, and saddle gear were stacked neatly by the door. Even the bed was made to perfection, looking strangely out of place with its military corners and taut covers. The cool precision of his room was echoed in his mood. Somehow, in the space of a few hours, Daniel had begun to draw away from her emotionally. He'd become the distant detached Pinkerton agent.

Daniel had pulled the rocker up to the window to catch the last pink rays of sunlight streaming through the lace curtain. On the floor around him lay the disassembled components of his Peacemaker revolver. He had apparently just finished cleaning his rifle as well. Susan watched as he wiped an oiled cloth along the Winchester's barrel and leaned it against the wall, then reached for the parts of the smaller weapon strewn at his feet.

"Preparing for war?" she teased.

"Maybe." His reply held no answering humor.

Susan stepped inside and, after a moment's deliberation, closed the door behind her. For the first time in over ten years, she did not wear the black uniform of a novice. Since she still felt conspicuous, with her bare head and "civilian" clothes, she had borrowed one of Esther's gray day dresses, but for all of the attention it had garnered from Daniel, she might as well have worn sackcloth.

"You didn't come to supper," she said.

"I wasn't hungry."

"Esther was worried."

He shrugged.

"She's gone back into town. Mr. Gibby has taken a turn for the worse, and Dr. Patterson needs her help. Donovan took her in the sleigh."

Daniel nodded to show he'd heard, but he still didn't speak.

"I brought you a tray." She set it on the dresser. "Chicken and dumplings. Your favorite."

"Thanks."

"Is something wrong?"

"No. Why?"

"You seem a little distant." He'd been so quiet and withdrawn all day, she wondered if she was the cause. Ever since they had returned to the orphanage and explained to the Reeds that Susan had decided to leave the order, Daniel had been especially reserved.

"Are you worried about what people will say now that I've left Saint Francis?" She waited, then added, "I don't want you to think that because I've left the convent you need to take care of me. I'll be fine. I've asked Esther and Donovan if I can stay here until I find another teaching position. They didn't appear to mind.''

"I'm sure they were delighted. They've missed you."

"Perhaps, but I can't help thinking I'm just another mouth to feed.'' That feeling grated her pride, but there was little else she could do for the time being.

Daniel began snapping the pieces of his revolver together. While he was bent over his task, she took a roll of muslin strips and a jar of ointment from the tray. "Essie told me I should check your wound and change the bandage.''

That comment captured his attention. He looked up at her. This time he didn't question the wisdom of the idea. He set his weapon aside and stood. "Fine. I assume you want the shirt off.''

For some strange reason Susan had the impression that *she,* and not his injury, would be under careful scrutiny.

"That would make my job easier.''

"Glad to oblige, but . . .'' He held up his palms to show her that he was covered with oil and grime.

"Oh. I see.'' Rosy patches stained Susan's cheeks, but she refused to cower away from the challenge Daniel had thrown down.

She reached for the buttons on his chambray shirt. One by one, she freed them from their holes, leaving a ribbon of bare flesh in her wake.

It had been days since she had seen him so intimately exposed. She had forgotten how quickly a glimpse of his chest could cause her heart to thud, her limbs to tremble. Daniel Crocker was a beautiful man. Firm, well-formed, muscular.

"Now what?'' Daniel asked, once the placket gaped open. He watched her in tense anticipation.

He'd never thought she would accept his challenge. He'd assumed she would back away, just as she had so many times in the past.

"I think my task would be easier if you took your shirt completely off."

Her blush of discomfiture deepened. He loved to see it. Her eyes sparkled like jewels. Her lips were unconsciously parted and inviting. But . . .

He retreated behind the emotional barriers he'd erected the day before when Susan had announced she'd left the order. He couldn't take advantage of her right now. She was vulnerable and a little lost. She didn't know where the future would take her. And the only thing Daniel knew for sure was that he could never have her.

Determined to appear unflustered, she walked behind him to take hold of his collar. "I'll help you remove this, since your hands are dirty." Her cool, schoolmarmish attitude deserted her the second her knuckles touched his skin. Darts of excitement skittered over her nerves like drops of water on a hot griddle.

Because she tried not to touch him, it took her several seconds to draw the shirt away from his shoulders. She could see the muscles contract beneath the sliding caress of the fabric, and the sight fascinated her. But she quickly abandoned the chore as soon as the fabric pooled around his hips, leaving his arms imprisoned in his sleeves.

As she circled him once again, she blurted, "You're very fit, Daniel."

He didn't answer, but she knew by the way he watched her so intently that he wasn't completely unaffected.

She bent to the strips of muslin wrapped low around his abdomen and discovered she had abandoned her efforts at disrobing Daniel much too soon.

Part of the bandage was still covered by the waist-band of his trousers.

"I don't suppose you could . . ." Her request died before it could even be uttered, and firming her resolve, she reached for the top button to his pants. Her bravado wavered, but she forced herself to continue.

He tried to stop her, but his arms were effectively pinned at his sides.

She ended any protest he might have made by meeting his gaze head-on and saying, "Don't, Daniel. Don't stop me. I need to do this. I need to know that I can." There was no denying the desperate edge to her words.

Though the stance of his body remained as hard and tensile as steel, she sensed that he had relented.

By the time the button gaped open and she had removed the bandage from his waist, Susan was wondering if she had accepted more of a challenge than she could handle. Her hands shook uncontrollably; her knees threatened to buckle.

She saw that Daniel's wound was healing quite nicely. The skin had knitted together and had lost most signs of infection. Only the angry edge around the cut and the string of black stitches testified to its fragile recovery.

"It looks better. Much better."

When Daniel would have spoken, she ignored him and began coating the area with one of Essie's ointments. Unconsciously, she let her fingers stroke him. Lovingly. Tenderly.

Daniel groaned. His hands balled into fists, and he fought to be free of the sleeves. "Susan, don't!"

His arms sprang loose and snapped around her back. Broad, oil-slick palms spread over her shoulder blades while his mouth swooped down to take her own.

Immediately her lips parted, and his tongue swept inside. Susan admitted to herself that this was exactly what she had been waiting for since she'd stepped outside the convent. She'd needed to be sure that she could enjoy Daniel's embrace without experiencing the guilt she'd always felt. She'd wanted to revel in the sensations he aroused without thinking about the spiritual consequences. And although the emotions that had stormed her prior to her resignation had been powerful, they seemed paltry compared to the rush of heat and light that stormed through her now. She felt no shame, only a rush of pleasure.

"I tried." He broke away from her and pressed a string of kisses down her throat. She gasped, never having known that particular area could be so sensitive. "I tried to stay away. I know you need time to adjust to all that's happened, and I know the last thing you need is the complication of someone like me in your life, but I can't stop what's happening. I can't leave you alone again."

She clung to him and pressed herself into the warmth of his broad chest. Like a starving person, she greedily consumed the sensual food he provided her.

"I need you," he whispered next to her ear.

"Yes."

"But I don't want to frighten you."

The black fear lingered on the edges of her consciousness, taunting her, tormenting her. "You won't."

He stroked her hair and tilted her head. "I could. And I probably will—but I need to know that you trust me enough to let me help you."

"Daniel, what are you saying?"

He trembled on the precipice between peril and safety, between total commitment and solitude.

"I want you."

Daniel rubbed her back, bringing her hips firmly

into contact with his own. Susan held still, afraid to move any closer, but unwilling to step back.

She felt so good in his arms that Daniel wondered how he had ever thought he could stay away from her. She belonged to him. She belonged *with* him.

Now he wanted to stay with her, to see each experience firsthand.

"Susan, I don't want you to stay here at the orphanage. I want you to come with me."

She opened her mouth, but couldn't speak. She didn't know exactly what Daniel was offering. She didn't know if he wanted a companion or simply felt sorry for her. But judging by the fire in his eyes and the familiar sweep of his hands on her hips, she had a fair idea.

"Do you trust me to take care of you?" he asked.

"Y-yes."

"Will you come with me?" He waited for her answer. If she refused, he didn't know what he would do, but he couldn't let her go. If she agreed, he would do anything, *anything*, to provide for her.

"Yes."

He wasn't sure he'd heard correctly. He'd been so afraid she would refuse, he'd almost missed her acceptance.

"Really?"

"Yes. Yes, I'll go with you."

He shouted in delight and hauled her close, lifting her off her feet. "You won't regret it, I promise. You and I have always made a good team. Tomorrow we'll . . ." He broke off and set her on the floor. "Damn, I forgot about Kutter."

"Kutter?"

"My boss. I was supposed to meet with him yesterday, but Braxton's message slipped my mind." Without warning, he released her and snatched his rifle and coat. "I'll be back in an hour, two at the most."

"But what—"

He caught her and pressed a quick heated kiss on her mouth. "Trust me," he said again. "I've got to talk to Kutter about resigning from my job with the Pinkertons."

"Resigning!"

"Then you and I will start making some plans."

"But, Daniel—"

He kissed her again, this time more slowly, lingeringly, sweetly. "I'll be back. You watch the house. Hem that pretty dress Essie gave you—I think I've ruined this one." He touched the curve of her cheek. "I don't ever want to see you in black or gray again, you hear?"

She grinned. "I hear."

She followed him onto the back stoop, receiving two more kisses for her effort. And as he rode into the night, she couldn't help thinking that for the first time in as long as she could remember, the anger had faded from Daniel's features and he appeared happy. Completely and utterly happy.

His joy lit a warm fire deep in her belly, a blaze that fought with the cool dregs of her fear.

18

He huddled in the cold, his hands numb, his feet nearly senseless. Days had passed since he'd encountered Gibby in the alchemist's shop, long endless days of silence and anticipation. In all that time no word had come of Crocker's weakening condition. Life had continued unaffected until finally he'd decided to check on the Pinkerton himself.

Diamond-chip stars shed splinters of light on the snow. He watched the orphanage. He waited, to no avail. Hours passed. Hours filled with a burning purpose. Then suddenly he had proof that Crocker had escaped the poison's effects once again: the Pinkerton emerged from the building like an avenging warrior. His stride was firm, his stance purposeful.

The pleasure on Crocker's face caused an ache to curl around the man's heart. No. *No!* Why had Crocker chosen not to take the powder? How could he have been so lucky—or so wise? By now he should have been weak and shaky, but judging by the sure way he mounted his horse and rode away, he had somehow discovered the entire plan.

The voices in the man's head began again, chastising him for his failure. A fury rose in him, so thick and black that he couldn't think. Too much pain had resulted from Crocker's sins. Something had to be done. He had planned on Daniel's weakened condition to sway the odds. Now he would have to revise his plans. He would have to employ every morsel of information he had gathered over the months to lure Crocker into his trap.

His limbs were immobile from the icy moisture that had seeped through his clothing, but he managed to push himself to his feet and stagger away from the barn.

His months of planning would serve him well. He knew everything there was to know about the Pinkerton: his hiding spots, his strategies, how he handled the pressures of his job, and what he did on his own time. He also knew how to bring Daniel to his knees. Crocker would pay dearly for each breath he took. This time the Pinkerton's little nun would serve as a tool. He would hurt her, hurting Daniel even more in the process.

In one week Baby Floyd would be brought into Ashton. On that same day Crocker would learn the meaning of vengeance and betrayal. He would suffer as no man had ever suffered. An eye for an eye. A tooth for a tooth.

Only then would he be allowed to die.

The stranger hobbled toward his mount. Stinging pins of feeling pricked at his legs but did not weaken his determination to see his plans through once and for all. The Pinkerton agent had bested him one too many times. Now he would drag Crocker into hell and beyond. He had already laid the groundwork. He had gathered an army of men. Tonight he would meet with them and revise his plans. Before the end of the week he would close the trap so quickly that Crocker would never foresee it, nor would he escape it once it was sprung.

Daniel cursed in impatience. With each mile that passed, he wished that his life could have been more like that of other men. He wished he could rise with the sun, spend his days on the land, and pass his evenings with a beautiful woman.

But now he planned to make that happen. With Susan. He didn't know why it had taken him so long to realize that they were meant to stay together. Perhaps he had needed her to leave the convent before allowing himself to think of such a thing. Now that she had done so, he couldn't push the idea from his mind.

There were a dozen things he needed to do to see their future secured. He would have to check on his land, find employment, buy stock and supplies. But first he had to sever his ties with the Pinkertons.

As he rode, Daniel damned every obstacle that stood in his way: the icy wind, the darkness, and most of all, Jedidiah Kutter for trying to pull him back into a world he wanted to forget.

He had to admit that even contemplating a change in his way of life scared him to death. He'd always lived alone, never depending on anyone but himself. But he couldn't go back to his old ways. He had to do this, now. While he still had the guts to throw his solitary existence away and learn to love a woman.

Hunching deeper into the coarse fur of his coat, he nudged his horse to a greater speed and rode through the trees to the main road. There he followed the double line of railroad tracks until he reached the fork where the Humboldt and Western ran east through a narrow pass and the Wasatch Territorial ran south.

The gelding galloped beneath the causeway built over the creekbed, and Daniel veered sharply to the left into a steep rocky canyon, following Braxton's directions. Pulling on the reins to slow his mount, Daniel moved quietly, cautiously. Once through the pass, he scanned the jumbled rocks around him with a care and suspicion that had become second nature.

When he reached a boulder that obstructed the trail, Daniel paused. Bringing his fingers to his lips, he issued four short whistles, then waited. When the signal was returned, he nudged Chief with his heels and carefully slid his rifle from the scabbard on his saddle.

Chief tossed his head, walking daintily around the rock and into a clearing. Daniel's eyes swept the icy canyon, darting to the dark shapes positioned on the rocks above him. Lifting his rifle in silent salute, Daniel acknowledged the Pinkertons who guarded the breach.

As he crossed the scant expanse of snow toward the ramshackle cabin butted against the sheer face of one rock wall, a figure stormed from the door and stood glowering at him from the top step.

"Damn it, Crocker! Where the hell have you been? I asked you to come yesterday."

Daniel ignored Jedidiah Kutter, bringing his gelding to a halt beside the stoop. He swung out of the saddle and secured the reins to a scrubby bush growing from beneath the steps.

"Well?" Kutter demanded impatiently.

Daniel refused to give the tall, barrel-chested man more than a cursory glance as he climbed the stoop and brushed past Kutter into the shack. "I got delayed." Not for the first time he felt irritated with Kutter for acting more like a warden than a boss.

The weak warmth of the cabin was welcome. Daniel tugged his gloves free with his teeth and strode over to the black iron stove in the corner. He took a chipped enamel mug from the shelf above his head, then poured himself a cup of coffee that had probably been brewing since morning.

"I was worried."

"I know, Kutter." Daniel gritted his teeth and spun to face the older man, then took a deep, calming drag of air, filling his lungs with the acrid scent of old coffee and woodsmoke. As quickly as it had come, his anger drained away. "I got here as soon as I could." He didn't bother to tell Kutter he'd forgotten all about the meeting. Daniel Crocker had never been careless, until a green-eyed beauty began to invade his every thought.

Kutter continued to watch him with the concerned scowl of a grouchy mother bear. He raked his gnarled hands through the curly hair that sprang out around his head like thousands of tiny corkscrews. Then he carefully combed the longer strands over the balding spot at the top of his skull. As if possessing a spirit of their own, the thin waves sprang back, leaving the red-brown skin of his scalp to show through.

"Come here. I want to show you something." Jedidiah Kutter visibly relaxed the tense set of his shoulders. With a jerk of his head, he gestured to the maps scattered on the table in the center of the room.

Daniel took a sip of the bitter brew in his cup, swearing aloud at its taste but savoring its heat. He was about to tell Kutter the truth, that he was leaving the profession now and wouldn't be back, but Kutter's serious mien kept the words inside him. Propping one hand on the rough table, he bent over the map spread on top of a jumbled pile of papers and weighted down with rocks.

"Floyd Dooley will be moved on Sunday."

"So soon?"

Kutter nodded. "He'll be brought in from Salt

Lake City on the Wasatch Territorial. The train will bypass Ashton"—as he spoke, Kutter used a crooked index finger to trace a route on the map—"and stop here, where the two railroads split."

Daniel nodded, taking another wary sip of his coffee. While he steeled himself against an urge to join the expedition, his mind automatically formed a picture of the terrain outside the canyon.

"We'll have men posted here"—Kutter pointed to the slopes above the fork—"and here." He stabbed the thick trees that lined the creekbed. "There will be six men in the boxcar with Dooley and six more scattered throughout the other cars."

Daniel pinned Kutter with a keen stare. "That's an awful lot of manpower for a simple prisoner transfer."

Kutter opened his mouth, then paused as if carefully choosing his words.

Comprehension dawned, and Daniel stiffened, setting his cup on the table and remarking softly, "Of all the brazen . . . You want the whole Dooley gang to ride right into your trap. And you're using Baby Floyd as bait."

Kutter's lips twisted. "Baby Floyd isn't our only drawing card, though I'm sure they'd bring a half dozen men to his rescue regardless of the circumstances. But I want the whole shebang. I want the whole damned Dooley clan to ride into our ambush so we can take care of them once and for all." Kutter lifted his head, his rheumy gray eyes direct. "And in order to do that, we've got to have another ace in the hole. You."

Cold seeped into Daniel's body. "What do you mean?" he asked slowly.

"Grant Dooley escaped from the Missouri prison two weeks ago."

Daniel froze.

"He'll be searching for the man who put him there," Kutter continued. "By now he's probably whipped his family into a frenzy. They won't be content with just saving their little brother if they know you'll be on their tail by sundown."

"I may not be one of the Dooleys' favorite people, but the whole clan won't show up to shoot me."

"We also leaked word that a shipment of dynamite will be brought through Ashton this week."

Damn. The Dooleys loved dynamite as much as little boys loved firecrackers. Blowing safes and trains and bridges to kingdom come just for the hell of it had become their trademark over the years. They would never be able to resist the lure of a whole crate of the stuff. Grant and Marvin Dooley wouldn't have to say much to persuade the rest of their family to use the explosives to destroy their arch rival. They would probably spend most of the week salivating over how many ways they could blow Daniel Crocker and the rest of the Pinkertons to bits.

And through it all Kutter intended to dangle Daniel in front of the Dooleys' noses like a worm wriggling on a hook. If Daniel had been told of the plan weeks ago, even days ago, he would have completed the assignment as he had any other in the past—maybe even relishing the knowledge that he could outsmart the Dooleys and see they were apprehended and brought to justice. But now there was Susan to worry about. And their future.

Daniel took his gloves out of his coat pocket and began tugging them over his hands. "No."

"What do you mean, 'no'?"

"I won't do it." He headed for the door.

"Crocker!"

Daniel paused.

"You can't leave, Crocker."

Daniel threw him a look over his shoulder. "Watch me."

"If you walk out of this assignment, I'll call in your note and you'll lose your land."

An ominous silence settled over the room. Daniel slowly turned, his expression steely. "You know as well as I do that the note is nearly paid off."

"Nearly, Daniel. Not completely."

Daniel felt a burst of fury and frustration. Damn it all to hell! For years he'd been saving almost every penny he earned to pay for the little spread of land not ten miles from where he now stood. A place of his own—something he'd never known. Five years ago, when the parcel he'd chosen had been about to be sold from under him, Kutter had offered to buy half and to allow Daniel to pay him back over time. And the debt was almost paid. Almost.

"That's blackmail, Kutter."

"That's right. Besides, if you don't help us put the Dooleys away for good, you'll live the rest of your life suspicious of every shadow. We've tried putting them in jail one by one, but damn it, they keep breaking each other out. It's time to take them all, in one fell swoop, then lock 'em away where the sun can't shine. I'm not above foreclosing on your land to do it. I could sell it and hire an army if I had to."

Daniel glared at his friend. Kutter couldn't do this to him. He knew how much the land meant to Daniel, how much he'd dreamed of it over the years.

But Kutter was also determined. And mule-headed. When he got a look like a bull about to charge, there was no stopping him.

"Do this job for me, Daniel, and the debt will be cleared—above and beyond your usual pay. I'll even throw in your first milk cow."

A gust of air escaped from Daniel's lungs. The offer was tempting. With a little extra money in his pocket, he and Susan would have the funds to buy livestock and make the necessary repairs. And the milk cow wouldn't hurt, either.

Just one job. One more job. "What exactly am I supposed to do?"

Kutter wasn't fool enough to believe Daniel had agreed to anything. Yet, Daniel could see that fact from the careful way the older man schooled his features.

"Make yourself as visible as possible for the next day or two. If anyone should ask, you're visiting family."

"Hell," Daniel whispered.

"Come Sunday, you'll assist in the transfer of a dangerous prisoner."

Daniel snorted aloud at that. Baby Floyd Dooley was a myopic, chuckleheaded piece of fluff. The only man Floyd had ever injured was himself.

But his brothers were killers.

"And then?"

"Then we'll apprehend Grant and Marvin Dooley . . . and go home."

Daniel shook his head in disbelief. "What makes you think the Dooleys will come after Floyd? Or the dynamite? Or me? They might decide it's not worth the effort."

"They'll come. Family honor."

"Honor like hell."

"Then let's say their shrew of a mother is not about to let her baby be hanged or to let you walk free."

That was one reason Daniel was prepared to believe.

"What makes you think they'll come to Ashton? Why not stop the train in Salt Lake or farther on?"

Kutter straightened. "This pass is the weakest spot

on the line. The Dooleys know we'll have to switch railroads in order to get Floyd back east.''

Daniel waited, knowing there was more to come.

"There have also been some strange things happening in Ashton.''

"What kinds of things?''

"Petty thefts of chickens from some of the farms, stolen horses, strangers asking odd questions about the railroad station and incoming train schedules. In town, the pharmacy was set on fire. The proprietor, a Mr. Gibby, was severely wounded. He has yet to regain consciousness.''

"And you think the Dooleys are responsible?''

"Maybe. Maybe not. But considering Grant's fondness for morphine, it's not an impossibility.''

Daniel carefully considered his options, but any way he looked at the situation, he didn't like it.

"What about the people at Benton House? My being involved in this will affect them.''

"They won't be in any danger. Grant Dooley isn't about to do anything that might ruin his chances of getting his brother back. His only hope is to organize an ambush when Floyd is moved from one rail line to another.''

Daniel wearily massaged the bridge of his nose. He was tired of all this. So tired. "Maybe you trust Dooley to leave the people at the orphanage alone, but I don't. I want your word that they'll be protected. Regardless.''

Kutter nodded. The tilt of his lips revealed his sense of impending victory. "You have it. I'll send a guard to the orphanage first thing in the morning.''

Daniel turned, his eyes narrowing to become dark slits. "And I want out,'' he stated lowly. "When this is all over, I leave the agency.''

Kutter seemed prepared to fight him, then conceded. "All right.''

Daniel's head dipped, showing his agreement to their plans. "I'll take a hotel room in town until this is all over."

"No."

Daniel's brows lifted and he shot Kutter a glare rife with warning.

"You can't leave Benton House. If you do, it will cause a whole lot of questions."

"Damn it to hell, you're asking me to jeopardize the lives of the people at the orphanage even more than you already have."

"I'm not asking you to do anything I haven't already planned to deal with!"

Daniel's chin jutted out at a stubborn angle.

"Go home, Daniel," Kutter urged softly, his voice taking on an almost fatherly tone. "Go back to your little girl."

Every muscle in Daniel's body grew taut. "What little girl?"

"The one you talk about when you're drunk and lonely. The one in the picture you keep hidden in your bags."

Daniel stormed from the cabin, jamming his hat on his head.

"Crocker!"

Daniel turned.

"I've got several men planted in town. One of them will contact you prior to the exchange. In the meantime . . . you take care."

Shrugging off the man's concern, Daniel yanked the reins from the bush and mounted his horse.

"Hey, Grant!"

The rough whisper reverberated through Grant Dooley's drug-induced euphoria. Silently cursing the man who had dared to disturb his fun, Grant eased his head from the prostitute's breast, grimacing when he met Marvin's hard-eyed stare.

"Get outta here, Marvin," Grant slurred. He dropped his head, nudging his chin into the woman's enormous cleavage and inhaled the odors of cheap perfume and sweat. Settling deeper into the moth-eaten settee, he slipped his hand beneath the woman's skirts.

"I thought you wanted to get back at Crocker—or was that just a lot of talk?"

"I said get out, Marvin!"

"She's alone. The Hurst girl is alone."

"So?"

"So I thought you wanted to even the score? Why can't we do something to her tonight? Why can't we sample Crocker's woman? Seems to me it would work in our favor. If we visit her tonight, he'll be mad—hoppin' mad. Men who are mad make mistakes."

It took an extreme effort of will, but Grant managed to prop open his eyelids. As Marvin's words sank into his cloudy head, his body tensed. He turned his head away from the woman's voluminous breasts so that he could squint up at the man who hovered above him. Then his eyes roamed around the smoky shack, which was crowded with Dooleys and two working women who moved from man to man hoping to relieve the Dooleys of whatever money could be found. After the stirring meeting they'd just had, the boys were rowdy and full of spite.

"Come on, Grant," Marvin cajoled. "Just you, me, Bart, and Nate. We could slip away without anybody noticin'. She's at the orphanage with those kids. Everyone else is in town."

Grant's lips curled in disgust, and his head dropped back into the pillow of womanly flesh. "Crocker's there by now."

"No. He's not."

"You're sure?"

"Hell, yes. His horse is still gone. I doubt he'll be back until dawn."

Grant began to laugh, a low, rich sound that echoed his enjoyment of the situation. Extricating himself from the clinging arms of the prostitute, he staggered to a chair where he'd looped his gun belt over the back.

"Round up Burt and Nate and meet me outside."

Marvin strode to the door, then stopped. When he turned, Grant caught an expression he hadn't seen in Marvin's face until now. Hate. Pure unadulterated hate. "I didn't haul my ass all over Wyoming Territory following that Pinkerton for nothing. I want a part in dragging him into hell."

Grant grinned. "Don't we all?" he quipped. "And like I've said before, that girl is the best way to do it."

19

Susan sat up in bed and tried to capture the sound that had awakened her. From far away she heard the muffled stamping of hooves and the snuffling of horses. She swept aside the covers and snatched her wrapper. An inexplicable urgency spurred her on. If Donovan and Essie had returned before dawn, that meant something must have happened to poor Mr. Gibby.

She hurried downstairs. Once in the foyer, she struck a match and touched it to the greedy kerosene-soaked wick of a glass lamp, then replaced the chimney. Since the sounds came from the drive at the front of the house, she hurried into the parlor, set the lamp on the table in front of the window, and lifted the curtain aside to stare into the pink-edged darkness. It was almost four-thirty. She'd gone to bed after midnight when Daniel still hadn't returned. Thinking he'd been detained by his superior, she hadn't worried. But now . . .

An arm snapped around her neck, and a rough hand clamped over her mouth, cutting off Susan's scream. Her fingers dug into the tight band that held her, trying to press back the acrid panic that was rapidly swelling in her throat.

Just stand still, little girlie. Stand still while we touch your mama's pretty skin.

Bucking wildly, Susan twisted in her captor's grip. Three dark male shapes entered the room. Apprehensively she watched their feverish expressions. She'd seen men look this way before, twenty years ago when the deserters had pushed her mother to the ground.

One gaunt, pockmarked man stepped forward, his mouth splitting into a slow smile. Susan flinched, but when she tried to escape the tight hold, the man who held her yanked her against his solid chest.

"You left one of the back windows unlocked," the pockmarked man chided. He made a clucking noise deep in his throat as he tugged his gloves off and slapped them against his thigh. "Careless. Very, very careless." The men on either side of him laughed softly.

Susan studied the three men in the flickering lamplight. Something about their faces and travel-stained clothing looked familiar. She'd seen these men before. Somewhere.

Susan moaned deep in her throat, squirming, but she could not escape. She wondered where Daniel could be.

"Nate." The leader made a motion toward the open door with his head. Behind him, a younger man—a boy, really—grinned and closed the door.

The gaunt man advanced. "Susan, isn't it?" When she didn't answer, the leader scowled. "I've heard Crocker talk about you. About the way you look in bed. How you like a man to be rough." He chuckled, a dry grating sound that rasped on her nerves. "Well, we can be rough."

A cry of outrage bubbled from her throat. The man shook his head, scolding her with mock concern. "You'd best not make a sound, you hear? There are children in the house. You wouldn't want to wake them."

Susan let out a low groan. The four men fairly reeked of the sour smell of whiskey. There was no one else in the house but the children. If she screamed and one of them came down to see this . . . She swallowed back the horror.

"That's better. Much, much better." The man nodded approvingly. With a slashing gesture, he motioned for his friends to move forward on either side, encircling her in a frighteningly male ring.

The pockmarked man's eyes glittered in the lamplight. "Now," he slurred, "I believe we have some unfinished business to attend to. Crocker has perfected the art of interfering in family business. I intend to return the favor."

He edged nearer, his thighs pressing into hers, his breath heavy with the stench of whiskey and some other, sickly odor that smelled very much like laudanum or opium. He cupped her chin, his fingers digging into her skin. Susan felt the sting of frustration and anger.

"I'm going to have you, Susan," he taunted. "You know that, don't you? I'm going to show you what it's like to be in the arms of a man." His breath was hot on her cheek. "The arms of a *real* man. When I've finished you'll beg for more. And when I can't give it to you, my brothers will take their turns."

Susan tried to block out the swirling blackness as ghosts from the past tumbled forward full force. Dear heaven! Wasn't there some way she could prevent this from happening? *Daniel*. What would Daniel have her do?

She sank her teeth into the hand of the man who held her, and he swore, releasing her. Suddenly she was free and running toward the doors leading into the hall.

The pockmarked man caught her wrists, whirled her to face him, then pinned her arms to her sides and savagely hauled her close to his chest.

His lips became hard. "Such eagerness. I like that in a woman."

Susan opened her mouth to scream, then remembered the children.

"That's right." He chuckled. "Remember those damned brats." He grasped the neck of her nightgown and pulled down, rending the garment in two. Crying out, Susan clutched at the torn halves, vainly trying to shield herself from her captors' lewd stares.

The clatter of hooves split the morning air.

The youngest man whirled toward the window. "Crocker," he muttered fiercely.

The leader snatched Susan closer to his body. When she tenaciously gripped the fabric over her breasts, he ripped a long tear down the back of her nightgown.

"So what?" he crowed. "There's four of us. He's not about to help her now."

"Damn it, Grant, the man's a Pinkerton," Nate warned.

"So what?" Grant took hold of Susan's shoulder and spun her around to face the other men. "What can he do?" He pulled her roughly against his hips. "Look at her. Do you want to give all this up simply because Crocker has made an untimely arrival?"

His brothers lost some of their alcohol-induced bravery and edged toward the window. "Now's not the time, Grant." The sound of hooves grew louder.

Nate parted the curtains and peered out into the darkness. "Damn it, he knows we're here! He's seen our horses. He's got the law on his side, Grant. No one's ever going to refute the word of a Pinkerton."

Grant turned her to face him and bent Susan's head back over his arm, grinding his lips to her own, crushing her mouth against her teeth. Susan sobbed, tasting her own blood. But when his tongue probed at her lips, she kept her jaw tightly clenched to prevent his savage invasion. Horror shuddered through her body. She felt herself losing control.

"Grant! Come on!"

Grant pushed her away, then backhanded her across the face, splitting her lip. Susan fell to the floor as he stumbled to the window. Behind her she heard the heavy footfalls of the man who had first held her. Warily she lifted her head, fear and anger filling her breast. The man stood above her, feet planted apart, his face filled with a burning, violent emotion as he stared at her battered face. The oddly flattened shape of his face caused the dim light to give him an evil cast, like some medieval dragon.

"Marvin!"

Executing a mocking bow, the man backed toward the window and escaped into the darkness as Grant gripped the sash.

"Don't think this is the end. I'll be back to collect," he rasped. "Go ahead and bed your Pinkerton. Crocker owes me for what he's done. I'll use you to make him pay. Again and again . . . and again." He climbed out the window and closed it with a sharp crash.

Susan lay on the floor, shivering violently amid the torn remnants of her nightgown. Dark, stagnant sobs lay trapped in her throat, burning her with their searing pressure. Through a haze of misery she heard

Daniel's boots pounding up the walk even as Grant and his men disappeared into the darkness.

The front door flew open. Daniel stood sharply etched in the doorway.

Susan cringed, shrinking into herself, attempting to disappear into the braided rug and polished pine boards. When Daniel stepped into the room, she leapt to her feet. An animal-like hiss escaped from her clenched teeth. "Don't touch me!"

Daniel's heart lurched. He stopped, his arms held wide as if to prove he wouldn't harm her. Very slowly he eased forward, but she retreated, pressing herself against the flocked wallpaper.

He fought to contain the fury raging through him. He couldn't let her see his anger, his thirst for vengeance. It would only scare her more. He noted the jagged edges of her gown and the rumpled fabric clutched to her waist. What had happened in those hours he'd been gone?

Cautiously, as if he were approaching a wild animal, Daniel drew the coat from his shoulders. When Susan flinched, he paused, his heart pounding. Then he held the jacket out toward her. Wordlessly she bunched her gaping gown with one fist while the other took the proffered garment and slipped it over her shoulders.

"Hell and damnation!" Daniel said. Her skin was covered with bruises. Her head reared and she shot a terrified glance in his direction. Knowing no way to allay her pain, he muttered harshly, "Damn them all to hell for hurting you."

At his outburst, some of her courage returned to stiffen her resolve.

"How did they get in?" Daniel rasped.

Her lashes trembled with the diamondlike glint of tears. She pointed to the window of the parlor. "Th-the back of the house."

Daniel silently berated himself for his own stupidity. He never should have left her alone. In his impatience to see Kutter, he'd left her without protection—something he knew better than to do. Then, instead of coming home immediately, he'd ridden to his spread of land.

"How badly did they . . . touch you?"

He longed to soothe her and fold her in his arms, but he knew that would be the worst thing he could do right now.

Susan's chin wobbled with her attempt at control. "He threatened to . . . to . . ."

Her words faltered into silence. In the dim lamplight her features were sharp and pinched, her skin ashen. Then her chest shook with a ragged breath.

"He hurt me, Daniel," she whispered. "He hurt me."

To Daniel's surprise, she moved toward him then, stopping inches away. As if unsure how her actions would be greeted, she lifted her arms and rested them lightly on his chest.

"He hurt me," she whispered again, slipping her hands up to his shoulders and circling his neck. "I've seen one of the men before. He stopped me a few days ago on my way to Ashton, but I didn't tell you. I should have told you. I didn't know who he was, but he was asking about the Pinkertons. I should have told you."

"Shh." Daniel pulled her into a gentle embrace. "Never again," he vowed. "Never again will anyone harm you."

She laid her head on his shoulder, her fingers digging into his back. But there was a difference in their embrace. In the past Daniel had always comforted her, shielding her from her own fears. This time her body trembled with an unmasked fury. A fury directed at the men who had been so cruel.

186

"I hate them, Daniel!" she whispered into his ear. "I hate them all for making me feel helpless and weak."

He traced the line of her spine disguised by the bulky fur of his coat. "I know, Susan. I know."

"I'll show them. I'll show them what it's like to be . . . afraid! And to *want* and to *need* and never be able to have."

"Shh."

"They'll be sorry, Daniel. They'll be sorry they ever tangled with me. I'll show them they can't hurt me. I'll show them I can be normal and . . . and loving. Just like any other woman." She drew back, and her eyes glittered in the dim light like bits of green glass. "They said they would come back. But if they do, they'll be sorry!"

Daniel sensed that Susan was right. The Dooleys would return. If not tonight, then tomorrow, or the next day. Once again they had been cheated of their pleasures. They weren't about to forget it or to let things rest.

His arms tightened around Susan, and he valiantly strove to keep his own fury at bay. The Dooleys would never hurt another hair on Susan's head. Daniel would see to that.

20

Esther closed the door to Mr. Gibby's bedroom and tiptoed into the sitting room beyond. "Donovan?" she coaxed, gently shaking her husband's shoulder.

Donovan awoke with a start. "What? What do you need?"

She rubbed his chest in a soothing manner. "Nothing. Why don't you go home? I'll need to stay here until this evening at the very least. Go get some sleep in a real bed."

He rubbed his eyes. "I can stay. I don't mind."

"Donovan, go home," she insisted. "Susan will need your help once the children wake up. Go."

Yawning, he pushed himself to his feet. "Nag, nag, nag," he teased, bending to kiss her. "I'll be back after breakfast."

Essie's face took on a distracted air. A frown settled between her brows.

"Essie?"

"Hmm?"

Donovan lifted her chin. "Is something wrong?"

She sighed. "Mr. Gibby is . . . not well."

He waited, sensing she had not said all she planned to.

"Donovan, before his wife's death, Mr. Gibby had been married for forty years. He has eight beautiful daughters scattered all over Wyoming and yet the name he calls out in his delirium is Daniel's."

"Not our Daniel."

"He calls out for Daniel," she insisted. "The Pinkerton."

Donovan froze in the act of lifting his hat. The couple exchanged a telling glance. No words needed to be said. They had been married too many years and had weathered too many storms together to have to speak their mind. Donovan knew Essie was concerned about Mr. Gibby's behavior. He didn't need to be told that she wanted him to investigate the pharmacist's strange remarks and try to make some sense of them.

"I don't think the fire was an accident, Donovan. Could Daniel have been involved somehow?"

"I'll take a lantern with me and swing by Mr. Gibby's store. It shouldn't take me long to look around a bit before I head home."

She stopped him and pulled him close. "Be careful. Please, please, be careful."

Daniel dipped a square of soft cotton into a basin of warm water and lifted it to the blood that trickled from the split in Susan's lip. When he touched the gaping skin, she recoiled.

"Which man did this to you?"

"Grant. They called him Grant."

"Bastard!" A white-hot fury blazed in his eyes when he realized that the Dooleys' assault on Susan had been a personal attack against him. He'd unwittingly put her in danger.

She grasped his wrist. Their gazes locked, and she stared at him with such fiery intensity that Daniel felt the anger fading from his body to be replaced by an unexpected wonder. What should have been a horrible scare had only intensified her determination to put the past behind her.

"Daniel?" He focused on the fullness of her lower lip. In the lamplight it was plunged in shadow, making it appear softer than velvet, smoother than satin. "Where have you been? I thought you would come home hours ago."

Still dressed in his shaggy coat, Susan looked tiny and defenseless . . . and inexplicably desirable.

"What?" he muttered abstractedly.

"Where have you been?"

Her eyes were so dark, so full of life, so vibrant.

"Out. I've been out."

Her grip became urgent. "You haven't changed your mind, have you? You still want me to . . . go with you?"

With that question, she relayed the extent of her fears and the breadth of her trust. He knew that if he told her to accompany him, remain his friend but never his lover, she would. The power she unwittingly offered him was both thrilling and terrifying.

Her skin was pale compared to his own, her hands soft and slender. "No, I haven't changed my mind."

"Then what's wrong?"

Her voice was husky, and like a shot of whiskey it burned its way over his nerve endings, spreading a trail of fire. Earlier he had accused Susan of wanting more out of life than what she had. Now he realized the comment applied to him as well. He not only wanted *more,* he wanted it all.

"Daniel?"

"Nothing's wrong. I met with my superior and told him about leaving the Pinkertons." He dropped the cloth into the pan of warm water. "I think it's time I settled down."

Susan held her breath. "What did he say?"

"I can leave after I help with one last assignment."

"What kind of assignment?"

He brushed the tangled auburn hair away from her face. "It's not important. I'll be done by the end of the week."

"Then you'll resign and leave Ashton?"

Daniel tore his eyes away from the vulnerability in her face. When he didn't immediately speak, Susan released him.

Since her nearness threatened to weaken his control, Daniel jumped to his feet and strode across the room. He pulled the curtain aside and stared out into the blackness. "I want . . . I'd like . . ." Why were the words so hard to say? Why were they dammed up in his throat like a lump of clay?

Daniel turned to face her, noting her earnest expression. But there was more than that. He saw steely determination as well. He paused, undecided. Was he being unfair? Would she be happier with another man?

She followed him and placed her small hand on his arm. Daniel nearly flinched. She had so much to give a man, if only he'd take the time to unlock her pain, to understand her needs and heal the wounds.

His fingers curled. Then, unable to stop himself, he stroked her cheek. She was so soft, so young—and so damned beautiful. Could he resist her vibrant beauty day after day, night after night, and give her the time she needed?

"I won't be a bother to you, Daniel. I can cook and clean."

"I want more."

She drew back, her lower lip slipping beneath her teeth. "Then you don't want me?"

"Oh, sweetheart, yes, I want you. All of you, everything you can give me." His voice was heavy with emotion. Yet he still hesitated, knowing once he'd spoken, the die would be cast and he could never withdraw the words. By even issuing his proposition, Daniel was abandoning every code he'd lived by since he'd left the orphanage fourteen years ago. He was putting himself in a position where someone would need him. Not just now, but for the rest of his life. In the past, whenever someone needed him, tragedy had struck. Annie had died because he'd loved her. And Mama. He'd even endangered Miss Essie long ago, when he'd tried to defend her and had killed a boy in a brawl. Daniel had begun to believe that bad luck followed him like a hungry shadow.

But he couldn't let Susan go.

His hand dropped to his side, and he watched her carefully, studying the tilt of her head, the taut line of her jaw. "Marry me."

Silence reigned in the room, marked only by the echo of Daniel's words as he waited and watched her reaction, seeing her shift from incredulity to wonder to doubt.

"Why, Daniel?"

The question startled him. He hadn't expected her to jump and squeal, exactly, but he hadn't anticipated this, either.

Why? What could he say? That he'd grown soft in the head and needy? That she'd wound herself like a morning glory around his heart?

Uncomfortable with revealing the truth, he said instead, "Because I always took care of you when you were little and now . . ." Hurt flared in her eyes.

He broke off and cursed under his breath. "No. That's not the reason."

"Then why?"

He felt something akin to pain slice through him when the coat slipped, exposing Susan's creamy shoulder. A shoulder that was soft and feminine and mottled with new bruises.

Daniel tenderly lifted the jacket back into place. With that single touch, his loins burned with the urgency of a schoolboy.

"Daniel?" There was no fear in her voice, only confusion.

As she stared at him with huge, startled eyes, Daniel knew that—more than anything else—he longed to see the moment when Susan awakened to passion and discovered life had much more to offer than the fear of the unknown.

He could not deny the overwhelming greed he felt to have her in his life, to be the man to free her. He knew that one day he would be punished for his greed. In the past he had always been punished for wanting.

But things are different now, a little voice inside him argued. He was older, wiser. He knew how to protect himself. And he could protect Susan, too. His streak of bad luck had ended when he followed Susan to Ashton. If something happened to him for wanting her, then he was willing to pay the price for a few sweet hours in her company. He'd been alone for so long. Surely, by helping to release her fears, he would satisfy any debt of happiness he might incur in heaven.

"Daniel, why would you want me to marry you?"

Her soft hand rested on his chest, and Daniel's stomach tightened. He had a sudden taste of the agony he would endure in the future. Susan might never know the passion of a woman. The fears locked deep inside her mind would not simply vanish because he willed them to. But that was a chance he was ready to take.

Daniel pulled her close, burying his face in the fullness of her hair. "You could have a new life with me, Susan. You can start fresh—be whatever you want to be."

"And you? Why would you want to saddle yourself with someone like me?"

"I'm not being saddled—"

"Why?"

"I've got my reasons."

"And if I'm free to be whatever I want, what will you become?"

He drew back, instinctively divining what she needed to know. If he became her husband, how much of one did he intend to be? He looked at her openly and honestly, allowing her to see only a hint of the incredible desire he felt. "Your husband. In every way."

"Daniel, I'm not like other women."

Evidently she knew there were still several emotional bridges for her to cross.

"No. You're not like other women." A pang of hurt was reflected in her eyes, and he hurried to add, "You're wonderful. I've never met anyone as good and honest as you, Susan. I'm not trying to say I'm worth your—"

"Daniel!"

"No, let me finish. I know I'm not the kind of man most women would allow at their tables, but I'll never hurt you, Susan. And as long as I'm alive, no one else will hurt you, either."

"So you're marrying me simply to protect me," she concluded. "I can take care of myself, Daniel. If that's your only reason, then—"

"No, Susan. That's not my only reason." He stroked her hair. Her beautiful silken hair.

"Why, Daniel?"

She was going to make him say it. She was going to make him humble himself and give her the whole truth. His throat worked and his mouth opened. "Because you need me and . . ."

He lifted his gaze, and Susan was stunned by what she found there. His eyes were those of a forgotten boy and a wary man.

Daniel's next words were all that Susan needed to plunge her into an unknown world and give her the courage to face her uncertainty and her fear.

"I think . . . I *know* I need you, too."

21

Susan's fingers closed over the locket that hung around her neck. She traced the worn engraving as she tiptoed down the back stairs, avoiding the treads that squeaked. In only a few minutes she would be a married woman.

To say that Donovan and the others at the orphanage had been surprised by their announcement was an understatement. Only Esther had seemed to regard them with a secret knowledge.

Immediately the older woman had begun to talk of a spring wedding. But Daniel adamantly refused to wait. He hadn't even been willing to delay the ceremony until the first of the reunion guests could arrive. With Susan's hand held tightly in his own, he'd insisted that they marry within three days. If no one approved, then they would elope.

Though Susan had regretted the fact that she couldn't be married in the chapel at Saint Francis, she hadn't protested. Her marriage to Daniel seemed like a fairy wish, an intangible bubble. She wasn't sure it could actually exist, and to speak about it too much might cause it to vanish. So she had begged Essie to agree and then had arranged for the local priest to marry them and invited Sister Mary Margaret and Max to join the family as witnesses. Though Max had been distraught to hear she would be marrying Daniel Crocker, Sister Mary Margaret had assured Susan that she would make sure he attended.

After twisting the knob on the guest room door, she slipped inside. "Daniel?"

Hearing the soft voice, Daniel turned from where he'd been glaring into the mirror and straightening his string tie. His obvious surprise quickly melted beneath a wave of pleasure. "You look beautiful." His comment was a bare wisp of sound.

Her hair was arranged in tumbling ringlets down her back. She had worn it loose especially for him. And she hadn't a shred of black on anywhere. The gown Esther had worked night and day to complete was a delicate cream color, as were her stockings, slippers, and petticoats.

She walked toward him, clutching the smooth fabric of her dress. "Esther came to my room a few minutes ago. We've been having a little talk." She looked away, embarrassed by what she intended to do and say, but she needed to reassure herself that she could be the kind of wife Daniel deserved. She needed to know that she could feel passion without fear.

"Is anything wrong?" he prompted.

"Daniel, I . . ."

"You're having second thoughts." His eyes became shuttered, taking on the ice blue sheen she hadn't seen in so long.

"No. I just need you to . . . Daniel, kiss me."

"What?"

"Do it. Please."

He grinned at her indulgently. "You can't wait for the ceremony?"

"Please, Daniel," she begged.

"And how would you like to be kissed? Like a friend? An acquaintance? A sister?"

"Don't tease."

He tried to appear serious, but the twitch at the corners of his lips gave him away. "I suppose you've decided to test the goods first? If that's the case, wouldn't you like more of an inspection? But then, you've seen almost all there is to see, haven't you?"

She threw her arms around his neck and pressed her lips to his, cutting off anything else he might have said.

No, she hadn't imagined how good it felt to have Daniel's lips on her own. How strong and safe he felt. How he made her believe she could conquer the world.

When he drew away, she smiled with satisfaction.

"Care to tell me what that was all about?"

"I needed to know I could . . . feel the things Essie told me about."

He pressed her palm to his chest, then eased it down, down. "You're free to feel anything you'd like."

"Daniel!"

Her face flamed and he chuckled, touching her chin and closing her mouth. "We'll continue this later. When we're alone and properly wed." Releasing her, he withdrew his watch and snapped open the lid. "We're late. I'll see if I can't put them off for a minute or two while you comb your hair."

The heat in his gaze chased away her last-minute fears. "We're going to be married, Susan," he stated decisively. "I'll see you in the parlor. Don't dally."

*   *   *

Less than fifteen minutes later Susan stood by Daniel's side. Around her stood the orphans in their Sunday best. One girl played the upright piano in the corner while another sang. Essie sniffled with delight. Sister Mary Margaret beamed and served as maid of honor while Donovan stood as best man. Max reluctantly held the rings, staring at Susan with huge betrayed eyes.

"Shall we begin?" Father Parker asked, looping his spectacles over his ears. "We are gathered here today . . ."

Susan memorized Daniel's tall, muscular form in his black dress suit and crisp white shirt. Without question, she'd made a wise decision. Strong, tall, and rugged, Daniel personified everything the West was supposed to breed into a man—courage, honor, and pride.

"More second thoughts?" Daniel murmured beneath the priest's counsel.

She squeezed his hand. "No."

The exchange of vows was brief. Through it all, Susan stood relaxed and calm, knowing she was doing the right thing. The cool weight of the gold band Daniel slid over her finger became a tangible symbol of their promises.

Father Parker finished the ceremony. "You may now kiss the bride."

Daniel bent to pull her into his powerful embrace, leaving Susan, the good father, and everyone else with no doubt that this would be a true marriage.

When he released her, Susan's heels sank to the floor. She touched her lips. He'd kissed her thoroughly, passionately. But instead of frightening her, he made her long for more.

The hall clock wheezed and ticked, filling the parlor with its rhythm and underlying the heavy silence that cloaked the two people who sat on the horsehair settee. Nearly a foot separated them, Susan guessed, but they were so aware of each other that they might as well have been sitting in each other's laps.

She peeked from beneath her lashes at the man who sat on her right. Although she had never seen Daniel at a loss, he was looking vaguely uncomfortable now. The last of their guests had left, and except for Father Parker who was snoring peacefully in the corner chair, they were alone. From the inner recesses of the house, they could hear Donovan settling the boys into bed and Essie returning the last few dishes to the hutch.

Susan wondered how long Daniel would wait before suggesting that they retire for the night. The tension in the room had become tangible and was beginning to crackle and pull taut. It was almost ten, and Daniel had yet to remove his jacket or loosen his tie, which only added to his stiffness. Susan wondered when he planned to release the buttons, shed his vest, his suspenders. And then . . .

A chill raced through her body, but she banished it by concentrating on the memory of the night she'd removed his shirt and tended to his wound. His skin had been warm then, and taut. And firm.

"Tired?"

Susan jumped when Daniel spoke to her for the first time in an hour. His expression was grim, but not with anger or frustration. It was something more. Something far more.

The moment had come.

"Yes. I am tired."

The clock wheezed a halfhearted chime. Ten o'clock.

"Daniel?"

"Yes?" His voice grew thick and rough.

She licked her lips to ease their dryness. "Daniel, Essie says that it doesn't have to be bad."

He cleared his throat. "What else did Essie tell you?"

"She told me . . . she told me that . . ." She could see a faint blush of color stain his cheeks and wondered if her own skin had turned fiery. "She told me that men almost always feel a pleasurable sensation." Images of a night so long ago rose to swim in front of her. Men laughing in drunken delight, calling out in raucous enjoyment.

As if he sensed her distress, Daniel touched her cheek. Closing her eyes, Susan concentrated on his finger as it slipped down her throat. Ruthlessly she clung to that point of contact. She *would* conquer her fears. She *would*.

Afraid that he might sense her nervousness and pull away, Susan continued. "Essie told me that a woman can feel good, too, Daniel. If she loves the man. And if he cares for her."

Daniel's Adam's apple bobbed as he swallowed. He tangled his hands in the ringlets that cascaded down her back. The fine hair at the back of her neck stood on end in response to his touch.

"Is that all you and Essie talked about?" he asked, his smooth voice not betraying his own quaking nerves.

"No. She said you were a big man and—"

"Sweet bloody hell!" he interjected swiftly, his voice still no louder than a whisper as he glanced at the supine Father Parker to see if he'd awakened and overheard. When he turned back, the lamplight stroked the blunt lines of his features, but Susan found only gentleness in his expression. "I take it there will be no secrets or surprises when I take you to bed."

Her heart bounded against her chest. He meant to make love to her. After an entire night of uncertainty, Susan had her answer.

"When?"

Her question startled him. He stood and walked to the window.

"When, Daniel?"

"Soon."

"Tonight?"

"I don't know. Go up to bed, Susan. I need to check on my horse and bed him down for the night."

Susan acquiesced, but then stopped and returned to his side. Clasping his arm for support, she rose on tiptoe to press her lips to his cheek. His eyes burned with some deep emotion she could not identify. Desire? Wonder?

"Good night." She took two steps, then rushed from the room.

Daniel watched her go, a knot of passion tightening his loins. He tried to still the urgency of his body. How was it that Susan's innocent gestures and words could inflame him more than the practiced seduction of an experienced woman?

Not bothering to put on his coat, Daniel escaped outside. He knew what Susan wanted of him tonight. And, heaven help him, he knew that the rest of the household expected the same thing. But Daniel admitted he was more nervous than he had ever been. His first attempt at lovemaking had been nothing compared to the indecision that flowed through him now.

The next few hours would set the tone not only for the rest of their marriage but also for the way Susan would feel about intimacy for the rest of her life. If he frightened her, she would learn to expect such a reaction. If he refused to touch her, she would think he found her lacking. Whatever he did, she could be affected for years to come. The thought was not only daunting, it was downright chilling.

Stepping into the mustiness of the barn, he settled Chief for the night, giving him an extra measure of oats. As he turned from the stall, he paused to slap the gelding on the rump.

"Well, boy," he murmured, "at least one of us will have an easy night of it." Daniel snorted ruefully before adding, "And it won't be me."

22

By the time Daniel finished in the barn and returned to the house, the clock was preparing to strike ten-thirty. The halls were dark. Father Parker had apparently awakened and gone home.

Daniel lit one of the lamps left on the hall table and fought the nervous churning of his stomach. Maybe Susan was already asleep. The day had been hectic, the evening long. Surely she felt the effects as much as he did.

He grasped the oak railing, paused, then with a burst of self-deprecation, strode down the hall to the guest room. He'd just wash up and gather a few clothes. Then he'd worry about how and when he'd go to Susan's room.

As he walked down the corridor, Daniel nearly swore aloud. Each plank of the floor heralded his progress. Every person in the house would know good and well where he was going and how long he stayed. And if the floors were this noisy, what kind of sounds would come from Susan's bed?

Daniel clamped his hand around the doorknob and twisted the brass ball as if to tear it from its escutcheon. He flung the door open and lifted the lamp.

Everything was gone from the room. His clothes. His saddlebags. Even the pitcher and basin that had stood on his dresser. With a sinking feeling, Daniel saw that the bed had been stripped and the mattress was rolled against the headboard.

"Daniel! What the hell are you doing here?"

Daniel jumped as if he'd been shot.

Donovan pushed away from the door to the boys' bedroom and padded barefoot down the hall. His shirt was unbuttoned, revealing a still-taut stomach. "Why aren't you upstairs?"

Daniel's mouth opened. Then closed. What could he say? He certainly couldn't tell Donovan that he'd been too yellow-livered to go to Susan's room. His *wife's* room. And he certainly wouldn't admit that he'd been considering spending another hour downstairs praying Susan would fall asleep before he joined her.

"I came to get my clothes," Daniel muttered, avoiding Donovan's twinkling eyes.

"I moved them. I knew you wouldn't have time. I thought the two of you would be more comfortable in Susan's room and away from the peephole. But I could move you back tomorrow if you'd like."

Suddenly Daniel felt like a prize stallion being sent out to breed with an audience waiting to watch.

"No. You're right." His voice sounded like the croak of a strangling frog. "After all, we'll only be staying a night or two anyway."

"Where will you be taking her?"

"My place." The floorboards squeaked beneath Daniel's feet as he retreated toward the back staircase. "Where it's quiet."

*　　*　　*

Susan walked to the far side of the bedroom. Stopping, she curled her toes against the cold floor, pressing one foot on top of the other and wrapping her arms around her body in an effort to get warm. She stared sightlessly out the window. Waiting. Worrying.

Minutes ago she'd stood at this same window and watched Daniel return from the barn, but then, instead of coming to her, he'd stayed downstairs. Her fingers pleated the fabric belt of her robe. He would come upstairs soon. He had to.

Didn't he?

Gnawing her lower lip, Susan frowned at her reflection in the window. She'd dressed in one of Essie's old wrappers and the voluminous linen nightgown Daniel had seen her in once before—the Dooleys had ruined her only other sleeping shift—and she was afraid that her attire was far from arousing. But her hair was neatly plaited and tied with a ribbon. Her skin glowed from a recent scrubbing, and her hands . . .
Well, her hands were freezing and trembling, and if he didn't come soon, she was going to—

The door burst open behind her.

She turned, coming face to face with Daniel. The door swung closed on its hinges, the lock snapping shut.

"I went to get my clothes."

"I see."

"They weren't there," he added.

"No?"

"No."

Nothing. She couldn't think of a thing to say.

"Donovan said he moved them in here."

"No."

"No, what?"

"No, he didn't move them in here. I thought they were downstairs."

Daniel frowned. "What in the hell did he do with my things?"

Silence.

"What do you need?" Susan asked, nervously wrapping the tie of her robe around her wrist.

"I don't need anything." At her startled look he hurried on, "I mean, I thought I'd wash first."

"Would you like a nightshirt?"

"What?"

"Donovan doesn't wear one, I don't think. But the boys might have something that would work."

"No. I don't want a nightshirt." When she blanched, he hurried on. "I mean . . ." He sighed. "Oh, hell."

He didn't speak for a long time. Susan gestured to the basin and pitcher on the nightstand. "I left you some water. It's still fairly warm."

"Yeah. Thanks." After a moment, he shrugged out of his jacket. Very carefully he laid it over the back of the rocker she'd moved into the corner of the room. Then he tugged at the string tie.

He was about to wash. In front of her. Here. In her room.

"Maybe you'd better get into bed. It's cold."

A rush of fear swept over her. "Should I take off my nightgown?"

"What!" Daniel faced her. "No. You're fine. Just fine." When she didn't move, he sighed. "Get under the covers. I don't want you catching your death."

"Which side?"

Daniel studied the single bed. There was no need to ask about sides. They'd be lucky if they found any room at all. "Doesn't matter."

Susan took off the wrapper and edged toward the bedstead. The quilts had already been turned down invitingly. The linens were cold next to her skin. She burrowed her legs beneath the sheets, heavy woolen blankets, and log cabin quilt. Bending her knees to her chest, she tucked her toes under her, pressing her back to the headboard and drawing the covers up to her chin. Though it was difficult on the narrow space, she managed to move far enough to one side to leave a sliver of room for Daniel.

Wryly Daniel noted that she'd taken the side closer to the door.

The next few minutes passed in an agony of self-consciousness for Daniel. He was no innocent with women. At the age of nine, he'd hidden in one of Pennsylvania's finest brothels. Soon he'd known all there was to know. At fifteen, he'd experimented with that knowledge firsthand. Since then he'd undressed in front of more females than he cared to remember.

But now . . . now he was disrobing in front of Susan. *His wife.* It was a sobering thought. As much as he might wonder at the phenomenon, Daniel's hands shook when he removed his tie and unbuttoned his shirt. After pausing only momentarily, he tugged the garment off. And shivered. Not from the temperature of the room but from Susan's penetrating stare.

Daniel sought to ignore the way she watched him pour water from the pitcher into the basin. But her scrutiny was like a hot finger sweeping down the crease of his spine.

Dipping his hands into the liquid, he rinsed his face and neck. What he'd thought would help him to control his sudden desires only served to intensify them. In the mirror over the dresser, he could see the way she eyed the moisture dripping onto his chest.

". . . a cloth on the—"

"What?" he interrupted.

Their gazes met and clung in the mirror.

"There's a cloth you can use. And I laid out your toiletries—Donovan did bring those." Her voice grew husky and snagged on his nerves like a callused hand.

He nodded and studied the rippled surface of the water. He'd best get this over with. Soon.

Quickly he splashed his chest and under his arms, unaware of the way the lamplight gleamed on his golden skin. But Susan was noticing it. Susan was conscious of the way each water-dappled muscle stretched and pulled when he moved. The moisture clung to the soft, silky patch of hair in the center of his chest. One wayward runnel broke loose of its silken trap to plunge down the crease in the center of his abdomen. When the droplet moved out of the area reflected in the looking glass, Susan pictured that drop plunging over the firm planes and pooling in the hollow of his navel.

Then he began to shave.

"I thought you didn't shave at night."

Daniel opened his mouth to respond, then closed it again. What could he say to that? She'd figure out soon enough that the sun did not cause his beard to grow, as he'd once told her. He could only imagine what thoughts would crowd into her head.

At long last Daniel finished his ablutions and looped the towel through the handle of the pitcher. Then he twisted the wick of the lamp until they were plunged into darkness. A darkness that should have been comforting. But was not. The blackness sizzled with tension.

Working quickly, Daniel shucked his boots, socks, and pants, leaving the bottoms of his long woolen underwear. At the edge of the bed he paused, seriously considering sleeping on the floor. But judging by the rustling of bedclothes, Susan had moved to the far side of the mattress and now lay poised, near falling.

Shutting his eyes, Daniel prayed for guidance.

Susan lay on her back, her hands at her sides, hugging the edge of the bed. Even so, when Daniel slid between the sheets, there was no avoiding the way his limbs tangled with hers. To her infinite relief, she discovered that he'd worn his drawers to bed, unlike the morning she'd caught him wearing only a sheet.

For long, awkward minutes, they lay next to each other trying not to move. Susan frantically wondered when it would begin. She could hear Daniel's breathing become more rapid. His skin increased in temperature while hers grew cold, icy.

Susan balled her fists in an attempt to garner her courage. "What do you want me to do?" she blurted.

Daniel had been hoping she'd fall asleep, but evidently that wasn't going to occur. "Why don't you . . ." He broke off, wincing at the sound of his own voice, full and heavy, in the darkness. Swallowing, he began again. "Why don't you come over here?"

After only a slight hesitation, he felt the mattress dip at his side. Lifting his arm, he drew her closer until her head rested in the crook of his shoulder. Her breast pressed intimately against his ribs. He could feel its weight, its fullness and it filled him with a pounding expectancy. A delirious, breathless energy.

Despite the heat being generated by their bodies beneath the covers, Susan started to shiver. Very slowly, because he'd always begun their embraces by caressing her face, Daniel skimmed his knuckles over the curve of her cheek. Her skin was silken. Irresistible. He wondered feverishly if the rest of her could possibly feel so sweet.

After some time Susan spoke again. "Daniel?"

"Hmm?" He could barely pull his thoughts into line. He was wondering how much longer he could go on like this, simply holding her, caressing her, but never allowing his passion free rein, never letting her to see how much he wanted her, needed her.

"What do I do next?"

The question nearly sent him over the edge. "Why don't you put your hand on my chest?"

He thought she would refuse. She had backed away so many times in the past. And he knew that if she could have guessed his thoughts, she'd have run screaming into the night. But shyly, hesitantly, she rested her palm on his breastbone. Her slender fingers seared his bare skin.

Time crept by. Susan continued to tremble in his arms, but less forcefully. Daniel could only pray that she would fall asleep soon, before he lost his ability to reason.

"Wouldn't you like to touch me, too, Daniel?"

Her words tore at his fragile control. Unable to resist his own desires, let alone the entreaty of her voice, he found he couldn't refuse.

Knowing he didn't trust himself to surrender to the invitation of her smooth flesh, he tugged at the grosgrain ribbon binding her hair. As he had wanted to for so long, Daniel freed the silken waves, combing them with his fingers and allowing them to spill over his chest. The soft strands tickled and tormented his skin. The fresh scents of rosewater and lavender filled his senses.

Growing bold at her own success, Susan slid her fingers across the firm span of his chest. Her palms molded each swell and hollow. Daniel groaned and tried to grasp the last shreds of sanity as she traced the faint swirls of hair across his breast, her fingers skidding across the taut skin until they rubbed over one masculine nipple.

Daniel felt a flare of heat and hunger at her tentative touch. Tilting her chin up, he took her mouth, greedily tasting, his tongue sweeping over her teeth, her lips. He rolled over, pinning her to the bed, one thigh shifting to rest on top of hers.

Her body had been made for his. He had never felt

so at home in another woman's arms. He wanted her so much. He yearned to have her arms wrapped around him, her body arching to meet his own.

He felt Susan quiver and shifted his body more securely over hers, thinking she was still cold. Then she shuddered again. A jagged sob escaped from her lips.

A sinking wave of self-loathing inundated him. He'd gone too far too fast.

She tried to pull away, but Daniel resolutely held her, speaking nonsense words to calm her. When she pushed against his chest with both hands, he held her face with his palms and forced her to look at him. In the moonwashed bedroom, she appeared frightened and ashamed.

"Don't. It's not your fault," he urged. "I went too quickly."

She covered her eyes with her hands. "I'm sorry." Twisting free of his embrace, she stumbled from the bed. Hurrying to the dresser, she lit the lamp. She had to dispel the darkness. The fear.

"Susan, stop running from me. We can work this out but only if you don't back away every time I upset you."

"Upset? Upset!" She turned on him, and the moonlight revealed the wildness of her features. "I can't do it. I can't!"

"Give it time."

"No! You don't understand. I thought once we were married, everything would be fine. But I can't let go of the past. When you touch me, the blackness spreads through me time and time again and I can't push it away!" The second she blurted her confession, Susan blanched. What a horrible thing to say to her bridegroom.

Daniel sat up in bed and raked his fingers through

his hair. The sheets pooled low over his hips, emphasizing his masculinity.

"I didn't marry you for sex, Susan. That's only one small portion of what goes on between a husband and wife." His tone held the frayed roughness of hurt and frustration.

"I shouldn't have married you at all."

She saw the color leave his skin.

"I knew that I would be punished if—" she stopped. She'd said too much.

"Punished?" Daniel swung from the bed and advanced.

She would have backed away from his fierce expression, but the dresser effectively prevented her escape.

Daniel captured her chin in his hand. "What have you got to be punished for? What have you done that's so horrible you think you deserve to be afraid?"

Vaguely she knew that he had taken her arms and tried to shake her. But thick clinging tendrils of darkness pulled her into the past, dredging up memories she had buried so deep they had festered and distorted.

Mama, Mama, I heard you call.

He was so big next to her. So male. He overpowered her, making her feel tiny and insignificant. Weak.

Helpless.

Just as those men had done.

The shadows crowded close. Dank smells and dark shapes filled the room. Gasping, she tried to focus on her husband, but Daniel's shape kept wavering, changing.

Mama!

Sobbing, she tried to free herself, but he held her fast. Distantly she heard him saying, "Tell me. Tell me what happened!"

She knew what he wanted. She had always known that one day she would have to confess her sins. But even now she shrank away from that course of action. No punishment could be worse than revealing to him what she had done.

"Tell me."

For the first time Susan consciously allowed herself to think of that night so long before. Her heart pounded in her chest as if fighting some overpowering force. It was so long ago. So long . . .

The room echoed with the phantom sounds of a woman's bitter sobs. And then the words tumbled from Susan's lips as she began to tell Daniel her story.

Fear ruled, just as it had so many years ago.

She heard thunder. Strange shouts. Papa was there somewhere. But it was Mama who jostled her awake. "Susan, I want you to run and hide in the cellar. A game! We're going to play a game."

She hugged her rag rabbit and scooted closer to the wall.

"Susan! Do as I say. You know what happens when you don't mind Mama."

She knew, she thought, as she darted a quick look at the painting of Jesus over her bed. God wouldn't love her if she disobeyed. She scrambled out of bed and hurried after her mother, wondering at the strange game.

Erin Hurst led her from the house and down the steps to the cellar. Big beams, bare of their winter stores, arched like arms overhead, and when Mama tried to go, Susan clasped her skirts. "Don't leave me here alone. Please don't leave me."

Erin bent to hug her close. "I love you, Susan. I love you." The thunder grew louder. Strange popping noises began, like those made by Papa's gun when they went hunting. "I want you to stay here. And don't come out! Not until I call for you. Do you understand me?"

Susan caught her mother's hand as she walked away. "Don't go, please."

"Susan!" A trace of panic tinged Mama's voice. "Do as you're told."

The cellar door slammed over Susan's head. She sobbed, gazing around in desperation. The thunder came again, sounding more like horses than an approaching storm. Susan stumbled up the rickety steps and pressed her ear to the trapdoor. She would do as she'd been told. She would be a good girl for Mama. Then, like the picture above her bed, Jesus would hold her on his lap and love her, and she wouldn't be punished.

Faintly she thought she detected her mother's voice. Was she calling? Was the game over? Once again she heard her mother's cries—more insistent this time. Fearing Mama needed her and would scold her if she didn't come, Susan climbed from the cellar.

She walked barefoot into the dark night and crept around the house. "Mama? Mama, I thought I heard you call."

At the edge of the house she stopped, gaping at the shape that lay on the ground in a pool of crimson. "Papa?" He was still. So . . . still. The man who stood over him ignored the fact that her father's life-less fingers still curled around the grip of a revolver. The stranger's knife gleamed with blood. He clutched her father's gold watch.

"Where's the rest?"

Susan cowered behind the corner of the house, unseen. Five other men circled her mother, taunting her, pushing her.

Mama sobbed, covering her face with her hands. "There's no more. No more!"

"Where's your money? You must have food!"

"There's nothing!"

The man with the knife kicked Susan's father and approached Erin. "Then we'll just have to take something else in exchange, won't we?"

"Mama!"

Her mother's hands dropped. Her face filled with terror. "Susan, go back!"

The man with the knife turned.

"Come here, little girl."

She took a step back.

"Little girl!"

The man with the knife wrapped an arm around her mother's neck and pressed the red-stained blade to her throat. "Come here or I'll cut her with this knife."

"No! Run, Susan!"

Susan turned to escape, slamming into another man. He lifted her, kicking and screaming, and carried her toward the tight knot of men. Roughly he set her in the center. When she dodged toward her mother, the man took her by one long braid and yanked her back.

"Just stand still, girlie. Stand still while we touch your mama's skin."

"Susan, close your eyes! You hear me? You close them tight. So tight you can't see the men or me."

Hesitating only a second, Susan obeyed. But she opened them once. She saw the men, their faces alight with lust, their expressions impatient as they taunted the man who lay upon her mother with a knife against her throat.

"Mama!"

The grunting man pushed away from Mama and came toward her, grinning, leering.

"So you want to play, too."

Screaming, Susan wriggled free from the group of

men. She ran to Papa. But he was dead and could not help her. Sobbing, hearing the men behind her, she grabbed the revolver with both hands. Lifting it wildly, she pulled the trigger, just as she'd seen her father do.

The gun jerked out of her hands. The shot went wild, the bullet striking one of the men in the chest. He tumbled to the ground and lay still.

"You little bitch!" the man's friend gasped, rolling the dead man onto his back so that his eyes stared sightlessly into the sky. "I'll show you what happens to little girls who interfere."

Behind him, Erin Hurst staggered to her knees, lifted a rock from the ground and brought it crashing down over the man's head.

"Run!"

Susan ran then. Ran and ran. She hid late into the night in the dank weeds surrounding the pond. Only after the rumble of the men's horses had disappeared into the heavy dawn did she force herself to return home. She went to her papa. But he was cold now.

Sobbing, she pushed herself to her feet and stumbled toward the second form in the grass. The face of the woman was barely recognizable, the body savaged. Susan could almost believe it was someone else . . . except for the hair. The bright red hair.

"Su . . ."

The word was a whisper, but Susan heard it. "Mama?" Clutching her mother's hands she bent low.

Erin managed to open one eye despite the swollen and battered flesh. Then when she caught sight of Susan, she looked away.

"Don't . . . look . . ."

"I didn't look, Mama, I didn't." But she had. She had not done as she'd been told. She would be punished.

Mama cried out, writhing on the ground. She pinned Susan in a wild clawlike grip. "Bring . . . me . . . gun." Susan shrank away, but Erin pulled her close. "No one can help me now . . . but . . . God." The one green eye that had escaped injury welled with tears despite the wreckage of her face. "I will . . . die . . . soon." The hands were desperate. Clawing. "I won't let you . . . watch."

"Mama?" She tried to touch her mother's face, her hands, but there was no place free from blood.

"Bring it!" Mama fiercely whispered, then panted for breath. "Do not disobey . . . me."

Leadenly, Susan went back to the body of her father and grabbed the revolver. She returned to Mama on legs that quaked.

"Give . . . it."

"No."

"Su . . . san . . . obey . . . me."

With a sob, Susan sank to her knees and threw the revolver to the ground.

Erin's fingers crawled, inch by inch, bit by bit. She encountered the grip but didn't have the strength to tug it toward her.

"Susan . . . I love . . . you." The one green eye was pressed shut. A tear slipped free to mingle with the blood. "Help . . . me."

Susan sobbed and backed away like a crab scuttling in the sand. "No!"

The black barrel gleamed on the ground next to her mother's distorted hand.

"Do not . . . disobey. Help . . . Then run . . . back to cellar. Please . . . help." The slit of a mouth that had once been lovely and had kissed Susan's cheek and whispered secrets in her ear opened, gasping for air to plead again. But no words emerged. That one green eye grew cloudy, lifeless. Dim.

"Mama?" The shape that no longer resembled her mother did not move.

Susan had disobeyed. She had not stayed in the cellar. She had not kept her eyes closed.

She had killed a man.

Crawling forward, she tried to shake Mama awake. But the flesh beneath her fingers felt odd. Unresponsive. "Mama! Answer me!" Horror threatened to consume her. She alone was responsible. If she had not disobeyed, her mother would have been safe. Her voice dropped to a painful whisper. *"Mama? Mama? Mama . . ."*

The bedroom echoed in silence. The air hung still. Silent.

In the aftermath of Susan's story Daniel didn't know what to say. What could anyone say? In all these years, no one had ever known, ever suspected, what had happened to Susan as a young girl. Though Susan's reaction to men had caused many people to surmise that she'd seen her mother being raped, no one had ever guessed that her scars were due to more. So much more. In her childish mind she had truly believed that if she'd obeyed her mother's commands, her family would not have been destroyed. For too long she'd carried the burden alone, thinking that God would demand a terrible penance of her for killing the deserter and for causing her parents' murder. That was probably why she had entered the convent—by serving God she had hoped to atone for her supposed sins.

But Daniel had stormed into her life, shaking that belief and drawing her away from her own tangled notion of justice. And now he had reopened the wounds. He had painfully resurrected the child in order to heal the woman.

Folding her close, Daniel absorbed her shuddering

sobs. And then, when the tears began, he rocked her, saying over and over, "It wasn't your fault, it wasn't your fault."

Lifting her face, he forced her to look at him. "Your mother loved you. She loved you. She would never have wanted you to feel such pain. When she asked you to obey, she only meant to protect you."

"I should have helped her! In the end she begged me to help her, but I didn't. I could have done something! If I'd behaved differently, if I'd obeyed her, she wouldn't have suffered. I should have found a way to ease her pain."

"You did, sweetheart, you did. You were with her at the end. She adored you. She loved you. She wanted to protect you. Neither she nor God would demand penance for what happened. Don't you see? Your mother could have lingered, but God took her. He took her so she wouldn't suffer. So *you* wouldn't suffer. He carried her spirit away to a place where she would be happy and free from pain. He never meant for you to torture yourself this way."

The words shimmered in the silence that followed.

"He took her," Susan echoed. Her hands clutched his shirt. She wanted, *needed,* to know that what Daniel said was true.

In her husband's eyes she found no disgust, no blame. Only a wealth of understanding. At one time she had thought that by becoming a nun she could atone for her part in her parents' death. But God hadn't demanded penance; Susan had. It had taken Daniel to make her see that.

"You haven't done anything wrong, sweetheart. You haven't done anything wrong."

She buried her head beneath his chin and wrapped her arms about his waist.

The wounds began to heal.

23

Timmy Libbley hid behind the water tower and watched. The freight train had pulled into Ashton at half past one in the morning. It would remain there, taking on supplies, for another quarter of an hour.

The young Pinkerton agent huddled in the cold and waited. Five minutes passed. Ten. The engine began to pant and gather energy.

As soon as the huge iron wheels ground into motion, Timmy swung into his saddle. Avoiding the shower of sparks being thrown from the track, he urged his mount into a gallop.

After taking the shortcut through the trees, he reined to a stop in front of Jedidiah Kutter.

"Did they take the bait and try to stop the train?"

"Nope. There wasn't a sign of a Dooley for miles."

Kutter swore, wrenching his hat from his head and swiping at his brow. "You're sure you planted the information about the dynamite with one of the Dooleys when you were in that saloon in Barryville?"

"Yes, sir."

"And the man appeared interested?"

"I'd say so. The whole clan started whooping and hollering."

"Then why didn't they come?" Kutter jammed his hat on. The original plan had been to lure some of the Dooleys out of hiding with a crate of dynamite, pick a few of them off, and follow them back to their camp, thus giving the Pinkertons the upper hand. Kutter had counted on knowing when the Dooleys planned to attack by having his own men follow them each step of the way. Now he had no more idea where they could be camped than he'd had a week ago.

Kutter signaled to one of the men who lingered next to the track. "Stop the train and retrieve the dynamite. No sense sending the explosives all the way back to Cheyenne."

Braxton Hill saluted, then swung the lantern from side to side. The locomotive grumbled in the distance, shuddered, and eventually squealed to a stop.

Braxton and his men rode up to the final boxcar and clambered aboard. A few seconds later they reappeared.

"Kutter!"

"Yeah."

"I think you'd better come here, sir."

"Damn, damn, damn." Kutter reined his horse toward the train. Timmy hesitantly followed.

"Well? What's the problem?"

Braxton hunkered down and eyed Timmy.

"You're sure no one tried to board the train at the station, boy?"

"I'm positive, sir."

"And you telegraphed the order for the dynamite *personally* and specified it was to be sent *without* fuses?"

Timmy paled. "I forgot to tell them about the fuses."

"Shit. Did you confirm that the dynamite was loaded at all?"

Timmy shifted uncomfortably in his saddle. "Y-yes, sir."

"Don't stammer!"

Timmy jumped at Kutter's rebuke. But Kutter soon lost interest in reprimanding him and glared at the wiry man squatting on the threshold of the boxcar. "Why all the questions?"

Braxton spit into the snow in disgust. "It's gone. The dynamite is gone."

Susan woke to find her head resting on Daniel's shoulder, her hair tangled between them. She blinked, staring at the bright patch of sunlight on the opposite wall. Then she gradually became aware that her arms hugged his waist and her nightgown rode high on her thighs.

But for once she felt no mortification, no guilt, no shame. Though the fear still lingered, deep inside her mind, the emotion was fainter now. Drawing upon the strength and absolution Daniel had offered her, she knew that she could one day be whole.

When she shifted, Daniel's fingers slipped into her hair, urging her to stay where she was. "Don't get up. Not yet. Just lie here and rest some more."

Surrendering, she lay in his arms, absorbing the heat of his body, the steady beat of his heart. Turning her head, she pressed a kiss to his collarbone.

He grew still beneath her.

"Last night . . ."

She pressed two fingers over his lips. "Thank you." Nothing more needed to be said. Her eyes conveyed her tacit message.

Bending close, she kissed his jaw, his chin, then touched her lips to his.

"Do you know," he stated hesitantly, "that when I first saw your hair loose, there was one thing that I wanted but thought I'd never have."

"What?"

He shifted, gradually, tenderly, until Susan lay across his chest. Their legs tangled intimately. Her lips were poised above his.

"Just once I wanted to have you lean over me with your hair falling around your shoulders so that I could hold you beneath a curtain of fire."

Delight spilled into her veins. Fear skittered away.

He urged her closer. Softly, gently, the tip of his nose skimmed her cheek, her nose, in a teasing caress. Then his mouth met hers. Susan did not back away. She buried the wispy remains of blackness and reveled in his embrace. Daniel's mouth became eager, then grew hungry. He completely possessed her with his kiss.

She clutched the pillow beneath his head, shutting out everything but the taste and smell of Daniel.

He was the one who drew away. His eyes darkened with passion. "We'll take things step by step."

"Yes," she replied breathlessly.

Proud of herself, Susan scrambled from the bed. Daniel didn't follow. Clasping his hands behind his head, he studied her every move. Momentarily daunted at the intimacy of having him watch her dress, Susan managed to slip her camisole and pantalets on beneath her nightdress. Her corset, however, proved to be a more difficult matter. Muttering under her breath, she tried to fasten the busk, but the laces had been tightened for her wedding and would have to be redone.

"Allow me."

Susan squealed when Daniel grasped the hem of

her gown and drew it over her head. Then he firmly turned her around and fastened her corset before handing her the butternut wool dress she'd folded over the arm of the rocker.

His gaze grew heated, fathomless, when his eyes met hers. He caressed the gentle slope of her shoulders.

She grew still.

He smiled.

Her eyes darkened.

His burned. Then he kissed her, long, slow, and wet.

When he lifted his head, she clutched her dress in a rumpled wad. When she managed to get into it at last, her cheeks flaming, he reached for his trousers and began to clothe himself. By the time he'd finished, Susan had neatly plaited her hair and fastened it with another ribbon.

In the mirror above the dresser, Susan watched Daniel approach. He tweaked her braid and pulled her to the door. "Give it time, Susan. Right now the only thing that should trouble you is what we'll have for breakfast."

After opening the door, he ushered her into the hall. On the opposite side of the threshold, blocking the corridor, lay a pile of Daniel's things.

"Donovan!" Daniel bellowed.

Susan began to laugh.

Sister Mary Margaret found Max at the huge kitchen table in the Ashton convent. He sat in his customary position, head down, arms protectively circling his plate as if he feared someone would take it—a habit he'd picked up during his two years in Andersonville prison during the war.

"Max?"

He didn't answer, but continued to stare morosely

225

into his cereal. Mary Margaret was relieved to find him in the kitchen. Since arriving in Ashton, he had taken to wandering the countryside, gathering treasures to put in his cigar box: rocks, bottles, matches, and twine.

"How would you like some raisins and honey in your oatmeal?" Usually the thought of such a treat would have brightened Max's week.

He barely moved.

Sighing, Mary Margaret took the seat beside him. "Max, Susan hasn't abandoned you. She's simply gone on to a new life."

He looked up at her, his expression tortured. "She was supposed to marry God."

Mary Margaret chafed his enormous work-worn hands. "Don't you want her to be happy?"

His lower lip jutted out in a sulky little-boy pout. "I didn't want her to leave."

"I know, Max. I know. But Daniel Crocker will be good to her. You'll see."

"Better'n God?" His chin trembled. His eyes filled with tears.

"Oh, Max," she murmured, feeling an echo of his pain. Gently she drew his grizzled head onto her shoulder. "She was a true friend to you, wasn't she? Someone special."

He nodded, clutching huge fistfuls of Mary Margaret's habit. "She has to come back. She has to! I've got to make her come back."

"She can't come back, Max. She doesn't belong in a convent anymore." Mary Margaret tried to think of a way to explain the situation in terms he could understand. "Do you remember the baby bird you found in the stables at the convent?"

"Ye-es."

"You were such a good friend to that baby bird,

Max. You nursed it and fed it and kept it warm. But what happened when it grew big?''

He refused to speak, even though she knew he remembered that little sparrow more clearly than he remembered his own departed family.

Mary Margaret continued, "He had never been around other birds. He didn't even know he was a bird. He used to hop around the yard or ride on your shoulder, but he couldn't fly. So what did you do, Max?"

He didn't respond.

"You were so wise. What did you do?"

"I—I took it out to the forest."

"Yes," she encouraged.

"I let it play with the other birds."

"And then what?"

He clutched her tighter, but there was no answer.

"You let him go, Max."

He sobbed.

"Let Susan go, Max."

"No-oo."

"Let her go."

He cried, his mouth open, eyes squeezed shut in abject misery. His giant's body shook with great heartrending sobs.

But Sister Mary Margaret rocked him back and forth like the child he was, knowing that someday soon Max would have to find a way to resign himself to the situation.

24

Susan stood shivering on the back stoop watching Daniel prepare his horse. A faint streak of light smudged the horizon, promising a cold winter day to come.

Instead of wearing his calfskin coat, Daniel had chosen a heavy canvas duster. Underneath, he'd dressed in denims, a chambray shirt, and another, shorter, fleece-lined black jacket. Susan understood that the clothes were, in a way, the uniform Daniel wore while working with the Pinkertons, since they allowed him to move quickly and silently.

"You could wait in the house," he said, noting her chattering teeth and pinched expression.

"No."

After another searching glance, he looped his saddlebags over Chief's rump.

Susan followed each motion he made with an outward show of dispassionate concern. Inside she was a quivering mass of nerves. Since their wedding night, she and Daniel had grown closer to each other than ever before.

Then, late Saturday night, one of Daniel's men had come to the orphanage and taken him away. Susan had waited impatiently while one hour melted into two. Then three. Daniel had returned, preoccupied and exuding an aura of quiet energy. But he would not tell her where he had been. Only that he had work to do the next day with the Pinkertons.

Later, in bed, he'd kissed her with a passion that startled and delighted her at the same time, then held her tightly against him, her head tucked under his chin. He'd remained motionless, silent, as if afraid he'd shatter the moment. As time passed, Susan began to fear his last assignment would be a dangerous one.

She had heard enough about the Pinkertons to know what Daniel would be facing in the next few hours. Here in the West, the Pinkertons had a reputation for relentlessly tracking their prey. They used whatever means necessary—usually violence.

Judging by Daniel's restlessness, Susan guessed that his assignment would bring him in contact with the Dooleys. Although she'd had no personal experience involving them, Susan knew they were ruthless. They'd been responsible for countless murders, countless fires.

And they killed.

Susan hadn't slept the entire night. She'd lain in Daniel's arms, listening to the sound of his steady breathing and the rhythmic beat of his heart. Over and over again she'd prayed to God and every saint in heaven to keep him safe. Her grasp on her own inner peace was nearly secure now, but if something were to happen to Daniel . . .

She couldn't bear to think of it. She didn't think

she could survive if something happened to him. She had grown to love him so deeply.

Love him.

She'd loved him forever, she supposed. First as a child—he'd been her idol, her protector, her friend, her confidant. But now she loved him in the most profound way that a woman could love a man. All that remained was to consummate that love.

Once, when he'd thought she was asleep, Daniel had slipped from the bed to stand at the window. Susan hesitated only briefly before joining him, encircling his waist and pressing her lips to the indentation of his spine. They'd stood that way for what seemed like hours, partaking of each other's strength and affection. But Daniel hadn't talked to her. He refused to speak of his job and what he anticipated would happen. She knew he meant to protect her, but his silence only made her worry more.

When dawn came, Daniel had donned a cloak of emotional distance along with his dark clothing. Sensing he needed to keep his mind on the hours ahead, Susan had brewed some coffee, then allowed him to tend silently to his affairs.

"I'll be back as soon as I can," Daniel said, breaking into her thoughts. He pulled on the cinch of his saddle and dropped the stirrup into place. "It'll be at least a day. Maybe two."

He looked up in time to see Susan nod. The air around them was frigid, each breath he took clouded in the air. But Susan had refused to stay inside. And he had needed to feel the strength of her presence so much that he hadn't forced the issue.

Her power over him astonished and amazed him. She had wrapped herself so firmly around his heart that he couldn't imagine life without her. Therein lay the problem he faced. For the first time he could remember, he feared the consequences of his job. He damned the danger, the random violence, the horror. He prayed that he could survive just one more day, that there wasn't a bullet with his name on it. Happiness lay within his grasp. But only if he could make his way back to safety.

In Susan's arms.

Susan clutched the shawl around her shoulders, but the loosely woven wool did little to keep her warm. She saw the spark of uncertainty in Daniel's eyes and wondered at its cause. "You'll be careful, won't you?"

The warm yellow glow spilling from the kitchen window slipped across his face, highlighting the strong line of his cheeks and jaw. Susan tried to memorize each crag and hollow and firmly imprint it on her mind.

When Daniel didn't immediately answer her, she took a step forward.

"No. Stay there." He crossed to climb the steps. "You don't even have your shoes on."

She lapped one bare foot over the other, but they'd long since grown numb from the cold. "I forgot."

"How you can forget your shoes when it's twelve degrees below zero, I'll never know." His tone was indulgent as he spanned her waist with his hands, lifted her off the bare boards, and set her down again on the tops of his boots.

Such a tiny act of consideration touched her more than hothouse roses or flowery words could ever have done. She wrapped her arms around the strong column of his waist and dug her fingers into the strength of his back.

"Please say you'll be careful," she said again. He hadn't answered her earlier, and she wanted his solemn word, even though she knew Daniel would have no real control over what happened to him in the next few hours.

"My men are well trained. They don't take a risk unless they have to." That wasn't what she'd wanted to hear, but she knew by his enigmatic expression that it was the best answer she was going to get.

Daniel sensed her disappointment, but what more could he say? He knew she wanted reassurances, but he found himself unable to make empty promises. It would be far more cruel to belittle her fears, only to have them come true.

Tentatively, knowing he must say his piece now, while he still had the time, Daniel said, "Promise me that if anything happens—"

"No! Don't you die on me, Daniel Crocker! I'll never speak to you again if you do."

Her illogical threat caused a ghost of a smile to tug at the corners of his mouth. "Nothing is going to happen to me. But just in case—"

"Don't you dare talk like that! You'll be back soon. You'll see."

"Just promise me you'll stay here with Essie and Donovan if anything should happen." He quickly added, "If I should be delayed or kept away for a while, I need to know you'll stay here where it's safe. Promise."

Knowing she had to say it, she repeated, "I promise." Susan wound her arms about his neck, rising on tiptoe to hug him close. She breathed deeply of his scent, plunged her fingers through his hair, needing to cherish everything about him. "Please," she begged, "be careful."

His arms swept around her, crushing her to the hard planes of his body. She welcomed the pressure and gloried in his possessiveness. How she'd grown to love this man!

Burying his face in the hollow of her neck, Daniel squeezed his eyes shut, trying to summon the strength to leave her. Regretfully, he let her go, bit by bit, inch by inch. He kissed her, softly, tenderly, reverently. "Get inside before you freeze solid," he added gruffly. Then, knowing he must go now or not at all, he broke away from her, strode down the steps, and mounted his horse.

"Be back in time for supper!" she called.

"Wear something pretty and colorful," he answered. "Pink or purple or red. You know how I love to see you in colors." For one fleeting second he paused and saluted. Then he grinned reassuringly and pulled on the reins, guiding Chief in a slow trot around the house and down the lane.

Despite the cold, Susan ran down the steps. "I love you, Daniel!"

But he must not have heard her, because he didn't pause, didn't turn. So Susan stood there for long, endless minutes until the clatter of hooves on the frozen lane melted into silence.

"Come back to me," she whispered into the gloom.

Daniel tugged his leather gloves firmly over his hands and cursed the bitter wind that pierced his clothes. Now more than ever he wanted to finish this job and move on to a different kind of life. He was tired of being suspicious, tired of being careful.

Tired of being angry at the world.

At the crest of a high hill, he brought Chief to a halt and stared across the rugged snow-carved landscape. Out there, just beyond the peak of the mountains, lay his land. Nearly every penny Daniel had earned with the Pinkertons had gone toward this parcel of earth and sky. There wouldn't be much money left in his savings to buy stock or fix up the house and outbuildings, but it didn't really matter. The land would be his.

If he closed his eyes, he could see each sweep of

earth, each twist and turn of the creek. He'd imagined it so many times that the vision in his imagination was almost more real than the parcel itself. Yet as he thought of it again there was a difference in the picture. Now the house he envisioned was warm and filled with laughter and light. There'd be chickens in the yard, a clothesline, someday maybe even a rope swing.

He would have all those things, he vowed silently. For the first time in his life he almost dared to believe that he could have a home. Not a house—a *home*.

Filled with a sense of urgency, Daniel pulled on the reins and galloped down the hill. The sooner he finished this job, the sooner he could return.

To Susan.

Max emerged from the screen of trees and stared at the shack in the woods. He'd come here several times, always waiting until the men disappeared, then foraging through their packs and boxes. He'd found such treasures here! Such pretty-colored things.

But the men and their toys were gone. Just like Susan.

Sighing, he continued on his journey. It had taken most of the night to escape Sister Mary Margaret, but he'd finally managed to gather a bundle of clothing and the box that held his treasures. Then he'd walked away from the convent. Soon he would find Susan and take her away with him.

Susan returned to her room and sank into the rocker, curling her feet beneath her. There was no sense in going back to bed. She was fully awake now and ready to begin her day. But as she gazed out the window, she found herself curiously loath to do anything but sit and watch the sun peeking from behind the craggy peaks of the mountains, kissing the slopes with its rosy warmth.

Susan stretched, amazed at the lethargic warmth that flowed in her veins. She'd never felt such a curious sensation before. Almost as if she was waiting for something. Something she'd wanted to happen for a long time.

Laughing softly at nothing in particular, she rose from the chair and stood in front of the dresser. Dropping the shawl, she pulled the fabric of her nightdress tight.

She'd seen the way Daniel had watched her this morning when she'd awakened him at dawn. There'd been hunger in his eyes. And passion. Soon he would make love to her.

The thought still had the power to flutter her nerves. But its force was blunted by the silky tingle of desire.

After smiling at her reflection in the mirror, Susan turned to see if there was anything at all in her wardrobe that might please her husband. Essie had given her a skirt, two blouses, and three gowns from her own supply.

Susan touched the sleeves of the violet suit Essie had insisted she take. Susan had tried to demur, stating that the ensemble with its basque-style jacket and intricate braided trim was much too extravagant for Essie to abandon. But Esther must have guessed that Susan had immediately fallen in love with the outfit, because she had refused to take it back. She'd insisted that Susan could wear it during the reunion later that week.

But Susan would wear it today. Just in case Daniel managed to come home early. He loved to see her wear colors.

* * *

Timmy Libbley galloped his horse up to the front of the queue of Pinkertons riding toward the split in the rail lines.

"Sir! Mr. K-Kutter, s-sir!"

Kutter stopped his mount and turned in the saddle to glare at the freckle-faced boy. "Damn it all to double danged hell, Timmy! If I've told you once, I've told you a hundred times. Do . . . not . . . *stutter!* And where the *hell* have you been. You were supposed to rendezvous with the rest of the group thirty minutes ago."

Timmy's mount shuddered to a halt in front of his superior. Libbley's face was beet red from his desperate ride. "But, Mr. Kutter, sir, I found their camp."

"Whose camp?"

"The Dooleys'. The Dooleys' camp! I stumbled on it early this morning when I took your orders to the guards you assigned to the orphanage."

"The hell you say! Are they still there?"

"Most of them have already abandoned camp. There were only two men still there when I found it. But I heard them planning"—he gulped and continued—"to take Miss Hurst. They're going to use her at the exchange to force Crocker into surrendering."

Kutter swore violently. "You!" He pointed to one of the men on the fringes of the group. "Go with Libbley here. I want you to ride back to the orphanage, get the girl, and the men who were assigned to guard her. Then I want you to hide her back at our headquarters. Don't let anyone near her and don't let her out of your sight until we come to fetch you. Understood?"

"Yes, sir!" The two men spoke in unison.

"Then get going! If the Dooleys capture her, we may as well kiss our foolproof plan good-bye."

"What if she won't come?"

Kutter glared at Timmy for daring to ask such a

fool question. "Lie to her, kidnap her, tell her Crocker's bleeding and calling her name—I don't care how you do it. Just get her out of there."

Daniel stamped his feet, attempting to return some semblance of feeling to his numbed extremities. Impatiently he watched as the rest of the Pinkertons moved into position. Kutter was the only man who dared to approach him. Once Daniel became involved in his work, he had a reputation for being single-minded, short-tempered, and relentless.

Tucking his hands under his arms, he paced in the square of tramped snow already formed by his continuous passage. "It's time?" he barked.

Behind him Kutter snapped open the lid of his watch.

"Yep, just six."

Over ten minutes remained until the train was scheduled to pass through.

"Any sign of the Dooleys?"

"Nope. Timmy thought he had a line on one or two of them," he added carefully, but did not elaborate. "I sent him into town to investigate."

"Everyone is in position?"

"Yep." Kutter took a cigar from his pocket and ran it through his fingers, over and over. He didn't light it for fear the scent of its smoke would carry too far. "I've got sentries stationed every mile all the way to Ashton. So far we've heard no word."

"No trouble with the rail lines?"

"None. Baby Floyd should arrive right on schedule."

"Good." Daniel squinted into the hazy glow of morning. The sun was just beginning to top the mountains, flooding the icy slopes with a brittle light. Not exactly the kind of weather a man would choose to spend cooped up in a boxcar with some idiot who'd been too dumb to refuse to ride with his brothers and too stupid to keep from getting caught.

From behind, Daniel heard Kutter take a deep breath. "Damn this waiting."

Though he didn't speak, Daniel seconded Kutter's lament with a nod. The air around him hung silent and still. The cracking pop of the creek grew muted as if in anticipation. There were no rustlings of animals, no plops of snow from heavy boughs. There was only the intensity of the men who waited, their breathing carefully controlled, their occasional comments hushed. Even Kutter's booming voice had grown quiet.

Kutter joined Daniel's silent perusal of the serpentine tracks stretching into the distance. He clamped the unlit cigar in his teeth. "I'm getting too damned old for this."

Despite Kutter's white hair, Daniel had never seen him as old. The thought of Kutter considering his own mortality made Daniel uncomfortable.

Kutter chomped on the cigar, then deftly shifted it to the other side of his mouth. "You know, I used to be like you." He cocked his head to regard Daniel with an impassive stare. "I was mean and hard and full of anger." His brows lifted as if in disbelief of how the years could have changed him so much. "But I never had a little girl like yours to show me just what I was missing."

Daniel frowned. "What the hell are you talking about?"

Kutter turned his head to squint at the narrow iron tracks. "Maybe you don't see it yet. But she's changed you. It's only been days, but she's made you . . ." Kutter grunted in embarrassment, then fumbled in his pocket and withdrew a crumpled scrap of paper. "Here. Take this."

Daniel scowled. "What is it?"

"The note on your land."

"You can give it to me later, when I've finished the job."

"No." Kutter nudged his arm. "Take it now. Call it a wedding present."

Daniel considered Kutter, then the paper he offered.

"Take it."

Daniel took the rumpled slip. He'd been dreaming of this for years, but now that it had come, he felt that he was severing his ties with a very old and dear friend. He tucked the note into his pocket. "Just don't think this gets you out of our arrangement. As soon as the Dooleys have been rounded up, I'll expect a milk cow, too."

Kutter chuckled, but his laughter was blunted when the air trembled in warning. The bare branches quivered at the muffled rumble and hiss of the approaching train—a train that was empty except for a few railroad personnel. Floyd's train would arrive only minutes behind this one.

"Crocker?"

"Yeah?"

"You're damned lucky, you know?"

In his pocket, Daniel's fist closed over the scrap of paper, crushing it into a ball. "Yeah. I know."

Daniel could only hope his luck would hold.

"Susan?"

"Yes, Carrie?"

The seven-year-old girl paused only long enough at the door to say "There's a man here to see you" before she scampered down the hall on her way outside to play.

Susan set aside the bowl she'd been drying and went to the door. A stranger waited on the stoop. Frowning at the way Carrie had left him to wait in the cold, Susan stepped into the chilly afternoon.

"Yes?"

The red-haired man turned, and Susan was immediately struck by the youthfulness of his features.

"Mrs. Crocker?"

Susan didn't recognize her new name. Then she felt a thrill of pleasure.

"Yes. I'm Susan Crocker."

The man, as if remembering his manners, swept the hat from his head and took a step toward her. There was a sense of urgency in the way he moved, and Susan immediately felt a twinge of alarm.

"Ma'am, I hate to be the one to bear bad news, but they asked me to come and get you."

"They?"

"Th-the Pinkertons, ma'am." He mauled his hat, staring down at the scuffed toes of his boots. "Something went wrong. They asked me to fetch you."

"What is it? What's happened? Daniel. Is he hurt?"

"If you could just come with me, ma'am. They'll explain everything there."

Spurred into action, Susan flew into the house, grabbed her cape from the hall rack and yelled, "Carrie! Tell Essie I've gone to get Daniel!"

She heard Carrie's faint "Yes, Susan." Then she rushed back outside, slamming the door behind her. She gestured to the barn. "If you can wait, I'll saddle a horse."

"Uh, no! No, ma'am. There's no time." He motioned to his mount. "If you'll take the saddle, I'll ride behind you."

"Certainly. Yes." She would do anything. Anything at all to get Daniel as quickly as possible.

The man jammed his hat on, solicitously taking her arm and leading her down the path to the front gate. Once there, he lifted her onto the gelding's back and mounted behind her.

Susan grasped the horse's mane as the Pinkerton took the reins, and turned the horse around. He dug his heels into the animal's side, and they galloped down the lane.

"How far do we have to go?"

"It won't be long. Then everything will be explained."

Max trudged to the top of the rise. Below, the orphanage buildings were scattered like blocks on a carpet of down. Miss Susan would be happy to see him!

Running now, he stumbled down the hill, intent on finding his friend. A shape appeared in the distance. He heard the pounding of hooves. Stopping, he dropped his bundle and waved his arms, recognizing Susan's flaming tresses.

"Susan! Stop for me, please! Susan!"

But the horse's pace didn't ease, didn't slow. The animal with its pair of riders galloped past.

Max turned in the snow to watch them disappear around the crook in the road. His chin trembled. "Why didn't you stop? Why didn't you stop?"

25

Donovan stepped outside the barn, squinting against the bright winter sky. He thought he'd heard a horse approach the house, but there was no one there.

Unease skittered through his frame. During the past few days he had grown more and more disturbed by things he'd seen in town. Ashton seemed to have attracted over a half dozen strangers who did little more all day than sit, gamble, and restlessly watch the roads. Donovan had spent enough time flirting with the wrong side of justice to know when he was looking at lawmen pretending to be laymen. And judging by Daniel's sudden disappearance early that morning, Donovan figured the Pinkertons must be up to something.

But what? And what did all of this have to do with Mr. Gibby?

Donovan had gone to the druggist's shop, just as he'd promised Essie, but he'd seen nothing suspicious about the charred wood and twisted beams.

Nothing to make him think the fire was anything more than an accident. Nothing except the eerie feeling of disquiet he'd experienced the minute he'd dismounted from his horse and surveyed the wreckage.

Since Mr. Gibby had begun to rouse, Donovan had tried to talk to him. But the man had mumbled on about Daniel and Pinkertons and poison, without making a bit of sense.

Shrugging off his odd mood, Donovan was about to return to his milking when he became aware of someone stumbling down the hill, a bundle clutched tightly in his arms. The identity of the giant man-child who had attended Susan's wedding could not be mistaken.

"Max?"

At the sound of his name, Max rushed toward him. "Please, you've got to go get her!" He clutched at Donovan's arms, his bundle spilling to the ground. Bits of bottle green glass, rocks, and other items tumbled free.

"Who, Max?"

"Susan. He's taken her away. She wouldn't have left that way; she would have stopped."

"Who, Max? Who took her?"

"He took her away from me. She would have stopped."

Donovan tried to calm the huge man, but he wouldn't be pacified. Something about his manner began to needle Donovan's own suspicions. Perhaps Donovan was chasing ideas that had no basis, but the bruises on Mr. Gibby's face and ribs looked more like the results of a beating than of a fire. And the way the man kept crying out about Daniel and poison? Donovan's instincts kept telling him there was something more—some important detail he already knew but hadn't seen the significance of. He kept thinking that at any minute all the information would fit together neatly like the pieces of a puzzle. In the meantime he didn't like having Susan mixed up in all of this.

"All right, Max. I'll go find her." Donovan bent to help the man pick up the items littering the ground. When he caught his first good look at Max's treasures, he froze. "Where did you get these?" he asked, collecting several narrow red cylinders.

"His men left them."

"Whose?"

"The devil's. They live next to the railroad tracks. By the creek near the old waterwheel."

Dynamite. Sweet bloody hell, the men Max had been spying on were hiding a load of dynamite. Donovan would have bet money that they were up to no good and that somehow the Pinkertons were involved.

Donovan cursed and ran for the barn. He had to find Daniel or one of his men and report what he'd found. Then he had to find Susan.

Susan gasped as the horse beneath her came to a stop in the middle of a stand of trees. She and her companion had followed the main road for a few miles. Then he'd reined the animal toward the mountain range, leading them into a small clearing in the midst of a copse of scrub oak and pine.

"Where's Daniel? I don't see him anywhere."

"We have to meet up with my partners first." He turned his horse to one side, put his fingers to his lips, and uttered three short whistles.

The air was brittle and cold, so thin and fragile that the slightest sound should have shattered the tense expectancy.

"Where are they?" Susan whispered.

"Soon, Mrs. Crocker. Soon."

The man's hand, which had rested on the pommel in front of her, shifted. Susan started when the redheaded boy touched her hand. Her jolt of stunned surprise intensified when the comforting pat became something far less innocent. His palm rubbed up her arm, cupped her shoulder. When Susan shifted away, he tangled his fingers in her hair and jerked her hard against his chest.

"You're a fool to love him," the boy whispered in her ear. The words dripped with hate. "He's a killer. A murderer. Do you know what he did to my brother?" When she didn't answer, he took a fistful of hair and yanked her head back. *Do you?*

Susan felt a jolt of alarm and then a surge of pure unadulterated fear. This man had not come to take her to Daniel. He had come to hurt her. To hurt Daniel. She could see it in the buried fanaticism deep in his eyes. She could hear it in the sharp edges of his voice.

Susan stared at the redheaded boy who'd come to fetch her. "Who are you?" An icy certainty began to settle in her limbs. She'd made a mistake. A horrible mistake. "You're not one of the Pinkertons, are you?" As soon as she uttered the words, the arms that supported her on the saddle wound around her body, preventing her escape.

"Timmy Beeb at your service, ma'am."

The name Beeb sent an icy wave of terror through her. Anyone who had lived in the territories knew of the Beeb brothers. Until last summer they had terrorized most of the Mountain West with their raping and pillaging.

Timmy's fingers clamped over her jaw and dug into her skin. "That's right. You know me now, don't you? Take a good hard look and remember my face. Your husband killed my brother. And for that I intend to drag you both into hell."

"He got her!"

The sound of another man's voice burst from the

quiet. Timmy released her, and the trees around them were suddenly alive with an army of men, all of them unkempt and smelling of sweat and contempt. Susan heard the snapping grate of a half dozen triggers being locked into place. Very slowly she turned. A frisson of fear raced down her spine when she found herself pinned in the sights of several shiny black revolvers.

One man separated himself from the group, and Susan immediately recognized the man who had attacked her days before. Grant Dooley. "So nice of you to join us, Mrs. Crocker," he offered with a grin. The sun gleamed off his pockmarked flesh. "I knew you could get her out from under the Pinkertons' noses, Timmy."

"No thanks to you," Timmy sneered. "You almost bungled the whole plan when you broke into the orphanage and tried to rape her. What a stupid, *stupid* stunt, Grant. I'd already met with you and your brothers and planned our strategy for the ambush. I even arranged for the dynamite to be stolen by a friend of mine and delivered to you. All you had to do was follow my orders. But no . . . you had to prove you were a man."

A flush tinged Grant's cheeks, but his mouth remained hard and implacable.

"Mount up!" Timmy yelled.

"What about the guards who were riding with you?" Grant asked. "Shouldn't we see to them first?"

Timmy gazed at him in disgust. "Unlike you, I don't make stupid mistakes, Grant. I slit their throats and left them by the creek to rot."

Fear curdled in Susan's breast at the calm, matter-of-fact manner in which Timmy related what he had done to the men. Her panic made it difficult to breathe, but Susan forced herself to keep her head as clear as possible. She had to think! Somehow she had to think!

"Get your gear and let's ride, Grant." Beeb's grip grew harsh. "And remember, we made a deal. You got the dynamite and all the information you needed about your brother's transfer. I get Daniel Crocker. He's mine."

As if to underscore Timmy's reminder, the low, throbbing roar of a locomotive could be heard in the distance.

Grant Dooley tipped his hat to the other man in silent acquiescence and swung into the saddle, knowing that he would find a way to double-cross Timmy Beeb. It galled him the way Timmy kept appearing at their camp and issuing orders on the best way to trap Daniel Crocker and free Floyd. Beeb had begun to think he owned the Dooleys—and to Grant's disgust, his brothers jumped to obey his commands.

But Grant didn't plan on following Timmy like a lamb to the slaughter. Beeb was trouble—perhaps even a little bit crazed. Grant would give him his lead until Floyd had been freed. Then Crocker would belong to the Dooleys.

Long before Floyd Dooley's train arrived, the ground rumbled. Daniel and his men melted into the shadows, waiting, watching.

But nothing happened.

The train, responding to a flagged signal from one of the Pinkertons, began to slow, groaning in protest. The air was filled with the heavy coal-tainted scent of steam. A tense expectation shimmered in the brittle air, threatening to explode into an inferno of nerves and raw tension.

And still nothing happened.

Daniel looked at Kutter, issuing a silent message. The man nodded. One of Kutter's men had leaked the information that Floyd would be transferred here. If the Dooleys were anywhere nearby—and the petty thievery occurring in Ashton over the last few days gave Kutter ample evidence they were—now would be the most advantageous time for them to appear. Daniel and his men were isolated in the narrow pass. It would be the perfect setting for an ambush.

Something had gone wrong.

Daniel's fingers grew taut around his rifle. The Dooleys should have come here. This was the most vulnerable spot in the line.

Straightening, he settled his hat over his brow and then, thinking swiftly and decisively, said, "We can't afford to wait any longer."

Kutter said, "I'll gather the fellows we've scattered in the rocks. We'll ride ahead through the pass along the road and signal you if we see anything up ahead. If they don't ambush us here, it means they've found a better spot."

"I'll take the rest of the men on the train with me. And, Kutter—"

The older man turned back, lifting one brow.

"You keep your eyes peeled, you hear? I don't want you walking blindly into one of their traps."

Kutter grinned. "And if I hear that little popgun of yours, I'll come running."

As Kutter strode away, Daniel gestured for the other Pinkertons to draw near. His gaze darted from man to man as he judged their strength. "We're going to have to do this job from the train. I'll need a dozen people scattered through the boxcars as well as six more to ride on top as guards. We can't let anything prevent Floyd from going to trial, even if it means letting his brothers go for now."

Around him, the guards began to jam their hands deeper into leather gloves and check their weapons. More than one slid a revolver beneath his coat or a knife into a sheath in his boot. Although they did not watch him as he spoke, Daniel knew they listened to each word with an intense concentration.

"Grover and Rueban, take your people and position them along the outside of the cars. At least one of you will need to ride up front."

"Rogers, Dicksen, you'll come with me. Hesse, take the other four and gather our mounts. I want them loaded onto the last boxcar in case something happens and we have to take Dooley through the canyon on horseback." His voice rose above the screeching rumble of the second train as it arrived and pulled to a stop.

"Let's go!"

The Pinkertons dispersed to their positions. Daniel lifted his rifle in a silent signal, and then he and his men emerged from the trees. The fine hair at the back of his neck rose. Until Floyd had been moved into the second train, Daniel would be out in the open, an easy target for anyone who might be watching.

The door to the boxcar slid open.

"Any trouble?" Daniel asked the whiskered Pinkerton who stepped into the aperture of the boxcar and surveyed the area, his gun at the ready.

After he was sure that no unaccountable shadows lurked in the trees, the man straightened and spit into the snow. "Not a peep," he answered tersely. "But then, my ears froze clear off halfway through Utah territory. Any sign of the Dooleys?"

"No. We're going ahead."

Backing into the shadowed interior of the car, the man shouted something and emerged a few minutes later with the prisoner surrounded by three other guards.

After the dimness of the boxcar, Floyd blinked at the bright winter light, raising his shackled arms to block the glare.

"Git down there, and no fussin', y'hear?" The Pinkerton prodded Floyd with the muzzle of his revolver.

Baby Floyd lowered his hands, revealing strands of milk white hair flopping over a narrow forehead. Round spectacles magnified his water blue eyes. He stared in bewilderment at the men who waited below him. His wrists inched down even more to reveal his bulb-tipped nose, thin lips, and round chin. His jaw was covered with peachlike fuzz the same downy color as his hair.

On either side of him, Daniel's men cocked and aimed their weapons. The whiskered Pinkerton jumped from the boxcar, and he and Daniel helped the other three men lift the shackled Dooley to the ground. Floyd stumbled over his chains and fell into the snow. With a frustrated sigh, Daniel pulled him upright.

For a split second, when Daniel met the prisoner's glance, there was a blazing light of hate and intelligence behind those watery blue eyes. Then Floyd blinked, and the blank-faced stare returned.

Digging the barrel of his rifle between the man's shoulders, Daniel prodded him toward the front of the train. "Move," Daniel ordered. It had always troubled him the way the Dooleys had been so over-protective of Floyd. In the past, Grant and Marvin had done most of the stealing and most of the killing, while Floyd had been kept isolated and well guarded.

Daniel's footsteps crunched in the snow. All the pieces were beginning to fit together. By allowing him that one unguarded glance, Floyd Dooley had revealed his secret: *he* was the leader of the Dooley gang. He was the brains.

So who was directing them now?

Floyd Dooley was quickly taken from the Wasatch Territorial to the boxcar of the second train. The

Humboldt and Western would carry the prisoner and his guards twelve miles through the winding pass and then continue east to Cheyenne.

Since the Dooleys had made no effort to release their brother here, the Pinkertons moved into position with a quiet haste. Their mounts had been loaded, and drawn away from the last car.

The Humboldt and Western's locomotive strained and shimmied, building up enough steam to roll its great iron wheels. Leaving the sliding door ajar, Daniel took his position by the opening. He steadied himself, gazing out at the stretch of dirty snow beside the tracks.

A flash of color appeared up ahead. Daniel stiffened and snapped his rifle into place as a horse and rider galloped onto the gravel shoulder and rushed past the locomotive and down the line of boxcars.

Automatically, Daniel cocked his weapon. One of his men went toward the opposite door and opened it just a crack, the others took their positions by Daniel.

The train was still moving slowly, barely inching along. The horseman came to a halt short of reaching the appropriate car and waved his arms.

"Hold your fire!" Daniel shouted, recognizing the man. "Hell and damnation, Donovan! Get out of here! Go home!"

Donovan didn't heed his warning. He dug his heels into his mount, stopping just short of the rails. At the last minute, he reached for the iron support at the side of the door. The momentum of the train caused him to swing free of his horse. Daniel grabbed his shirt and hauled him inside.

The train heaved, gaining speed. Swearing, Daniel considered dumping Donovan back onto the ground, but they were moving too fast now, and the snowy banks were littered with rocks as they neared the creek.

Furious, Daniel took Donovan's collar, hauling him upright. "Damn it! What do you think you're doing here?"

Donovan noted the other figures in the boxcar, and his eyes stopped on Baby Floyd. "The Dooleys. That's what this is all about." Donovan had seen their pictures posted in the sheriff's office, and he'd read the reports of their raids in the newspapers. He took another gulp of air and returned his attention to Daniel. "Luckily, Max saw you riding out of Ashton in the direction of the tracks early this morning."

"Max? What's wrong?" Daniel demanded roughly, already sensing, already growing chilled from the unspoken message in Donovan's features.

"Someone came to the house and took Susan. I tried to follow him and found three Pinkertons lying on the creek bank. Their throats had been cut. The man who took Susan must have been one of the Dooleys."

In the corner of the boxcar Floyd Dooley began to laugh.

Susan cried out when Timmy Beeb jerked his horse to a stop beneath the wooden bridge, throwing her forward. From above, on the curving mountain road, came the sound of galloping horses. Timmy drew a knife from his boot and pressed the blade to Susan's throat.

"Not a sound," he said next to her ear.

Susan's heart began to pound in her chest, ricocheting off the tight band of her ribs. Familiar black memories rose to the fore, but she refused to allow them to take hold. Somehow, with Daniel's help, she had purged herself of those images, and they no longer had the power to haunt her. She alone controlled her destiny and her fears. And by heaven she would find a way to free herself and warn Daniel.

The hooves echoed overhead, reverberating hollowly on the wooden planks. Then they continued on. Beeb waited long, endless seconds, then nodded in satisfaction. "They'll be halfway to Nebraska before they notice they've passed the very person they're looking for."

Cautiously Timmy led the rest of the men from beneath the bridge and along the creek bank until he encountered the railroad trestle spanning the gulch. "We haven't got much time." He seemed to sniff the air for the approach of the train, then turned to spear one of the Dooleys with an iron-willed stare. "You! Set the dynamite under the trestle there. Do it just like I told you or you'll blow us all to kingdom come." He pointed to another man. "You put the charges on the hillside about a mile back. As soon as you light the fuses, join us in the center. Grant, you take the girl up into the trees next to the tracks." Timmy smiled slowly. A crooked, feral smile. "That way she won't miss the fireworks." He stroked her hair, and she shrank away in revulsion.

"You see, we're going to trap your husband," he explained in much the same tone he might have used to explain a difficult procedure to a youngster. "We'll wait until the train rounds the bend, and then we'll blow the rocks free in front of them, and the timber in back, trapping them in between." His easy grin suddenly died. "Take her, damn it!"

Grant Dooley yanked Susan free from the saddle and tugged her toward the hillside.

"Grant!"

Grant turned in time to catch the coil of rope Timmy threw in his direction.

"Tie her up first. We wouldn't want her to escape. Would we?" The last was a clear warning.

Grant's jaw hardened at the slight. He tugged her

arms behind her and wound the heavy rope around her wrists. He pushed her forward. "Get going!"

Following her as if she were a puppy on a leash, Grant poked and prodded her back, forcing Susan to climb the steep, slippery slope despite the hampering folds of her skirts. All the while she kept searching for some avenue of escape, some way of dodging free. If she could just pull the rope loose and kick Grant down the hill, she could get away.

"Don't even think it," Grant warned when she edged toward the icy bluff. He pulled her across the railroad tracks and into the brush beyond, then led her to a boulder beneath a tree and pushed her down. The icy air seeped through her clothes. Since she'd been dressed for a day indoors, she was already numb from the cold. Her cloak provided scant protection from the elements, and the violet suit she wore was no barrier against the brittle cold.

"Grant!"

"What!"

"Leave her there and get into the trees."

Grant wavered, ready to defy Timmy's orders. Then his rebellion visibly melted and he threw the rope on the ground and stamped away. Although he longed to wrap his hands around Timmy's neck, he knew that would have to wait.

Susan clenched her fingers behind her and twisted her hands, but they were bound too tightly to slip free.

Timmy waded through the snow, sank down on one knee, and pointed the barrel of his revolver at the bridge of her nose. "Don't try anything stupid. I'll gag you and tie you down if I have to." He stroked her lower lip with the barrel of his weapon. "But I'd rather not do that."

Beeb stood. "You really are a pretty little thing. And you've got spirit, more than I gave you credit for." He shook his head, clucking in regret. "I'm almost sorry I'm going to have to make you a widow."

The voices called to him—shouting, commanding—and Timmy Beeb retreated. Soon justice would be served. He had built a trap that Crocker would not escape, and the Pinkerton would be punished. An eye for an eye, a tooth for a tooth. He chortled in delight as he melted into the thick undergrowth. Soon he would reveal himself to his enemy, but he felt no fear, only triumph.

The game had ended. Timmy Beeb had won. And before the day was through, he would see to it that Crocker died and went to hell.

26

The first explosion rocked the boxcar, throwing Daniel, Donovan, and the Pinkertons to the floor. Almost simultaneously another explosion rumbled from behind. The train screeched to a halt.

"Ambush!" someone shouted from overhead.

Daniel's hands curled around his rifle, but he didn't rise. "Stay down!" he ordered. A barrage of bullets pummeled the upper regions of the boxcar, smacking into the wood with a dull thudding sound. Evidently the Dooleys were trying to pick off the Pinkertons clinging to the top of the train.

Daniel inched closer to the partly open door and looked outside. A cover of trees and shrubs kept him from pinpointing the location of the men who were firing at them, but what he could see made him shudder. He and his men had fallen into the perfect trap. The serpentine railroad tracks formed a U-shaped curve. The iron rails had been blown away on either end of the turn, causing the locomotive and the first three boxcars to be thrown over on their sides and jammed together like a child's toy.

Damn it! He should have known the Dooleys would try something like this farther up the line. He should have taken the time to have Kutter report back to him before moving Floyd at all. But he'd blindly continued, too impatient to finish his last assignment to take the proper precautions.

Soon after the hail of gunfire had begun, it petered out, leaving only the returning volleys from the Pinkertons on the train. Daniel grew wary, cautious. "Hold your fire!" he shouted.

The noise dwindled to an occasional pop. Then nothing. The air echoed with the sounds of scudding timbers and heavy rocks, which had been dislodged by the blast and continued to slide down the gulch into the creek below. The air became heavy and thick with the smell of smoke and steam. And something more. Something else tainted the breeze with a desperate edge.

Daniel knew their situation was critical. The train had been sealed inside the rubble as effectively as if a pair of giant hands had descended to hold the cars in place. Kutter had probably heard the blast, but he could be miles away by now. Daniel couldn't count on his immediate intervention.

"Damn, damn, *damn!*" Daniel slapped his hand on the floor. "They've outsmarted us again." He turned to see Dooley's reaction to the tumult.

A lump of dread sank into Daniel's stomach. Floyd Dooley sat upright in the corner of the boxcar staring sightlessly in Daniel's direction as if accusing him. A bright stain of blood ran from a scarlet patch in his temple.

Half bending, half running, Daniel hurried toward the far side of the railway car. Before he reached the other man, he knew Floyd Dooley was dead. And there'd be hell to pay. Soon.

Panic clawed at Daniel. Then he felt a ruthless fury.

"Is he—"

"Dead," Daniel affirmed.

"They'll be wanting Dooley bad," one grizzled man stated needlessly.

"And alive," Daniel muttered.

But there had been no way to prevent the outlaw's death. The unexpected attack that had surprised the Pinkertons had resulted in Floyd's being murdered by his own family.

"What are we going to do?"

Daniel gazed blindly at the half opened door, trying to think. "I don't know. Right now they have the advantage. We're going to have to wait and see what they want and how they planned to get Floyd out of this mess." Daniel didn't mention that he feared his wife would somehow be involved in forcing the issue.

"Crocker!"

The shout came from the edge of the trees.

"I know you're in there, Crocker."

Keeping himself concealed, Daniel readied his weapon and crept toward the doorway. He'd easily recognized Grant Dooley's gravelly voice.

"What do you want?"

"Just a little exchange," the voice called. "Something you have . . . for something we have."

Praying he could buy a little time, Daniel forced himself to laugh. "Don't tell me you're willing to give yourself up in order to get your brother back."

"No, I got something better in mind. And if you'd like to see it, I'd be glad to show you. Just tell your men on top of the train to throw down their arms."

"You think I'm stupid, Dooley?"

"No. Which is exactly why I think you'll do it."

"Daniel, no!"

Daniel heard Susan's voice. No. No! Why hadn't he protected her? Why had he thought that he could love her and still keep her safe? Hadn't he learned his lesson with Mama—and Annie? Hadn't he learned that if he dared to love someone, his love would bring death.

"Do as you're told, Crocker, and she won't get hurt."

"Damn it, you'd better not have touched her!"

"Just do it, Crocker! Tell your men to throw down their arms."

Years of training and instinct played sharply against Daniel's need to see Susan safe and away from harm. He pressed his back to the wall of the boxcar. "Do it," he ordered his men. "Do what they say!"

There was a second of hesitation. He could feel the surprise spreading from one man to another. Never before had Daniel put anything ahead of his job. He'd ruthlessly drawn the line between business and things that were better left private. But now he was crossing that line for the sake of a civilian. A woman.

One by one Daniel heard his men's rifles and revolvers slithering across the top of the train and dropping with a clacking sound off the tops of the boxcars.

"That's right!" the voice crowed from the edge of the woods. "And now the men inside. Tell them to throw out their arms."

Jerking his head in affirmation, Daniel motioned for the men in the boxcar to throw their guns into the snow.

"Get those Pinkertons to step into the doorway of the boxcars so I can see what they're doing."

"I won't endanger my men," Daniel shouted back. "Not until I see if you've hurt her."

The man laughed—a harsh, grating sound that

made Daniel cringe when he thought of his wife at Grant Dooley's mercy.

"You're smarter than I give you credit for, Crocker."

There was a rustle of leaves, a whisper of brush, and then as Daniel peeked out of the car he saw Susan step into a tiny clearing not fifteen yards away.

Her gaze met and clung to his, reassuring him that she was unharmed. Daniel pushed back the fear, focusing instead, with a fierce pang of pride, on the defiant light in her eyes. Her chin tilted at a militant angle, and she bravely walked into the clearing. Grant Dooley stood just behind her, covering her mouth with one hand, the other holding a gun at her temple.

"All right, Crocker. Show me your men."

When Donovan would have stood as well, Daniel motioned for him to stay hidden. Earlier, when Grant had ordered the men to throw out their arms, Daniel had tossed his revolver into the pile with the others. Now he carefully set his rifle against the wall of the boxcar in silent command to the older man, who watched. Then Daniel stepped into the opening, lifting his hands wide and knowing his fate would be left to Donovan and the firearms his men had managed to hide from the Dooleys.

Grant laughed, signaling for his companions to move away from the trees. "Did we surprise you, Crocker? I know you counted on having the Dooleys ride into your little trap. But you didn't count on us being as smart as we really are. We got ourselves a spy."

As if on cue, a redheaded, freckle-faced youngster rode into view. Daniel knew him. He'd nearly killed the man months ago when he'd caught him and his brother after a pillaging and raping spree in Utah Territory. If Mackie Beeb had been dangerous, Timothy Beeb was twice as deadly. Mackie killed for money; Timmy Beeb killed for sport. Rumor had it a streak of madness ran in the family. But if that was the case, Timmy Beeb was sane enough to know how to use it to his advantage.

Daniel didn't speak. He merely clenched his hands into tight fists and stared at the woman standing in the snow who had come to mean so much to him. A woman he had placed in so much danger.

"And now," Grant ordered. "Now you're going to have your men step down."

When Daniel moved to join the others who were jumping to the ground, Grant shouted, "No, not you, Crocker! You'll stay there to bring my brother out. Then, after you're done, I've promised Beeb he can have you. Seems he hates you worse than we do."

Daniel remained where he was while the rest of the Pinkertons were herded away from the train by the Dooley gang. When they had been taken to a clearing twenty or thirty yards away from the rails, Grant edged forward. He was still covering Susan's mouth; but he hadn't masked her eyes, and Daniel could tell she was about to try something desperate.

He tried to discourage her by an infinitesimal shake of his head, but she continued to will him to believe in her. At that moment Daniel saw that Susan's arms had been tied in back of her and Grant held the rope in the palm of his gun hand.

In a flash Daniel knew what Susan planned to do, and by heaven he thought it might work.

"Get my brother, Crocker!" Dooley shouted, clearly worried by Daniel's hesitation in responding to his orders.

Daniel ducked into the shadows and turned to the man who hid there. "Donovan, I don't know what will happen in the next few minutes. I hope your shooting is as deadly as it used to be."

"I think I'd do better to concentrate on my throwing arm." He reached into his pockets and pulled out four sticks of dynamite. "Max took a roundabout route through the Dooley hideout on his way to the orphanage. I found these as well as fuses and caps in his box of treasures."

Daniel stared at him. "Great bloody hell." A slow excitement began to build. Donovan might have found a way to turn things to the Pinkertons' advantage.

"Do you think you can throw those far enough into the trees to avoid killing anyone, yet still create enough of a diversion for me and my men to take cover?"

"You bet."

His own hands shook with nerves, but Daniel managed to show Donovan how to prepare the sticks, then gave him a tin of matches from his duster pocket. "Make sure you throw them into the trees so you don't blow us all to bits."

"Crocker! I've had enough of your stalling!"

Casting a glance at the dead man who had caused him all this trouble, Daniel shot Donovan a look of encouragement, took a deep breath, and dived out of the boxcar.

Rolling onto the ground, he reached for the nearest weapon. The dirt to one side of him exploded in a roar as a stick of dynamite landed in the bushes. The Dooleys stood stunned for a split second. Long enough for Daniel and his men to take their positions. Lifting the revolver, Daniel pointed it at Grant just as Susan bit down hard on her captive's thumb, then ducked and jerked on the rope.

A barrage of gunfire came from the Pinkertons who had immediately dropped to the ground and drawn their hidden weapons. Their position to one side of Daniel kept him out of their line of fire, yet gave them ample opportunity to pin most of the Dooley gang in their sights. The screams of dying men began to pepper the chaotic din.

Daniel heard Donovan yell, and then another piece of land exploded. Grant aimed, but his shot went wild, the bullet winging Daniel's shoulder. Daniel fired at the first man to lift his weapon—Marvin Dooley, who stood only a few feet away. Then he ran forward, threw Susan behind the shield of his body, and aimed his gun at Grant Dooley's head. The hammer clicked on an empty chamber.

Simultaneously the air was filled with the sounds of battle as Kutter and his men galloped over the summit of the hill and down into the gulch.

Grant swung his foot, knocking the revolver out of Daniel's hand. Daniel dived into Susan, rolling her to the ground and covering her with his own body as Grant took aim. But another round of rifle shots splatted into the snow at Grant's feet. He ran into the cover of scrub and trees. "Where's Marvin?" he shouted at Beeb who had run for cover at the first hint of trouble.

"Dead." Beeb dug his heels to the flanks of his horse.

Looking back, Grant saw his brother's lifeless form in the snow. Dazed, he mounted and followed Beeb into the hills.

Susan struggled to escape the heavy weight that had her pinned to the ground. "Daniel?" She rolled him over. Pushing aside the thick fabric of his coat, and clawing at the layers beneath, she finally found his wound. She gasped at the bright patch of scarlet spreading from his upper arm.

His eyes flickered and opened. They filled with caution and an instinct for survival, and he grasped the back of her neck, pulling her to the ground even as his body twisted to cover her and his hands fumbled to reload his revolver.

"Daniel? Are you all right?"

"Shh." His exhaled warning was shaky. Cautiously he lifted his head. Some men were gathering a few of the Dooleys. Others scrambled to remove their mounts from the train. He sat up, and Susan knelt beside him.

Kutter's horse cantered toward them and came to an abrupt stop just inches away from where they sat.

"Floyd and Marvin Dooley are dead," Daniel stated bluntly. "And your new man, Timmy, is one of the Beebs—Mackie Beeb's avenging brother."

"That bastard!" Kutter's face creased in frustration, and he swore. Seeing Susan, he muttered an apology. "Does Grant know his brothers have gone to their Maker?"

"I'm sure he knows about Marvin, but not about Floyd." Daniel winced as he gestured to the boxcar. The movement reminded him of the dull pain throbbing in his shoulder. "I don't think so."

Kutter's gaze swung from one end of the train to the other, taking in the red-stained snow and the chaos surrounding the Pinkertons gathering their horses in preparation for the hunt. "We've got to find Grant and Timmy Beeb before they disappear into the high country. The Dooleys are bad enough, but I don't relish the idea of having them combine forces with a Beeb. Mixing the two families together is like mixing fire and kerosene."

Daniel tried to rise. Susan helped him when he wavered. "I'll just get my horse."

"Hell, man, you don't think you're going to ride after them?"

"It's my job!"

Kutter leaned out of his saddle, spearing him with

a fierce gaze. "Not anymore, it's not," he snapped. "As of now you are officially discharged."

"Damn it, Kutter, I—"

"No! You listen to me, Daniel. Until now I've enjoyed seeing you take your own lead. It's done me good more than once. But right now I'm putting my foot down. Grant Dooley's been after you for years. Once he finds out his brothers are dead and his cousins have been apprehended, your life won't be worth spit. I can't even begin to imagine what Timmy Beeb would do to you if he found you." He stabbed him with an emphatic finger. "I am ordering the two of you to get the hell out of here, Crocker. You know how I feel about involving civilians in Pinkerton business. If you won't leave for me, then do it for her." Kutter gestured to Susan with his chin.

As if suddenly becoming aware of her presence, Daniel grew quiet.

"I want you to take him away," Kutter ordered Susan softly, his tone low and not to be disputed. "Get a horse from the boxcar and leave as fast as you can. And by God, you two had better find yourselves a good place to hide until this is all over."

Susan nodded in understanding and, leaving Daniel's side, hurried toward the train. Not bothering to ask permission, she grasped the reins of the horse being led down the ramp, recognizing it as the one Daniel always rode. Despite the disgruntled look she received from the man who had been trying to unload the animal for himself, Susan tugged the mount back to Daniel.

Daniel looked at her, obviously debating whether he should follow his ingrained sense of duty to his men or stay with Susan.

Reaching his side, she stared up at him. As she searched his pale, tension-carved face, she knew just how close she had come to losing him. "We're going home, Daniel. Your job here is finished."

Bit by bit his defiance drained away. Curling his fingers around her neck, he dipped his head to seal her lips with a tender kiss, letting her taste of the fear and panic that had held him in their grip since he'd seen her in Grant's clutches. "Yes. We'll go home."

He swung onto the horse, then reached out to help her up behind him. Her arms curled around his waist and she buried her cheek in his neck, savoring the strength of his body.

"You know where to find me," Daniel said to Kutter, holding the reins firmly to calm his jittery horse.

The older man nodded. "I'll be in touch in the next day or so. I might even bring a cow."

Daniel's lips twitched in a slight smile. "Thanks," he said. Both men knew he wasn't referring to livestock, but to the fact that Kutter had released him from his duties and understood his need to see Susan safely hidden away.

Kutter's face creased in an uncomfortable frown even as his eyes twinkled with unabashed delight. "Get out of here," he ordered gruffly. "And make sure you're not followed."

One of Daniel's men returned to give him his revolver. Daniel shoved the weapon into his holster, lifted the reins, and trotted toward the gulch.

Once they were away from the ambush site and moving through the trees, Susan spoke up. "Your wound?"

"Just a crease," Daniel replied. "We can tend to it as soon as we get back."

She nuzzled her face into his uninjured shoulder and squeezed him. He returned the pressure, using his free hand to clasp her arm.

Up ahead, the trees rustled. Daniel pulled on the

reins, drew his revolver, and held it in a steady deadly aim on the unknown intruder.

A familiar figure edged his horse onto the road.

"Donovan!" Susan cried, shocked to find the man here.

Daniel relaxed. "Good work, Donovan."

Donovan threw him a mocking salute. "My pleasure. Where you headed?"

"I think it's best if we disappear for a day or two."

"Good. Don't worry about anything at Benton House; we'll be fine. I'll alert the town about the Dooleys on my way back." He gave Daniel his rifle. "You're going to need this, boy."

Daniel slid the rifle into the scabbard on his saddle.

"You two be careful now," Donovan urged. Then he directed his horse toward the orphanage and disappeared down the road.

He grew preoccupied as he urged Chief toward the mouth of the pass. Once they had reached the edge of the canyon, Daniel waited in a concealing screen of trees until he was satisfied that no one lurked anywhere near. Then he prodded the horse into a gallop, heading north, following the line of the mountains and the crooked path of the creek.

After a few miles, Susan asked, "Where are we going?"

"Trapper Pass."

27

Susan didn't ask any more questions. She sensed Daniel's urgency and desire to hide them safely away from prying eyes.

Since she'd expected to ride for some time, perhaps long into the night, she was surprised when Daniel guided Chief into a narrow pass through the mountains. He rode over a shallow frozen creek and ascended a small hill. There, nestled in the valley below, stood a small frame house and a barn. In the late afternoon sunshine the buildings rested in shadows, their shapes warm and welcoming.

Susan was almost hesitant to inquire, "Daniel, where are we?"

He spoke softly, but his voice rang with quiet pride. "Home."

"Home? Is this your place?"

"I bought the spread with the help of a friend about five years ago. My debt to him was paid today."

"Five years?" she echoed weakly. "Why didn't

you say something? Why didn't you ever live here until now?''

His fingers curved around her knee in a reassuring caress. "Because I expected to return as the conquering hero," he stated ruefully. "But I made a living out of killing—first in the cavalry, then with the Pinkertons. I didn't want to come back with blood on my hands." His mouth tightened. "I wanted to show people I'd made something of myself, that I wasn't a homeless brat abandoned in the alleys of Bentonburg, Pennsylvania."

"We never thought that, Daniel."

"I did."

At last Susan understood that part of Daniel's hardness came from the image of himself that he'd been nurturing inside his mind since childhood. He believed himself to be unworthy of love, so he thought everyone else felt the same way.

"You could have stayed here all these years."

He smiled and twisted in the saddle to meet her gaze, his eyes warm and heated in a way Susan had rarely seen. "If it hadn't been for you," he continued, "I probably never would have found the courage to stay here."

He smiled, and Susan hugged his waist with all the fervor and passion that had been growing inside her. Turning, he nudged Chief forward, heading for the buildings in the center of the clearing.

He led the gelding to the barn, stopping to allow Susan to slide to the ground. After following suit, he jerked open the doors. A musty smell still lingered inside. Although he'd come here several times in the last few days to prepare for Susan's arrival, a faint air of neglect still clung to the place, a result of the years without an owner and Daniel's infrequent visits.

But there was nothing another batch of fresh straw

and a little spring air couldn't take care of, he thought with satisfaction. Once the warmer weather came, he'd replace some of the posts that had been gnawed at by horses boarded inside during the winter. Then in time he'd install new pulleys and ropes in the loft. With a load of hay and some animals, the place would look and smell almost new.

After rubbing Chief down, Daniel looked up to find Susan waiting for him in the doorway.

"We really should get you inside and take care of that wound."

"Fine." He grasped his Winchester, then held out his hand. "Welcome home, Mrs. Crocker."

Together they walked toward the house. When she saw the building that would become her home, she felt a thrill of delight. Susan knew she could make a life for herself here with Daniel and perhaps their children—something she had dreamed about but had never really hoped to attain, until Daniel reentered her life.

"The house isn't much right now, I'm afraid. It's been out of use for a while. I've come here once or twice in the last few days to clean a few things, but it's still a little rickety. Maybe soon we can afford to give it a coat of whitewash . . . and I'm pretty handy with a hammer."

"Daniel, it's lovely."

"It is something, isn't it?" Whooping, he swept her into his arms, sucking in his breath at the yanking pain in his shoulder and setting her back on the ground. He swore and touched the flesh wound.

"Where's the key?" She smiled at his effort.

"Left breast pocket."

She burrowed her numbed fingers beneath his coat, savoring the warmth of his skin as she tunneled beneath the buttoned flap of his work shirt and withdrew the watch chain.

"The key with the worn etchings," Daniel instructed.

Susan noted the brass designs on the base of the key had been rubbed smooth, as if they had been caressed, over and over again, in unconscious devotion.

The latch gave way with a grating rasp, demonstrating its lack of attention in the last few years. The swollen back door resisted her push, and Daniel kicked it until it flew open and slammed against the inside wall.

She stepped inside the kitchen, and he followed, setting his revolver and rifle on the counter of the hutch. The room was dim due to the boarded windows, but enough light entered through the cracks between the slats to illuminate the tiny area.

Susan gazed about her, not noticing the cobwebs Daniel had missed in the corners, the secondhand furniture, or the musty closed-in smell. She envisioned how it would look after a more thorough cleaning, with curtains at the windows and a fresh tin countertop on the hutch.

"It doesn't look like much now," Daniel said.

"It's beautiful."

"I didn't really have time to get things ready for you. I managed to scrape off most of the dust and scrub down the furniture . . . and I brought in a few things." Daniel hesitated like a little boy, obviously wanting to please her. "There's a pantry here"—he crossed to throw open a door to a tiny two-by-two closet—"and through there is a bedroom."

Susan joined him at the second door and looked in at the small unfurnished room. Then Daniel was darting toward the middle of the kitchen.

"We've got a root cellar, with a trapdoor right in the house, not outside!" He pounded on the hollow spot with his heel, then grasped her arm and pulled her into the hall. "This will be the parlor," he said, motioning to a small room at the front of the house.

The windows promised a wealth of light once the protective planks were removed and the panes cleaned.

"And this"—he hesitated, then opened the final door—"is another bedroom."

Peeking around his shoulder, Susan saw that, except for the kitchen, it was the only room in the house with furniture. A dresser stood next to one wall, complete with a porcelain pitcher and basin. The rest of the small space was filled with an iron bed. Evidently Daniel had bought it on one of his trips. It now stood resplendent with fresh linens and a quilted comforter.

" 'Course there's still a lot to be done. I'd hoped to finish before you came."

"I'm glad you didn't finish. I'll enjoy helping you get it ready."

He smiled, drawing her into his arms. She allowed herself the luxury for only a moment, then pulled back. "Your shoulder."

She took him to the kitchen and pushed Daniel into a rickety green chair—which, besides the battered table and hutch, was the only piece of furniture in the room. "We're going to bandage that wound right now," she stated firmly.

"No turpentine."

"No turpentine."

Susan helped him take off the duster, then his coat and shirt. A streak of blood creased his shoulder. Lifting her skirts, she unbuttoned her petticoat and allowed it to drop to the floor. Daniel watched with one brow lifted in teasing inquiry.

She blushed. "Where can I get some water?"

Daniel gestured to the pantry. "A pump was piped into the house, but not to the kitchen. I primed it a few days ago."

A pail hung from the neck of the pump, and she filled the container with water, then returned. Using the top of her petticoat, she cleansed his skin, glad to see that while he had lost some blood, the wound was only superficial. She ripped the ruffle off her petticoat and snapped the gathering threads, making a long, narrow strip of cotton. She then proceeded to wrap the makeshift bandage around his shoulder, binding the wound.

"That should do until we can get to the orphanage and find you a proper dressing."

He lifted his arm, testing the muscle. He winced at the twinge of pain, but his smile of pleasure congratulated her on her efforts. Due to the chill of the air, he slipped his arms back into the shirt.

Susan urged Daniel back into the bedroom and settled him on the edge of the mattress. "You just sit here. I'm going to pump some more water so that both of us can wash. I want you to rest until I get back."

Susan returned to the kitchen, retrieving the pail she'd used earlier. Crossing to the door, she dumped the soiled water into the snow, then went to the pump and filled the container with clear water. Humming beneath her breath, she set the bucket on the table and returned to the chilly porch to remove a few sticks of wood from the stack piled against the outer wall. After shutting herself into the relative warmth of the kitchen again, she dodged into the parlor, where she'd seen a fireplace.

"Daniel?" Since she could find no matches, she went back into the bedroom to ask Daniel where he had hidden them.

She found him fast asleep on the bed. It appeared the events of the day, combined with the shock of his wound, had proved to be more than his body could handle.

Shivering, Susan foraged through the drawers in the hutch until she discovered a tin of matches. Crow-ing with success, she took the bucket and hurried to the parlor and lit a fire.

Soon she had enough of a blaze to heat the water and allow her to wash. After scrubbing her skin clean, she grimaced in distaste when forced to don her suit again. The purple fabric was streaked with mud, and the snow had caused some of the dyed braid to bleed.

Emotionally and physically drained after all that had happened since that morning, Susan gathered up Daniel's coat and padded barefoot into the bedroom. She climbed upon the bed, nestling up to her husband and wrapping her arms around his waist as if to assure herself that he was warm and safe.

Daniel awoke with a start. Turning his head, he found Susan studying him with such adoration in her eyes that his chest swelled.

She removed the watch from his pocket and lifted the lid. "It's barely six. You've been asleep less than an hour. You should try to rest."

Daniel rubbed one hand over his face, attempting to still the adrenaline that continued to race through him after all that had happened. He kept telling himself it was over, but his mind and body refused to believe that. After ten years with the Pinkertons he was finding it difficult to leave that life behind and move on to another.

"How's the wound?"

He flexed his arm. There was a dull throb in his shoulder and he could feel the muscles growing stiff, but he was alive and he'd survived worse. No doubt he'd survive this, too.

"It's just a twinge. It'll be better in no time."

They lay for long minutes in peaceful silence. Then Susan's stomach growled and she giggled. "I don't suppose that among the things you tucked away in this house there might be some food?"

"As a matter of fact . . ."

He found a tin of beans and another of peaches. They spread one of the blankets on the parlor floor and ate their meal straight from the cans. They used Daniel's knife as a makeshift utensil, since he had neglected to bring plates or flatware.

When they finished, Susan's fingers were sticky, but her appetite was satisfied. "So what are you going to do now that you're not a Pinkerton?" she asked.

"I thought I'd raise stock and some horses. My years in the cavalry and with the Pinkertons have made me a good judge of horseflesh, and I think I can earn a living at it. For both of us."

She liked the sound of that. *Both of us*.

Daniel edged closer. "I hope you'll be happy here, Susan. It might get lonely. Sometimes the pass isolates us from Ashton in the winter."

"Then we'll never have to worry about privacy." Her gaze flicked to his lips, wondering when he would kiss her.

Daniel kept talking, avoiding that look. "In the spring it will be muddy and the road will be impassable."

"So we'll have no unwelcome guests."

Daniel didn't continue. He couldn't. Susan's hair spilled about her shoulders. Her eyes gleamed like deep summer streams. She was so beautiful, he wondered how much longer he could wait until she became his in every way.

When Daniel remained silent, Susan added, "You've forgotten summer, Daniel. In summer we'll be shaded by the hills, and a fresh breeze will cool the house. Then in autumn the leaves will explode with color, and we'll be protected from the first chill of winter."

He touched one of her fingers, then moved on to the next. Her skin was so soft, so smooth, so enticing. "I'm offering you a hard life, Susan. There won't be a lot of money at first."

"I don't need money."

"For a while I won't be able to hire any help."

"I'll help."

"And this house is small and cramped. It may be years before we can build an addition."

"I don't want another room, Daniel."

He abandoned his examination of her hand and looked up. What he saw in her gaze made him pause. Need. Desire.

"I have everything I need. Right here," she said. "You'll see. We'll be happy. So happy."

The expression on his face told her clearly that he didn't know if he should believe her. He'd lived his whole life alone—and now that there was someone to share it, he felt he wasn't offering her enough.

She leaned forward. "This house and this land are more than I ever dreamed of having, Daniel. But I'd give them up in a second if my having them meant I'd never have you."

Her voice grew husky as she remembered the moment when Grant Dooley had stood above them, his revolver aimed at Daniel's head.

"I've been followed by a damn unlucky star. Until now," Daniel whispered. "I don't deserve you."

She shook her head, still not understanding why he couldn't see that she didn't care about his past—not when they had a future. Together.

"Why not, Daniel?"

He didn't answer. He merely twisted to plant a kiss in the center of her palm. Susan made a fist as if she could capture the warmth of his lips.

In a lithe, simple movement, Daniel turned her away from him and drew her back against his chest, closing his arms around her waist. They remained that way for some time, watching the slivers of light from the boarded windows crawl across the floor as dusk fell and darkness closed in upon them.

"I'm anxious to see what this place will look like with the boards off and the windows cleaned," Susan whispered into the comfortable silence. Daniel's arms tightened in response. "We'll be happy here. We'll have a home that's safe and full of love."

Love. That word scared the hell out of Daniel. And after the events of the day, he wasn't so sure he could keep Susan safe, either.

A frown marred Susan's brow as he pulled away from her and stood. He strode across the room, stopped at one of the windows, and braced himself against the wall.

Susan climbed to her feet and walked toward him, laying her hand on his arm. The muscles were tense, taut. "What's wrong?"

"I failed you today."

"I don't understand."

"I didn't keep you safe."

"You couldn't have prevented what happened."

"But I should have! Don't you see? I should have taken care of you!"

Susan sensed that something more than the Dooleys lay beneath his tension. "What is it? Something else is bothering you. What?"

"Nothing." The word was formed on a single breath of air.

Susan forced him to look at her. His eyes were dark, tormented.

"Tell me," she urged softly. "I hate to see you so worried. I told you my secrets. I told you everything."

Silence blanketed the room, broken only by the

soft crackle of the fire in the grate. Daniel's head tilted back, and he held his breath in his chest.

"I don't want anything to happen to you," he said.

"Nothing will happen. I lo—"

He placed his fingers over her lips. "Don't say that!" He caressed her mouth. "Please don't love me, Susan."

"I don't understand."

"Everyone who has ever loved me has died, Susan. And I won't have you die."

Susan would have smiled at the idiotic statement if he had not remained so solemn.

"You don't honestly believe that, do you?"

"You never knew how I came to be at the orphanage, did you, Susan?" He backed away, releasing her. "By all the rules of heaven, I never should have been an orphan." He laughed, and the sound was bitter. "I was the ninth child in a family of ten. My father was a drunken bastard who couldn't leave my mother alone long enough for her to be out of the birthing bed before he planted another baby in her."

Susan winced at Daniel's crude words, but did not interrupt.

"Every baby was a boy. After I was born, Mama thought she'd had her last child. Until Annie. Little Annie." His voice grew gentle. "Damn, she was pretty. From the very first. But Mama never really knew."

Daniel took a deep, tormented breath. "I was the only one home when she began to bleed. I tried to help her, but there was nothing I could do." He swallowed. "I promised to take care of Annie," Daniel said quickly, clearing his throat.

"After Mama died, my father grew worse and worse. When the war broke out, most of my brothers ran off to join the army. One day I walked into the house to find my father shaking Annie and making her cry. I yelled at him and kicked him. After that, I wouldn't leave her alone with him. I took her everywhere with me. About a month passed. Then Pa took us into town and told us to wait for him there. He never came back.''

Daniel's head dipped. "We went to Bentonburg. For a time we stayed in one of the brothels. The daughter of one of the women there hid us, but when we were discovered, we had to leave again. One night I went to find us something to eat. I'd hidden Annie in a basket in the bushes outside of town. She was sleeping. I knew I could return and . . .''

Susan steeled herself against the pain in Daniel's voice. She had to let him continue. She had to let him purge himself of the hurt inside just as he had allowed her to purge her own guilt.

"A couple found her there. They took her home, thinking she'd been abandoned. When I discovered where she'd been taken, I decided it would be . . . best . . . to let them have her. She was just a baby . . . a baby." His hands grew rigid, the knuckles gleaming starkly in the firelight. "Two nights later I found her battered body in the street. They'd beaten her and left her for dead.''

Susan fought back a cry of distress. How had Daniel borne this for so long? How had he shouldered the pain and guilt that must have crushed his young soul? He couldn't have been much more than a baby himself.

Susan circled his waist with her arms, resting her cheek on his chest. He returned the embrace, but his body remained tense. She never would have guessed at the burden he'd carried . . . and continued to carry.

"Annie needed me. Annie loved me. And I let her down, just as I'd let Mama down.''

"It wasn't your fault," she whispered. She lifted

her head. "Do you hear me, Daniel Crocker? It wasn't your fault your sister died, just as it wasn't mine that Mama died. You taught me that. You aren't cursed or damned, or whatever you want to call it. Your love did not kill your mother or your sister." When he tried to back away, she would not release him. "And your devotion will not kill me."

He turned his head, but she made him look at her. "I love you, Daniel Crocker," she stated slowly, emphatically. "And I will spend the rest of my life loving you. A long and happy life."

28

Daniel's body remained tense, alert. A muscle flexed in his jaw.

Susan stepped back. "Believe me, Daniel." There was no hesitation, no nervousness, no fear, as she slipped the top button of her suit free. "I love you, Daniel."

She faltered only once, then slid the second button loose, exposing a wedge of creamy feminine skin.

Daniel swallowed. "Susan, don't you see—"

"I love you."

The next button nudged through its hole. Daniel gaped at her in astonishment. He'd grown so used to being the partner in control, the tempter, he had never thought their roles would ever be reversed. The mere idea of being seduced by his own wife caused a licking heat to begin at his nerve endings and work its way to the very core of his body.

"Susan," he moaned, incapable of saying more.

With each inch of exposed flesh, she told him of

her love, her trust. Soon the basque jacket yawned open, revealing the undergarments beneath. A delicate batiste corset cover hid the rigid stays of her corset. But Daniel could see firsthand how the foundation garment cinched her waist and pushed her breasts against the fragile restraint of the tatted yoke of her camisole.

Then she pushed the bodice from her shoulders, exposing the bare flesh of her arms and shoulders. She stood still, her head proud, her eyes glittering with lines of molten gold and green.

"I won't leave you, Daniel. Ever." The bodice dropped from her fingers to the floor.

Susan knew by his expression that Daniel had assumed she would stop here. He was sure her courage would flag. But Susan continued to undress. Her nimble fingers worked the fastenings of her corset cover. As each shell-like disk slipped free, she could see the hurt little boy buried inside Daniel being taken over by the man he'd become.

The soft batiste garment fell to the floor. As Daniel stared at the fullness of her breasts, a spark of fear deep inside Susan's head threatened her courage. But it was quickly doused by her overwhelming desire to be loved by her husband. Daniel needed her. She needed him. Their lovemaking would be beautiful, exciting, and rich. She knew he would be gentle, and she wanted to surprise him with the depth of her own passion.

Sinuously she pushed her skirts and petticoats down over her hips. One by one she released the metal hooks on her corset, exposing the wrinkled fabric of her camisole beneath. "Tonight you won't get out of your husbandly duties, Daniel."

Daniel experienced a flare of heat at her words. She was so delicate, so beautiful. Yet, who would have thought she could become such a siren. This was how Adam must have felt. If Eve had looked at him with half the urgency and love he saw shining from Susan's eyes, he would have taken the apple much more quickly.

"You make me feel things I didn't know were possible, Daniel."

A sensuous coil tightened low in his belly as she toyed with the satin ribbon woven through the crocheted beading that edged the yoke. He could only watch as that ribbon slipped free, so slowly, so teasingly, that he thought he would die from the suspense.

Didn't she know what she was doing to him? Didn't she know his control was threatening to explode?

"Tell me you love me, Daniel." Susan tugged. The ribbon grew taut, pulling the fabric of the camisole away from her chest. With each inch of progress, the material gaped more, revealing the firm swells of her breasts.

"You will tell me one day," she whispered. "Someday soon."

A low growl bled from Daniel's throat. He couldn't bear any more. She didn't have to prove anything to him. Not now. Not ever again.

If she had been any other woman, he would have scooped her into his arms and stormed into the bedroom. He would have spent his passion fiercely and quickly. But he couldn't do that. Not with her.

"Don't, Susan. You don't have to do this." He wished she would stop. Now. While he still had the power to summon some small shred of control.

Susan merely smiled at him. The air had grown so taut, so silent. "Yes. I do."

He had abandoned all pretense of looking at her face. He was staring at her breasts, making them feel heavy, making them ache for his touch. Susan focused on the warmth his look ignited in her body . . .

and her soul. She wanted him. She needed him. She would have him. Tonight.

Her hands trembled, then lifted to his chest, brushing over the smooth fabric of his shirt and around his neck. Standing on tiptoe, she brought her mouth up until it hesitated only a fraction of an inch from his own. She could feel Daniel's ragged breath on her cheek.

When he drew her close, she closed her eyelids. "Please, Daniel." She touched her lips to his. She employed all of the techniques he had taught her about kissing. She sipped, she tasted, she nibbled. And with each kiss she felt desire grow and blossom inside her. Her body arched against him until Daniel took her weight, melding his hips to hers so she could feel the evidence of his arousal.

Groaning in painful delight, she forced herself to back away. Not in fear this time, not in haste, but in a tormenting feminine invitation.

Smiling, she backed toward the bedroom. Her skin was feverish, her face flushed. Knowing what it would take to push Daniel over the edge, she lifted her arms and began to unbraid her hair, totally aware of the way her actions caused her breasts to lift in a brazen manner.

"Make love to me, Daniel," she murmured huskily. "Please."

Not waiting to witness the answer in his eyes, she turned, affording him a glimpse of her delectable backside through the slit in her drawers. Daniel moaned aloud when the camisole dropped to the floor behind her as she disappeared around the door.

He couldn't resist. Heaven help him, he knew she might lose her courage again, but he couldn't back away.

"Sweetheart?" He strode into the hall.

Her pantalets lay on the smooth pine boards halfway to the bedroom.

Daniel hesitated. His heart was pounding with a murderous force, its beat centered somewhere in the base of his loins. He wiped his hand nervously over his mouth, then stepped into the bedroom.

The lamp was low. Susan lay on the bed, the covers drawn over her breasts. He could tell some of her bravado had slipped by the way she trembled, but she still gazed at him with blatant hunger.

Daniel cleared his throat, unable to turn away. He wanted to know what she looked like. Beneath the covers. Bare. The mere thought aroused him to the point of pain.

"Please," she whispered.

"Please what?"

"Please make love to me."

He could only nod.

"When?" she asked, repeating the question she'd asked so many times.

"Soon."

"When?"

He pulled the shirttails from his trousers, striving to leash his passion just a little longer. "Now."

As she had the night he'd bathed, Susan watched him strip the shirt from his shoulders. He bared himself much more quickly than she had done in the other room. He tore his arms from the sleeves and dropped the garment on the floor. In the dim light the bandage gleamed starkly next to his skin. Swiftly he began unbuttoning his trousers.

"Essie said that a man could—"

"Damn, I don't want to hear what Essie told you," Daniel bit out between clenched teeth.

Susan giggled nervously. "Why not?"

"Because she apparently told you too much."

At the sound of her silky laughter, Daniel tore the

buttons loose, wondering how long he would last. Each time he looked at his wife, all his passions raged. But he had to hold on long enough to bring his wife to an answering pitch of ecstasy.

With a self-consciousness that he found disconcerting, Daniel pushed his trousers to the floor. Then he approached the bed and sat on the edge. When he reached out to turn down the wick of the lamp, she stopped him, her fingertips feather-light on his arm. The blanket slipped, and Daniel felt her breasts rubbing his shoulder blades. He fought to think of something—anything but the pounding urgency of his own body.

"No, leave it," she murmured in his ear.

"I don't want to frighten you."

She grew still against him, and he could feel a shiver course through her. Nerves or anticipation? he wondered. But soon she pressed her lips to his skin and smiled. "You won't ever frighten me."

Uncertainly, Daniel unbuttoned his underdrawers and stood away from the edge of the bed. From behind, he heard her settling back on the pillows, but he could feel her watching him as surely as if her scrutiny were a hot finger tracing the crease in his spine.

He slipped the woolen underdrawers to the floor, then stood with his back to her, praying he would not shock her when he turned around. For he was more than ready for her.

"Daniel?"

"What?"

"Come to bed."

He debated his choices. He could turn and have her stare. Or he could sit down on the mattress and hope that he could cover himself before she got an eyeful.

"Daniel."

Daniel sank down on the edge of the bed. He reached blindly behind him for the covers. He encountered a bare arm, the skin soft and smooth and utterly feminine. He twisted in surprise. As he had feared, her eyes immediately dropped to look at him.

"Oh." The word was only a whisper of sound, but it clearly revealed her thoughts.

Her gaze bounced back up to his face.

"Maybe we should wait, Susan."

Her fingers covered his lips. "Shh." Her hand slid around his neck, and she pulled him down until he lay half over her body. He groaned silently at the contact of her breasts on the muscles of his chest, her knee to his hip.

"Make love to me, Daniel."

"You're sure?"

"Yes. Oh, yes."

The last was a hungry growl of impatience.

Knowing he must touch her or die, Daniel swooped to take her lips in a searing kiss. She tasted of peaches and passion. As his tongue swept into the velvety hollows, she clutched at his shoulder, trying to draw him closer, to absorb him into her very flesh.

He lifted his head, gasping for breath, trying to tear his mind away from the innocent torment her fingers aroused.

"Daniel?"

"Mmm?"

"Touch me."

He rubbed his thumb over her jaw. "I *am* touching you."

She shook her head. "Not my face."

At her words the fire inside him exploded into a raging inferno. He burned so hot that he feared his touch would sear her. But then her small fingers curled around his wrist, guiding his hand down her chest and filling his palm with her breast. Her eyes flickered closed, her head dropped back on the pillows in open delight.

"Essie was—"

Daniel crushed his lips to hers. He didn't know how much longer he could wait. She was making him crazy. Unwittingly Susan enticed him to the melting point by testing her courage. Yet, if he didn't take the time to ensure that she was ready for him . . .

Susan moaned, her hips straining. Slowly, carefully, Daniel stroked her and loved her with his hands and mouth, bringing her to a fever pitch, all the while attempting to ignore his own pain. He had to make this night one she would remember with pleasure, not with fear.

"What, Daniel? What do I do next?"

Her warmth and the sweet innocence of her responses were his undoing. Her hand curved around his hip to settle in the hollow of his back. He clenched his jaw, willing himself not to think of the overwhelming delight she brought him.

He framed her face with his hands. "Trust me?"

She nodded.

"I'll try to hold off until . . ."

"Until what?"

Despite his torment, Daniel grinned. "Evidently Essie didn't tell you *everything*."

Slowly he settled himself between her thighs. She was so small, so tiny, he feared she would not be able to accommodate him. His knees nudged at her legs until they parted.

Unable to say the words of love that trembled on the tip of his tongue, Daniel dipped his head to kiss her eyes shut so that she would not watch.

His hand swept down to stroke her gently into readiness. Then, carefully, he entered her a little way only. Susan gasped, shrinking away. Daniel withdrew.

"No," he groaned. "Lie still. You're so tight."

Her hands clung to his shoulders. Her nails bit into his skin. Once again Daniel entered her, thrusting a little farther into her warmth, this time allowing her to adjust to his body. Then, in one smooth movement, he plunged into the velvet softness and broke the barrier between them.

Susan dug her nails into his back, holding him close and burying her head in the curve of his neck. Her teeth were wet and slick on his skin.

"Is it over? The pain?"

He nodded and fought for control, fought to think of anything but his wife and her rough, hurt voice.

Then he felt her smile against his shoulder. "I thought it would be worse."

At her words, Daniel felt a burst of pride, a rush of adoration. "It can be better," he assured, hoping he could hold off long enough to give her the pleasure she deserved.

"Really?"

He drew back, meeting her emerald gaze. "Really."

"Show me."

Restored by her limitless faith in him, Daniel began a rhythm as old as time. Slowly, achingly, he taught her a woman's passion, just as he had longed to do since the day he'd seen her picture, the day he'd kissed her at the academy, the day he'd made her his wife.

Together they moved toward the same goal, their lips meeting and breaking away, seeking and slipping free. Then, just when Daniel thought he would not be able to hold back any longer, Susan gasped. Her muscles shuddered and tightened around him, immediately bringing him to his own explosive release.

She cried out. He heard the ecstasy in each syllable. Passion spilled over them both as their bodies strained, trembled, then fell into a blissful oblivion.

Long endless minutes passed before Daniel could gather his wits enough to lift himself up on his forearms. He brushed the moist hair from her face. At first he thought she might already have fallen asleep, but she smiled, and her lashes flickered.

"Daniel?"

"Hmm?"

Her expression held all of the adoration that Daniel had tried to run from for so many years.

"I love you."

29

Timmy Beeb cantered toward the yawning cave where he and the Dooleys had camped the night before. His horse was breathing hard from the steep climb up the side of the mountain. Below, he could see an occasional flash of sunlight on metal. Nearly twenty-four hours had passed, and the Pinkertons were still hot on their trail.

Shooting an impatient glance at the men in the valley who stuck to them like ticks to a hound, Beeb glared at his companions. A few of Grant's cousins had managed to follow them into the hills. After mere hours of sleep, Beeb had followed the counsel of the voices in his head and had taken a horse. Under the cover of the black midnight shadows, he had returned to the site of the ambush to see if Crocker was still in charge. He had learned that Daniel had been sent away. Now Beeb was ready to ride.

"Get up! We're moving out."

Beeb noted the way Grant ambled toward his

mount, drinking from a half-full bottle of liquor to ease the ache in his belly and the pain in his body. It was obvious he had missed his daily portion of morphine. In a few hours he would be shaking and pale. Beeb snickered, not about to tell Grant he had the bottle of morphine powder he'd taken from Gibby stashed in his saddlebags.

One by one the remaining men mounted their horses. A tall slender Dooley was not quite so biddable, however. He gazed at Timmy in baleful rebellion. "Why?"

In response, Beeb whipped his revolver from his gun belt and aimed it at the bridge of the man's nose. He fired.

"Any other questions?"

The three men who remained watched in horror. Timmy laughed aloud at their pinched features. They were all a bunch of rabbits. They didn't even have enough gumption to run, not realizing they were mere hours away from meeting their Maker. Beeb didn't intend to take them with him when he went into hiding, and he didn't intend to leave any witnesses. He would keep the Dooleys long enough to sacrifice their hides to the Pinkertons. Then he would go. Alone.

"Where are you taking us now?" Grant asked, his tone carefully modulated lest it offend Beeb's hair-trigger temper. He had plans of his own where Beeb was concerned.

"Back to Ashton."

Grant's eyes sparkled. "You mean you'll help us get Floyd?"

Beeb's lips curled in disgust. "He's dead! Your brother is *dead*."

Grant stared at the other man in disbelief. In the space of twenty-four hours, his family had dwindled to nothing. Nothing! He wanted to blame Crocker. His soul ached to lay his miseries at the Pinkerton's door, but he knew Beeb was more to blame than anyone. It was Beeb who'd lured them into his plan. Grant never should have listened when Beeb approached him and his kin in that saloon in Barryville and tempted them with a scheme to free Floyd and capture Crocker at the same time. But the whole thing had seemed so perfect.

"How did Floyd die?"

Beeb grinned in genuine delight, setting Grant's teeth on edge. "I don't know. I saw them lifting him from the boxcar this morning. Floyd was probably dead before we left. Bet you Crocker put a bullet through his head."

Grant's hands curled into fists. When he didn't speak, Beeb continued to taunt him. "Don't you understand? Crocker is responsible for everything that happened. That bastard did this to you."

Grant was beginning to believe differently, but for the moment there was nothing he could do. Crocker would die. Beeb would see to that. Then Grant would see to Beeb.

"Mount up!" Timmy yelled.

"Where are we going?"

"Have you forgotten already? I know everything about Crocker—his habits, his fears, his weaknesses. I even know where he is."

Daniel's eyes snapped open; sleep deserted him. He grew tense, not knowing exactly what had disturbed him. He waited, listening to the quiet of the morning. When he heard nothing further, he willed his muscles to relax and the pounding of his heart to slow to a more normal rate.

Slowly his body responded. Even more slowly his mind. Nothing had happened. Nothing at all. He was just jittery. And after all that had occurred the last few days, who could blame him?

Managing to reassure himself, Daniel yawned and stretched, rolling onto his side. He encountered soft, feminine skin. Susan.

A smile curved his lips. She was so beautiful. So warm. So passionate.

Daniel tried to settle back into sleep, but couldn't. There was something—some niggling worry—pressing in the back of his brain. He would go out to the barn and check his horse, make sure everything was all right. Then he'd return to her side.

He paused only for a second, then eased from the bed and ran his fingers through his hair. He fondly regarded his wife and found himself looking forward to the years and years to come when he would see the same sight each morning. She had taught him to laugh, to love. And to dream.

Pulling on his underdrawers, socks, and shirt, he fastened a handful of buttons, then dragged on his trousers and boots. Silently he left the room, collecting his rifle from the kitchen counter in response to years of habit, and crossed to the door. Stepping out into the cold, he allowed his eyes to roam in a fascinated caress over his land.

Heavy clouds scudded against the jutting faces of the mountains, their thick fleecy weight promising snow and warmer weather. Spring would come soon enough. Susan would love it here. They would make a home equal to no other, the kind he'd never had as a child and the kind he had never dreamed of having. They would be happy and—

Something warned Daniel long before he heard the sounds. His head jerked up. Four horsemen loomed in sharp relief against the hillside.

A pang of angry bitterness settled into Daniel's soul and he whirled and ran into the house. Even as he rushed through the kitchen and into the bedroom, he could hear the muffled sound of approaching hooves. They'd seen him out on the porch.

"Susan!"

She was already sitting up in bed, her hair tumbling around her shoulders in chaotic fiery waves. "What is it? What's wrong?"

"The Dooleys," he rasped. "Get dressed. We've got to get you away from here. I'll put you on the horse. I want you to ride to the orphanage."

"No, Daniel."

"Susan, listen to me!" He threw her clothes into her lap. Since his Peacemaker was still in the kitchen, he searched one of the drawers in the dresser and withdrew a second revolver that he'd hidden beneath a pile of shirts. "I won't have anything happen to you! You'll go where it's safe!"

"Only if you come."

"Susan, if they see me with you they'll follow! Now get up!"

She looked at him in frustrated silence, then began to fumble into her clothes, easing her skirt and jacket over her bare skin and fastening the garment. As soon as she was completely dressed, Daniel pulled her into the kitchen. Once at the door, he knew it was already too late. The four men were only fifty feet away from the house. There was no way she could run to the barn without being seen.

"Quick! Hide in the cellar, and don't come out until I come for you. Understand?"

Daniel shoved the table aside, not allowing himself to waver when the color drained from Susan's skin. He knew he was triggering old memories, but he couldn't think of anything else to do.

"Daniel, no! I'm staying here with you. If we're going to fight, we'll fight together."

"Susan, do as I say!" He lifted the trapdoor and carried her protesting form to the opening. Forcibly he led her down the steps into the cellar. When she shouted at him and refused to go, Daniel cupped her cheeks with his hands and gave her one long kiss, letting her feel all the tenderness and love she had taught him to give in the past weeks.

"Please, Susan," he begged. "Please, just do what I ask."

He pressed the revolver into her hands, and an unspoken message flashed between them. Then he was pushing her deeper into the dark cellar and closing the trapdoor over her head. Susan cringed when the scrape of the table being moved over the trapdoor filled her ears. She scrambled up the stairs to pound on the planks.

"Daniel!"

He didn't answer.

Darn it! He couldn't do this to her! He couldn't! This was her home, too. And she could shoot. She could! She could defend herself against the Dooleys just as well as he. He wasn't going to leave her helpless and afraid, the way her mother had done. This time Susan intended to fight.

She pounded until her skin was raw, screaming for Daniel to let her out. From above she could hear him lifting the windows and smacking the butt of his rifle on the planks that covered them from the outside. Muffled shouts and curses were coming from the Dooleys, but she was too well insulated to make them out. Sporadic gunfire sounded above her. Susan's heart beat in her ears; her limbs grew numb. She had to get out. She had to! She couldn't let him protect her this way. She had to help him.

With all the strength she had left, she slammed her shoulder against the trapdoor until it began to move—ever so slightly—and she knew she was causing the table to skitter out of the way.

Again and again she banged until the heels of her

hands were bruised and bloody. But with each jarring smack, the door moved a little farther and a little farther, until the table skidded out of the way and the trapdoor popped open far enough to allow her a glimpse of the kitchen.

She scrambled out of the opening, then cursed when the hatch slammed shut on her skirts. Reaching behind her, she jerked them loose, not heeding the rending sound of her dress tearing. Wildly she gazed around her, searching for the man she loved. Then she noted the back door was open. Daniel was kneeling behind a snowbank in the yard firing at the men who lay amid the scrub surrounding the house. One man already lay crumpled on the frozen ground near Grant while two others fired their weapons over the top of the well casing.

Daniel ducked, then ran and crouched behind a water barrel by the barn. Susan knew he was trying to lure the men away from the house and the sound of her pounding.

Damning the man's foolish sense of honor and his pigheaded stubbornness, she held the gun more firmly. It was heavy in her palms and strangely familiar. She knew how it worked, she knew how to cock the hammer and pull the trigger—she'd even killed a man. And she was willing to do it again if it would help the man she loved, just as she had tried to help her mother.

Pausing only enough to see that the chambers were loaded, she raced outside in time to see Timmy Beeb spring from the brush and run for the stables, his revolver aimed at Daniel's head.

"No!" she shouted.

Beeb looked at her, and for one split second, his aim wavered. She lifted her gun and fired. He jerked, the bullet striking his chest as his finger closed over his own trigger.

A raw scream burst from Susan's throat when the bullet plowed through her shoulder, slamming her body backwards, knocking her head on the steps. In dazed awareness, everything began to move slowly . . . slowly. Her fingers relaxed. The revolver tumbled from her grasp. She heard someone calling her, the cry filling her senses with the horrible sound of loss. Her hand automatically went to her head, feeling the exploding pain where she'd struck the step. And somewhere, from a great distance, she saw Daniel racing toward her.

A low moan ripped from her throat. She clutched thick handfuls of snow, but she didn't acknowledge the icy temperature as the pain spread through her body like a numbing wave.

She saw him. She saw Daniel bend over her.

"K-kiss me?" she begged. She tried to smile. Tried to reassure him that everything would be all right.

Daniel closed his eyes, and she thought she saw a gleaming track of wetness leak from his lashes. Then he pressed his lips to her own. Susan sighed. How she loved this man! How she would love him for the rest of her days.

Then, as if her body had found all that it needed, she drifted into a cool, welcoming darkness.

Daniel felt the strength draining from her body even as he held her. In disbelief, he held her limp body close, pressing her to his heart. His throat worked.

"Shoot him!"

Daniel's head shot up. From across the scant distance that separated him, he saw Timmy Beeb writhing on the ground, clutching his chest where Susan had wounded him.

"Kill him, damn it!" Beeb shouted again. "An eye for an eye! Can't you hear the voices? They're shouting for you to get rid of the devil's seed once and for all.''

Daniel saw two other men crouch at the corner of the barn—Grant Dooley and his cousin Nate.

Nate lifted his gun, but in a move Daniel had not expected, Grant's hand snapped out and stopped him. ''Let Beeb do his own murdering. He's the one who hatched this idiot plan in the first place. He's the one who got Floyd and Marvin killed. He murdered Bart in cold blood.''

The muted thump of hooves and the jingle of bridles pierced the air.

Nate blanched. ''The Pinkertons. They've heard the shots and they're coming!'' He scooped his revolver from the snow and strode to his horse.

Beeb watched him leave with half-crazed eyes. ''Where are you going?''

Nate glared at him in disgust and disbelief. ''I'm getting out, damn it! I'm not sitting here like a rat in a trap, waiting for them to ride down on me.'' He mounted and fled to a sheltering screen of trees.

Daniel's eye caught a sudden flash of movement. Timmy Beeb lunged in the snow for the revolver that had tumbled out of his reach. Daniel saw him lift it, saw him pull back the hammer.

An explosion split the silence. Beeb wavered and fell face down in the snow.

Holding the still smoking revolver, Grant Dooley regarded Daniel for some time. ''That wasn't for you,'' he said. ''That was for Floyd. And Marvin. And Bart.'' Then he ran for his horse and swung into the saddle.

In the aftermath of the gun battle, the approach of the Pinkertons was quiet, ghostly, the sounds concealed by the drifts of powder. Daniel watched in numbed detachment as Grant rushed past the body of Timmy Beeb lying crumpled in the snow, his fingers still curled around his revolver, his face contorted in the throes of death.

The Pinkertons rode by, heading in the Dooleys' direction, but as Daniel watched the two men being apprehended once and for all, he felt nothing. No distaste, no remorse, not even gratitude that Grant had spared his life. His body curled protectively over the woman he held. His wife.

Don't let her die! his heart cried out. *Dear God, don't spare me again to see death take someone I love.*

His brow creased in a frown. She was growing cold. So cold.

Gently, tenderly, he lifted her in his arms and carried her into the house. Crossing to the bedroom, he laid her on the mattress and drew the blanket over her. Then, after kissing her cheek, he hurried into the kitchen to fetch water and the torn petticoat Susan had left on the table.

He stripped her dress from her body and bathed her wound. Her skin grew ashen, cool. Daniel tried not to think of what he would do if she died. As Mama had died. And Annie.

"Susan? Hang on. Please hang on," Daniel crooned softly. Susan was so small, so frail in his arms. She wasn't made to withstand the pain he'd brought to her. The fear.

"Susan? Susan, can you hear me?" He scooped her up and held her against his chest, rocking her softly. "Listen to me. I still have so many things to tell you, to show you." He took a deep, ragged breath. "There's a fresh spring up on the hill. During the summer it's cool and sweet, and the banks are lined with wild watercress." His voice grew raw. "And the big oak tree . . . in the backyard. I thought I'd hang a rope swing on that thick branch."

Her arms hung limp at her sides, mocking his memories of the way she'd touched him. Held him.

"I never told you how much I loved you, did I?" he whispered. "I thought if I never said the words, I could protect you. Keep you . . . safe."

His throat closed over a burning knot of pain as he breathed in her scent and remembered her joy.

Time crawled by, but Daniel remained oblivious to its passage. At some point, much later, Kutter came into the room. "I sent for the doctor."

Daniel didn't hear him. He merely rocked Susan in his arms, murmuring soft incoherent phrases in her ear.

Kutter approached him and rested a hand on Daniel's shoulder. "Daniel?"

Startled, Daniel looked up.

"The doctor's here," Kutter repeated. His fingers tightened. "She'll be fine, son. You and I both know that the hero always gets shot in the shoulder. And the hero always lives." Kutter's lips twitched in a weak smile of encouragement.

Daniel laid Susan back on the pillows. Compared to the pallor of her skin, the fire of her hair seemed to have diminished, as if foretelling what was to come. Annie's gold locket gleamed dully next to her skin.

Daniel smoothed the thick waves away from her face. She didn't move, didn't react. He bent and pressed his mouth to her ear. "I love you," he whispered. He brushed his lips over hers. Then, at Kutter's urging, he stood and left the bedroom.

The doctor stayed in the room for a long time. Daniel waited, not daring to hope.

At long last the older man returned, offering Daniel a heartening smile. "She'll be right as rain in a day or two, you wait and see. The bullet went clean through, near as I can tell. Just keep her warm and let her rest."

Relief coursed through Daniel, and he grinned. "Thank you. Thank you!"

But by morning Susan had still not awakened. By the following nightfall, she was feverish and delirious.

Sometime during the day, Essie arrived, then Donovan. They tried to get Daniel to eat, tried to get him to sleep, but he couldn't bring himself to step away from the bed even for a single minute.

The next morning the doctor was summoned again. This time when he stepped from the room his expression was grim. "Her condition has been complicated by the blow she sustained to the head," he stated slowly. "In addition, she has signs of an infection. I believe a piece of the bullet is embedded in her chest." His expression grew sober. "The only alternative is to operate, but with possible injuries to the brain, she may not recover from the shock to her system."

Daniel barely registered the way Essie's face blanched or the way Donovan clasped her hand. Daniel grew still. Silent. Essie turned and spoke to him. He could hear the words lapping over him in relentless waves, but he paid them no mind. He was seeing a tiny infant, her jaw shattered, her body broken.

"Daniel?" Essie shook his arm. "It's your choice."

He swallowed past the lump in his throat.

Please. Can you help her?

"Daniel?"

He tore free from the memories to see Essie regarding him with concern.

"Do whatever you have to do," he whispered. "But I can't watch. Sweet heaven, don't ask me to watch." Incapable of saying anything more, Daniel walked to the door. Donovan patted his shoulder, but did not follow, and for that Daniel was grateful.

Don't love. Don't need.

Mother needed me. Annie needed me. And I let them both down.

Don't love me, Susan. Don't need me.

I've been followed by a damned unlucky star. Until now.

Daniel walked into the musty warmth of the barn. He gathered his shovel from the first stall, then went back outside.

The snow sighed beneath his feet in silent condemnation. The icy moisture sank through his clothes. Cloudy memories tumbled through his head. Annie, Belle and the social club, the Benton House Memorial Orphanage, the cavalry, the Pinkertons. Susan.

I love you, Daniel . . . love you . . . love you. . . .

The shovel bit into the ice and snow. The harsh squeak filled his ears, and Daniel saw another hillside, another grave. He forced himself to take another jabbing scoop. Then another and another, until he was striking bare frozen earth. And still he continued, even though the icy ground would not give way beneath the blade.

You make me feel things I didn't know were possible.

You'll see, Daniel. We'll be happy. So happy.

A sob tore through his chest, and Daniel sank to his knees. His head arched back, and his mouth opened in a silent cry. Inwardly he cursed God and the fates for requiring yet another sacrifice of him, another price for loving.

"No!" His shout tore through the winter stillness and echoed against the brittle hills, shattering the silence. "Damn it all to hell, no." As a boy he'd dug a narrow trough in the earth and enshrouded his sister in his only coat. Then, dry-eyed, he'd left her to rest for eternity in the dark ground. But he would *not* do the same for Susan! He would not let her die! Not when spring was so near and he needed her so much.

Ruthlessly he threw the shovel away and watched as it skidded across the snow. Dropping his head, Daniel gasped deep lungfuls of air. He would *make* her live. Somehow.

Pushing himself upright, Daniel turned.

Behind him a huge giant of a man waited in the snow. "Where is she?" he said. "Where's Susan?"

Daniel approached him. He didn't really know what to say to Max. Susan had told Daniel about him. She'd said he was special. Like a child.

"She's sick, Max."

"Sick?" He looked at Daniel with wide, uncomprehending eyes. "But I need her."

Wordlessly Daniel put his arm around the older man's shoulder and led him back to the house. "We're going to make her better, Max. We both need her."

In the hours that followed, Daniel closed himself in the parlor and tried to ignore the sounds coming from the kitchen where Susan had been laid out on the table. He and Max sat in silence, their backs against the wall, until Donovan entered the room again.

"The doctor has finished. We need you to help carry her."

After squeezing Max's shoulder reassuringly, Daniel went into the kitchen. Ignoring the blood that stained the floor and the table, he approached his wife. When Donovan would have helped, he waved him away. He lifted her slight form, carried her into the bedroom, and tucked her beneath the blankets.

The doctor looked in on her once more before leaving. "I wish I could give her something for the pain, but with Gibby's place burned to the ground, I haven't got much of a supply on hand."

"I've got some morphine in my saddlebags."

"Give her just a bit. Not much."

"Thanks, Doc." Daniel clapped the man on the back and walked him as far as the bedroom door. Then he took the vial of white powder from his bags and shook a little into the tin mug of water Essie had left on the nightstand.

Donovan stepped inside the doorway. "Doc gave her something for the pain?"

"No. He told me to use the morphine powder Gibby filled for me."

Donovan nodded. "It'll do the trick. I remember doling it out to my men during the war and they . . ." His words trailed off. His brow furrowed.

Daniel held the cup to Susan's lips.

"No. Daniel, no!"

Donovan lunged across the room, knocking the cup from Daniel's hand.

"What the hell?"

Donovan snatched the vial from the nightstand, sniffed the bottle, and scowled. "Poison. That's what Gibby was trying to say." His eyes glittered. "I'm no expert on drugs, but I'd bet my money this isn't straight morphine."

Daniel swore, wondering how much longer Beeb would continue to threaten his family. He could only hope his efforts would not end in Susan's death.

As dusk bled into total darkness, Daniel cared for his wife. Minutes stretched into hours. Hours into days. Days into eternities. Each night Daniel lit the lamps and talked to Susan, hoping to woo her from her unnatural sleep. His voice became hoarse from overuse, but still he continued. When she grew chill, he lay by her side, warming her. When she became feverish, he bathed her skin with water from the pump. Over and over he whispered words of encouragement and love, searching her face for a glimmer of improvement, of strength.

Each day the doctor visited. Each day he returned

from the bedroom, regretfully shaking his head. Esther offered her strength and comfort. And Donovan. There was nothing they could do. Nothing Daniel could do. But wait. And pray.

As the nights grew long, and one day stretched into two, then three, Daniel grew more and more afraid. He paused in drawing the covers up to her chin. A weariness flooded his body, and he fought the tide of despair that washed over him.

Kneeling at her bedside, he rested his head on her breast, his arms winding around her waist. He didn't know how much longer he could continue to hope.

Huge sobs racked his body, tearing from his chest where they had been lodged for so long. His body shook, and he clutched her slender body when he found himself fearing that, after all his efforts, she would still die. From deep inside him, hidden wells of grief burst, painful reminders of all that he had tried to forget, all that he had buried.

"Daniel?"

He grew still, the blood in his veins seeming to freeze.

Very slowly he lifted his head. Susan blinked at him in confusion, her brow creasing.

"Why . . . are you . . . crying?"

He stared hard, willing himself to believe this was no illusion, or that if it was, he would never awaken.

Her body trembled with weariness, but inch by inch her hand crept across the covers to grasp his fingers.

"D-Daniel?"

Another sob tore from Daniel's throat even as a smile of triumph split his mouth.

"Wh-what's . . . wrong?"

He shook his head, wiping away the tears that continued to fall. "Not a thing. Not a damned thing."

She attempted to grin, but her expression was still a little confused.

He tried to stand, to get Essie and Donovan, to send word to Kutter, Max, the doctor.

"Stay?"

The rest of the world melted away beneath the power of her gaze.

"I love you, Susan," he whispered gruffly.

She smiled. "I knew . . . you would tell me someday . . . soon."

Knowing she was still weak and tired, Daniel slid into the bed beside her, then pulled her close enough to rest her head on his shoulder. Her hand curled over his chest, and he buried his fingers in her hair.

"Susan?" A peace settled in his soul at the sound of her name and the nudging response of her hand on his skin. "Did I tell you we have a freshwater spring on the hill? And in the summer . . ."

Epilogue

Ashton, Wyoming Territory
April 6, 1889

A low grumble of thunder tumbled across the valley floor, bringing the thick scent of rain.

Susan shifted, yawning and sliding her hand across the covers in search of her husband's warm length. When her hand encountered only cool sheets and tousled pillows, she opened her eyes.

Midnight shadows enveloped the room in a warm velvet cloak. Intermittent flashes of lightning splashed the bed with a hazy glow. Susan lay back, listening to the patter of the rain, waiting for Daniel to return.

Another good-natured rumble of thunder echoed overhead, and Susan smiled. The rain would wash away the last patches of snow on the upper slopes. Then the forsythia and lilacs would bloom.

Allowing thoughts of spring to fill her senses with the phantom scent of grass and flowers, Susan lay in bed watching the play of lightning and rain on the ceiling. Several minutes passed, and when there was still no sign of Daniel, she slipped from under the covers and picked up her wrapper. The smooth, polished floorboards were cool beneath her bare feet as she padded across the room. She opened the door, and the low murmur of Daniel's voice told her where she would find him.

Susan's lips tilted in an indulgent smile, and she shrugged into her wrapper, fastening the tie over the faint protruding swell of her abdomen. Silently she moved to the door of the little bedroom. There she paused.

The two occupants remained unaware of her presence. Daniel's frame seemed incongruous on the child's tiny bed. But there was nothing incongruous about the young girl he held tenderly in his arms or the expression of love on his face.

Susan leaned against the door, watching her husband's broad, work-hardened palm stroking their daughter's tousled copper braids. Soft shushing noises whispered from his throat.

At another grumble of thunder, Annabelle clung to his shoulders, damp trails of tears still streaking her cheeks.

"Still scared?"

Susan barely caught Daniel's low query.

Annabelle's chest swelled in a ragged breath. "I don't like . . . thunder."

"Shh . . ." Daniel drew her closer, wiping the tears from her face. "It's all right to be afraid," he murmured. "Everyone is afraid of something at one time or another."

"Even you, Papa?"

Susan gripped the neckline of her wrapper. The slight movement caused Daniel's glance to settle on her face.

"Even me." Daniel's voice was oddly husky. "But I learned that when people love you, there's nothing to fear." His arms tightened around Annabelle's tiny body. From above the child's head, his eyes clung to Susan's, burning with a love and adoration that had grown stronger over the years, never waning.

"Never forget how much your mother and I love you, Annabelle, and you'll always be safe." His voice grew thick with emotion. "Love never dies."

Holding fast to her husband's strong gaze, Susan knew that somehow—together—they had weathered the storms of their past to journey into a bright shining future. The distant sound of thunder would no longer hold a threat, but only the promise of cool, refreshing rains.

Kathryn Lynn Davis

SING TO ME OF DREAMS

The *New York Times* bestselling author of *Too Deep For Tears* brings us a rich, sensuous novel filled with the intimate yearnings and passions of a turbulent family, their lovers and friends, and the one extraordinary woman, Saylah, who enters their lives.

There is a future I do not seek, but which will come to be, just the same...

With these words echoing in her heart, Saylah sets off on a journey that will take her through all the mysteries of the human heart—from a tranquil life of simple joys to the world of white settlers in the lush, unspoiled Pacific Northwest.

Available in Paperback from Pocket Books

POCKET
B O O K S

408-01

A Captivating New Novel of Passion and Pride in the
Bestselling Tradition of *A Knight In Shining Armor*

JUDE DEVERAUX

ETERNITY

The saga of the Montgomery family continues in
the stunning new novel from the *New York Times*
bestselling author Jude Deveraux.

Carrie Montgomery had never had to fight for
anything—until she met the most wonderful, most
exasperating man. Savor the romance and
adventure as they discover if their love can last for
all ETERNITY.

Available in Paperback from Pocket Star Books in February 1992

POCKET
STAR
BOOKS